A SECRET WISH

As Mary read through the figures, she could feel Paul's breath warm on her cheek. This sensation affected her even more powerfully than the touch of his arm had done a moment before. She'd always been aware of him in a physical sense, but now that awareness was heightened to a nearly unbearable degree. He shifted lightly on the sofa and as he did, his leg touched hers for a brief instant. Brief as it was, that touch seemed to set Mary's whole body trembling.

"Well, all seems to be in order here," Paul said, shutting the ledger and smiling at Mary. "You keep accounts as admirably as you do everything else, Miss Grant. Have you anything more to show me?"

Mary picked up the last of the ledgers and handed it to Paul. She admired his profile as he bent over the book. A lock of hair hung over his forehead, accenting its noble form. Beneath the fine arch of his brow, his vivid blue eyes were narrowed in concentration as he studied the columns of numbers.

Mary's gaze dwelt caressingly on these details before her eyes came to rest upon his mouth. As she stared at it, Mary found herself imagining what it would feel like to be kissed by that mouth. She could imagine Paul's arms around her, crushing her close against him, her whole body aflame with excitement as he slowly lowered his lips to hers. . . .

Books by Joy Reed

AN INCONVENIENT ENGAGEMENT

TWELFTH NIGHT

THE SEDUCTION OF LADY CARROLL

MIDSUMMER MOON

LORD WYLAND TAKES A WIFE

Published by Zebra Books

LORD WYLAND TAKES A WIFE

JOY REED

Zebra Books
Kensington Publishing Corp.
http://www.zebrabooks.com

ZEBRA BOOKS are published by

Kensington Publishing Corp.
850 Third Avenue
New York, NY 10022

First Printing: October, 1997
10 9 8 7 6 5 4 3 2 1

Printed in the United States of America

for my husband

One

For the twentieth time that evening, Paul Wycliff picked up the letter that was lying on the table in front of him and read it through.

He was a tall, strongly built gentleman in his late twenties, fair-haired, blue-eyed, and good-looking to a degree which his female acquaintance united in calling indecent. Good-looking he certainly was, but good looks were not his only asset. A close observer might have read character in his clear-cut mouth, determination in his strong, square jaw, and intelligence in the vivid blue eyes that looked out beneath his handsome brow. Yet at the moment, the brow was contracted in a frown, and there was a look both sad and stern in Paul's eyes as he looked down at the letter in his hand.

The letter read:

March 2, 1814

Dear Paul,

I have received your letter of this date and, after long and painful deliberation, find myself with no choice but to accept the second of the two alternatives you offer. You will guess with what reluctance I take this drastic step. Yet I would not do so, were I not firmly convinced that in the long run, it would tend toward your greater happiness.

You know well my feelings on the subject of a marriage

between us. I have never made a secret of them, and I am still as determined as ever not to subject you to the ills that would attend so disproportionate a match as ours would be. I must therefore take the painful step of dissolving the relationship between us. Enclosed are your letters to me; I beg that you will return mine to you at your earliest convenience. Please believe that I shall continue to think of you with affection and shall ever regard myself as,

> Your most sincere friend and well-wisher,
> Cecelia de Lacey

There was a bitter smile on Paul's lips as he read through this letter. Nothing could have been more noble than the sentiments it propounded, but Paul had reason to believe that the motives which had inspired it were a good deal less noble.

He had first made the acquaintance of Cecelia, Lady de Lacey, seven years ago. At that time he had been only twenty-one, newly graduated from Oxford and on the verge of taking orders for the church. Since his teens, it had been an understood thing between Paul and his father that Paul should adopt the church as his profession. Paul's father had often avowed his intention of buying a property and settling down, and it was his hope to find one with a church living attached so that Paul would have some occupation to work at until the property should pass into his own hands.

"It don't do for young men to be brought up in idleness," he often told Paul solemnly. "I know that to my cost, for I was never bred up to any profession, and I've always been an idle, useless kind of fellow. I did well enough when your mother was alive, but now she's gone I don't seem to accomplish much of anything."

There was but too much truth in these words, as Paul had reason to know. His father was a kind-hearted, well-intentioned, thoroughly amiable man, but he was also weak and terminally indecisive. When he had been fatally injured in a carriage accident during the last year of Paul's Oxford studies, the promised estate and living had yet to materialize.

On his deathbed, Mr. Wycliff had apologized for his failings with his customary humility. But he had been urgent in two things: that Paul should complete his studies at Oxford, and that he should use the monies that would come to him on his father's death to buy the estate his father had always intended to bequeath him. This was the last conversation Paul was ever to have with his father, and it naturally made a great impression on him. As soon as his father's obsequies were complete, he had returned to Oxford, taken up his studies with renewed zeal, and ended by matriculating with a Double First.

There had been satisfaction in obtaining this honor, but when it had been achieved, Paul had found himself at loose ends. From boyhood on, he had unquestioningly accepted his father's plan that he was destined for Holy Orders. Indeed, he had entered into the plan with enthusiasm and had conscientiously prepared himself for his future vocation by applying himself to his studies both religious and secular, and by conducting himself in his personal life as he felt a future clergyman ought to behave.

Now, for the first time, he found himself questioning his vocation to the church. It had been one thing to study for Holy Orders when there had been a prospect of a family living to fill and when there had been at least an ostensible need for him to support himself. Now, however, there was no such need. His father had been born the Honourable Andrew Wycliff, younger son of the Right Honourable Earl of Wyland. And though Mr. Wycliff had had little to do with the more exalted members of his family since his marriage to Paul's mother, he had nevertheless gleaned sufficient of the family fortune previous to that event to support him comfortably during his lifetime and to leave Paul very well provided for after his death.

Paul, indeed, was in some doubt as to whether his father would even have wished him to become a clergyman under the present circumstances. Mr. Wycliff had obviously been anxious that Paul complete his studies, but his concern had not extended to the taking of Holy Orders. He had rather seemed to imply that he expected Paul to buy an estate and live as a landed gentleman. But Paul had no heart for buying estates just then. In some strange way, in the weeks following his graduation from Oxford, he felt as though he were only just beginning to realize the fact of his father's death.

It had not been so bad while he had had his studies to occupy him. In fact, he had frequently congratulated himself during the last few months that he was bearing up very well under the shock of his loss. Now, however, he realized that the shock had only been postponed. He felt tired and melancholy, unfit alike for employment or diversion. A friend, seeing Paul's state of mind, had kindly invited him to accompany him on a trip to London. Paul had accepted the invitation, and it was there, at an assembly in Mayfair, that he had first made the acquaintance of Lady de Lacey.

Lady de Lacey had been in her early thirties then and in the first stages of mourning her husband, an elderly knight. Perhaps it was the sight of her sitting sadly apart from the other merrymakers in her somber black dress that had first drawn Paul to her, or perhaps it was only her undoubted beauty, which was calculated to draw attention to itself no matter how somberly she was dressed. In any case, Paul had been immediately and powerfully smitten. Lady de Lacey, for her part, had seemed equally smitten, and the progress of their love affair had been rapid. They had been barely two weeks acquainted when Paul had first proposed she marry him.

"Marry you," Lady de Lacey had repeated with a melancholy smile. "Oh, Paul, if only it could be. But I love you too well to let you make such a sacrifice as that. For it *would* be a sacrifice, my love: indeed, it would. You are young, with your whole life ahead of you—"

"And I want to spend it with you, Cecelia," Paul had interrupted passionately. "How can you say it would be a sacrifice for me to marry you? It would be much more of a sacrifice to give you up. You must know that I could never be happy without you now that I've met you. And I thought you felt the same about me."

"Oh, but I do, Paul. It's only that I'm older than you and see the disadvantages that would attend our marrying, as well as the advantages. What do you suppose people would say if they saw such a blighted creature as myself, tying herself to a young man like you, in the prime of life?"

Paul, with youthful impetuosity, had roundly damned the opinions of other people. "It doesn't matter what they think, or what anyone thinks," he had said hotly. "It's only you and I that matter, Cecelia. And it seems to me that if you cared as much for me as I care for you, you wouldn't give a rap for the opinions of anyone else."

At this, Lady de Lacey had dissolved into tears. Paul had immediately begged pardon for having spoken so harshly. "Indeed, indeed, I know you care for me, Cecelia," he had said with contrition. "I'm a blackguard for saying such things to you—"

"No, you're not a blackguard, Paul," Lady de Lacey had said, wiping her eyes and giving him another melancholy smile. "And indeed I do care for you, more than you can imagine. But I can't marry you, Paul. It's not only the difference in our ages. The thing is, Paul, that I've been married before—and not happily married, either. Sir Henry was often very unkind to me. I know, of course, that *you* would never be unkind to me," she added hastily, as Paul opened his mouth to protest. "But it seems as though I just couldn't take the risk. You must try to understand my feelings, my love. After Sir Henry died, I made up my mind never to marry again."

"So we must part?" Paul had said, in an agonized voice. "Are you saying I can never see you again?"

Lady de Lacey had given him a long, meditative look. "No, I'm not saying that, Paul," she had said, slowly and carefully. "We cannot marry, but I see no reason why we cannot go on seeing each other."

"But you say we cannot marry. What would be the point of it? You must know I can't go on like this, Cecelia. It would drive me mad to see you and know you are never to be mine—to try to pretend you are merely a friend when you mean so much more to me. I believe I would rather leave London forever and be done with it than endure that kind of torture."

There had been almost a smile on Lady de Lacey's lips as she had listened to this passionate effusion. "Oh, Paul, you *are* young, aren't you?" she had said. "It's only the young who see things in black and white. You must know, Paul, that there are friends and *friends*. Even if we do not marry, there is no reason why we cannot go on loving each other."

It had been some time before Paul had understood her meaning. When he had, he had been as shocked as though an angel from heaven had proposed an illicit liaison. Whatever had been the late Mr. Wycliff's failings, he had always been a moral man and had instilled in his son a deep respect for conventional standards of right and wrong. This respect had been intensified by Paul's training for the Church, so that at first, he could not listen to Lady de Lacey's proposals with anything but consternation.

Lady de Lacey had persevered, however. In the gentlest tones, she pointed out the advantages such a relationship would hold for them both. "And indeed, people do not make so much of those old moral conventions nowadays, you know, Paul. I'm sure the Prince Regent makes no secret of his relationship with Lady Hertford, and I could name you a dozen other couples who are on terms of intimacy with each other and yet are married to someone else. That is very bad, of course," she added swiftly, seeing Paul's look of revulsion. "But in our case, there are no someone elses to be considered. It would be only us, and if we choose to dispense with convention and consider ourselves committed to each other without the benefit of a marriage license, whom would we be hurting? No one, Paul: no one at all."

That there were fallacies in these arguments Paul could readily discern, but he found himself succumbing to them all the same. It was one thing to reject temptation in the abstract; quite another when it came in the form of a beautiful woman and was so much in accord with his own inclinations. And so it was that he found himself plunged into a relationship with Lady de Lacey that resembled marriage in all its particulars, yet was no marriage at all in the sterner eyes of the Church and State.

At the beginning of this relationship, Paul had been careful to do nothing that might compromise Lady de Lacey's reputation in the eyes of the world. He had taken lodgings in London when he had first come up with his friend, and these lodgings he kept up, despite Lady de Lacey's urgings that he abandon them and move in with her. During his visits to her house in Harley Street, he kept a tight check on his speech and behavior as long as her servants were about, and he always took care to leave her at an hour that, if not precisely decent of itself, still allowed of a decent interpretation. In public he treated her with the same respectful formality he would have accorded to any lady of her age and rank, and among his masculine acquaintance he stoutly maintained the fiction that she was only a friend.

It had been some months before he had become aware that Lady de Lacey was steadily undermining his efforts on her behalf. She addressed him with devastating frankness in front of her friends and servants, did not hesitate to kiss or caress him in public, and in general seemed eager to publish the true state of relations between her and her young lover.

Once the first shock of this realization was past, Paul had gradually become reconciled to the situation. By the time he had been acquainted with Lady de Lacey a year, he was regularly spending the night at her house and could demand breakfast or bath water from her servants the next morning without looking or feeling in the least self-conscious. They, in turn, treated him with affectionate respect, as though he were some favored young relative of Lady de Lacey instead of something a good deal more equivocal. In public it was the same. He and Lady de Lacey were treated as an acknowledged couple, and on the few occasions he attended social functions without her, he might be sure of being hailed by someone of her acquaintance anxious to inquire after her health.

Although Paul was thus outwardly reconciled to this state of affairs, inwardly it continued to bother him a great deal. At intervals he renewed his proposal of marriage to Lady de Lacey, hoping that their relationship had now progressed to such a point that she might consider making it official. This Lady de Lacey was never willing to do, however. She would treat the matter as a joke, telling him he had no business tying himself up to an old woman like herself. If he persevered in his proposals, she would take refuge in tears as she had before.

Paul soon saw the wisdom of not pressing the issue too far. But still he continued to hope his mistress might one day consent to regularize their union. With this goal in mind, he made a point of renewing his proposals whenever the moment seemed favorable. As far as he could see, his best hope in this regard was that Lady de Lacey might one day become pregnant. If there were a child's welfare to be considered, Paul reasoned hopefully, she could hardly refuse to let him give it (and her) the protection of his name. But either Lady de Lacey was incapable of bearing children, or, as Paul gradually came to suspect, she was too *au fait* with the ways of the world to allow an ill-timed pregnancy to disrupt her comfortable way of life. At all events, no pregnancy had come, and the relations between her and Paul had continued as before.

Yet in spite of this continuity, it was inevitable that their relationship should undergo a few changes over time. The first fiery ardor of their love gradually cooled and was replaced by a less fevered but still warm affection. This affection had seemed to continue more or less unabated on Lady de Lacey's part, but in the last year or two Paul had become aware of a change in his own feelings, an increasing dissatisfaction that had come to taint every aspect of their relationship in his eyes.

He had attributed this at first to his dissatisfaction with the irregular aspects of their union. This irregularity had never en-

tirely ceased to irk him, although he had done his best to quiet
the voice of his conscience by use of the same platitudes that
Lady de Lacey was so fond of voicing. But with such an upbringing and such an education as his had been, it was inevitable
that some feeling of guilt should persist. Still, as time went on,
Paul grew increasingly confident that this alone was not responsible for his growing sense of dissatisfaction. The truth, when
he finally brought himself to admit it, was that as he had become
better acquainted with his goddess, he had discovered her to
have feet of clay.

The realization had not come upon him all at once. He had
tried to shut his eyes to it for a long time, but with the two of
them living upon such intimate terms, it was inevitable that the
true light of her character should dawn upon him sooner or
later. Lady de Lacey was a liar. She lied incessantly about small
matters, and on occasion about larger ones. For the most part
her lies were of the small and harmless variety, but even these
Paul felt to be an affront to his understanding.

"Oh, Paul, I've been such a lazy creature this afternoon. I
haven't stirred from the house," was her gay greeting to him on
one occasion, when he had seen her only a few hours before
coming out of a milliner's shop on Bond Street. Or, "Oh, Paul,
I hope you will excuse me from going to Lady Fulton's with
you this evening. I have one of my stupid headaches coming
on and shall have to spend the evening in bed," she had told
him, looking touchingly wan. Yet when Paul had returned early
from Lady Fulton's party, full of concern for her condition, he
had found her garbed in full evening dress and seated in the
drawing room with several of her friends, laughing and talking
with great animation.

It was not the fact that she preferred to stay home with her
friends rather than attend a party with him that rankled, as Paul
assured himself. It was not even the fact that she had found it
necessary to lie about her preference. But the mere fact that she
had lied about such a small matter cast doubt on every other
statement she had ever made. Looked at in this light, even her

affection for him became suspect. This was more especially the case as by this time that affection was beginning to appear a little worn around the edges.

"So I said I was to go to the Englewoods'. I daresay I did say so, but at the last moment I changed my mind and decided to go to Brights' instead. Is that such a terrible thing?" she had snapped on one occasion, when Paul had caught her out in another deception.

"It is when I had planned to meet you at the Englewoods'," he had replied, striving to keep his temper. "I think you might have let me know, Cecelia, rather than letting me cool my heels in St. James's Square for the best part of an hour. And if you were at the Brights', how is it that Lord Dunbury brought you home in his carriage?"

"Lord Dunbury was calling upon Alfred Bright and kindly offered to take me home, as you were not there to do so. Indeed, now that I think of it, I am quite sure I told you I was going to the Brights', Paul. You must simply have forgotten and gone to the Englewoods' instead."

This was such a palpable fiction that Paul would not dignify it with any reply. After spending a few more minutes vainly trying to coax him into a good humor, Lady de Lacey had abandoned her efforts and flounced off in a huff. The situation had produced a distinct coolness between them. Paul had stayed away from Harley Street for several days, but he had no reason to suppose Lady de Lacey felt the lack of his company during that time. According to several witnesses whose credibility he had no reason to doubt, his place had been filled most satisfactorily by Lord Dunbury.

Lord Dunbury was a young nobleman of large fortune who had come recently to Town in company with his mother and sister. He was pleasant, well-mannered, and tolerably good-looking, but it was his youth which was his outstanding characteristic, for he still lacked some months of being of age.

Paul, upon making Lord Dunbury's acquaintance, had been irresistibly reminded of his own youthful self seven years ago, when he had first come to London. This resemblance had caused Paul to treat the young nobleman with great kindness and consideration at first, but his sympathies had suffered a shock when he had discovered that he and Lord Dunbury bore yet another point of resemblance. For Lord Dunbury, on making Lady de Lacey's acquaintance, had instantly fallen head over heels in love with her. And despite the disparity in their ages, it had become more and more apparent to Paul that Lady de Lacey was inclined to encourage his suit.

In such a situation, Paul hardly knew how to behave. He felt it ridiculous to be jealous of a boy scarcely out of his teens, but there was no denying that Lady de Lacey was giving him ample cause for jealousy. The subject was avidly discussed among the members of the *ton,* and though most of them were not inconsiderate enough to discuss it in Paul's presence, he could not avoid hearing some part of what was being said. Overall, opinions seemed to be pretty well divided as to whether Lord Dunbury would make, or be allowed to make, an offer of marriage to Lady de Lacey, but almost no one seemed to doubt that she would accept him if he did.

"Dunbury's a viscount, y'know," had been the remark of one worldly wise gentleman whom Paul had overheard discussing the matter at White's that very afternoon. "It's not an old title as such things go, but a viscount's a viscount after all, and she can't afford to be too particular in her situation."

"Of course, Dunbury's pretty well off for brass, too," had suggested another gentleman, who formed one of the first gentleman's audience.

"Aye, but it's the title that'll clinch the matter," asserted the first gentleman. "She'll snap him up in a trice, mark my words. Everybody knows she married de Lacey for *his* title. I don't expect she'll hesitate to trade it for a better one, even if it means robbing the cradle."

Paul's first reaction to this speech had been a wave of hot anger. For a moment he had considered confronting the worldly wise gentleman and forcing him to recant his words, by means

of his fists if necessary. But his anger soon gave way to a mood
of calmer reflection. The gentleman, in voicing his opinion, had
only been giving the consensus of society, a consensus that was
fully supported by Lady de Lacey's actions. Paul himself could
not but own it. Collecting his hat and walking stick from White's
doorman, he had left the club and wandered the streets of London for the best part of two hours, meditating all the while on
the intolerable position which Lady de Lacey's behavior had
put him in.

His meditations, though painful, had eventually borne fruit
in the form of a resolution. Returning to his lodgings, he had
sat down and written a letter to Lady de Lacey. He was careful
not to give way to anger in his letter, but had merely outlined
the situation as it appeared to him without dwelling on his in-
juries. He concluded by asking Lady de Lacey one last time to
marry him. If she still felt she could not, he added in a post-
script, he thought it was time they should consider parting ways,
rather than continuing with a relationship that was becoming
unsatisfactory to them both.

On rereading this letter, Paul found it had rather the air of
an ultimatum. He decided to send it anyway, however, for
whether Lady de Lacey accepted or rejected his offer mattered
little to him at this point. He wanted only to have the matter
settled definitely one way or another after so many months of
living in limbo. Indeed, as he had paced back and forth across
his sitting room waiting for a reply to his letter, it had occurred
to him more than once that he was not altogether sure what
kind of response he really wanted.

The response, such as it was, had come soon enough. And
now, as Paul looked down at the letter in his hand, he was struck
by the strange mixture of emotions he felt within his heart.
Some feeling of sadness was inevitable, of course, after the
dissolution of a love affair of such long standing. Yet in a way,
he felt almost as much relieved as saddened. In a flash of self-
intuition, he recognized that in sending his ultimatum to Lady

de Lacey, he had perhaps been unconsciously hoping for this very outcome.

Now that release had come, however, he scarcely knew what to do with his newfound freedom. He had the idea that gentlemen usually consoled themselves with strong drink and masculine company in these situations, but he had little inclination for company just then and none at all for strong drink. Exploring his inner sensations curiously, he discovered that he felt more hungry than anything else. This was hardly surprising, for he had had nothing to eat since early that morning. It was past ten o'clock now, too late for dinner, but Paul felt he would be the better for a sandwich or two. Reaching his hand to the bell-rope, he was just about to pull it when the door opened and his valet came into the sitting room.

"You are a veritable conjurer, Smithson," said Paul, smiling at the man. "How is it that you always seem to know when I am about to ring for you?"

Smithson, a thin, upright man of about thirty with sleek dark hair and an extremely correct demeanor, looked modestly pleased by these words. "Indeed, sir, I was not aware you wanted me," he said. "My appearance is entirely coincidental. I came to deliver an express which has just arrived for you. It would appear to be a matter of some urgency. The messenger who brought it said he was instructed to wait for a reply."

"An express?" repeated Paul in surprise. It occurred to him suddenly that Lady de Lacey might have repented of her first decision and sent another letter giving consent to his proposal of marriage. Such a thrill of horror went through him at this idea as to give him a tolerably clear picture of his own feelings. Making an effort to conceal his consternation, he picked up the letter which Smithson was offering him on a silver salver.

Two

A single glance at the letter was enough to relieve Paul's apprehensions. It was directed to him in a handwriting very different from Lady de Lacey's flowery script, and the superscription bore a Yorkshire address. On closer examination, he discovered that it was an address not unknown to him.

"Why, this comes from Wycliff," he said, looking up from the letter with surprise.

"Yes, so I observed, sir," said Smithson. He hesitated briefly, then added in a wooden voice, "I presumed it was a communication from your uncle, Lord Wyland."

Paul frowned and looked at the letter again. He felt almost reluctant to open it. The few communications he had received from his uncle during his lifetime had not been of a nature to inspire him with a desire to receive any more.

Lord Wyland, ninth Earl of Wyland and Baron Wycliff, was Paul's father's elder brother. Although older than Mr. Wycliff by only a year or two, he possessed a personality that was at once stronger and less endearing than his younger brother's. Lord Wyland was a grim, rigid, humorless man, prone to condemn anyone whose nature differed from his own and prone especially to condemn any fancied immorality which he perceived in the conduct of those around him. The moral and religious principles which Paul's father had possessed in a more moderate degree had been transmuted in him into a kind of fanaticism. Yet his fanaticism was not of a consistent kind, for while preaching on one hand the virtues of humility and the vanity of worldly wealth and rank, he had still been able to roundly condemn his brother for marrying Paul's mother, a young lady of no family or fortune who was earning her living as a governess in the home of one of his neighbors.

As a general rule, Paul's father was the most biddable of men, but on this occasion he had shown unexpected spirit. He had not only married Paul's mother in the teeth of his brother's opposition, but had defended her right to be treated by Lord Wyland with all the honor due her position. And when Lord Wyland had failed to comply in this regard, Mr. Wycliff had abruptly removed his bride and himself from his brother's home and had signified his intention of returning there no more.

From that time on, relations between the two brothers had been strained. It had not been until the death of Paul's mother that Lord Wyland had made any effort to extend an olive branch to his brother. On that occasion, his motives probably had more to do with concern for the succession than a simple Christian desire to reconcile with his brother. Lord Wyland's own wife had died only a few years before, leaving him a childless widower, and it was natural that in these circumstances he should seek to be on good terms with those who stood next in line to inherit his title and estate. So he had written a stiff letter to Paul's father consoling him on the death of his wife and had included in the same letter an invitation for Paul to visit him at his estate in Yorkshire.

Paul had not wanted to accept the invitation. He had been sixteen then, of an age to resent his uncle's treatment of his mother, and the circumstance of his having so recently lost that mother made him all the more determined to have nothing to do with the man who had so signally failed to appreciate her merits. But on this occasion, as on the occasion of his marriage, Mr. Wycliff had been unexpectedly firm.

"You know you're heir presumptive to the title after me, my boy," he had told Paul solemnly. "And Wyland knows I'm not likely to outlive him by more than a year or two. As things stand now, it's Carlton House to a Charley's shelter you'll come into the whole business when he cuts up. Might as well go up to Yorkshire and see what he's got in mind for you. You needn't stay but a week or two if you don't like it, but it'd probably do you good to get away from here for a bit. It's a gloomy place, now your mother's gone," Mr. Wycliff had finished, with a slight catch in his voice.

Reluctant as Paul was to accept these arguments, he was obliged to admit that there was much sense in what his father said. A few days later he had embarked on the long journey to Wycliff in Yorkshire. Wycliff was not his uncle's only estate, or even his principal one; that honor belonged to Wyland Park, Lord Wyland's seat in Wiltshire. But it was at Wycliff that Lord Wyland preferred to reside when able to follow his own inclinations.

As a residence Wycliff had much to recommend it, in a historical sense at least. It had been the original seat of the Wycliffs when they had been mere barons struggling to hold onto their property in the wake of the Norman conquest. The house had been a castle originally, but this structure had been all but destroyed in the War of the Roses. Subsequent generations of Wycliffs had laboriously built it into a manor house of some size and splendor, only to see it fall prey to Cromwell's men during the Civil War.

For the duration of the war and the ensuing Commonwealth, Wycliff had languished vacant and in disrepair. But as soon as the Monarchy had been restored—and with it the fortunes of the Wycliffs—the then Lord Wycliff had confidently undertaken to build it up again. Consequently, the house as it stood now contained elements of the Norman, the Tudor, and the baroque, not to mention sundry renovations added by later owners in various other styles. By rights this should have given it a wildly heterogeneous appearance, but in fact it presented a facade of unexpected unity, chiefly because the same gray limestone had been used to carry out all of its multitudinous additions. It was not a friendly looking house, however. The first time Paul had seen it, looming grimly on its rocky outcrop high above the sea, he had begun to suspect what it was that made it his uncle's residence of choice.

The interior of the house had proved little more welcoming than its exterior. Paul preserved a memory of cold, dark, cheerless rooms that were either inconveniently large and drafty or uncomfortably small and cramped. Neither was his uncle's hospitality such as to mitigate the discomforts of his home. After Paul had spent two weeks being harangued morning and evening at family prayers and being lectured between times about rentals, agriculture, and property management, he was very glad to bring the visit to an end.

The visit had never been repeated. Soon afterwards, Paul's father had received a letter from his brother, informing him that he was about to marry again. Lord Wyland's second union had proved more fruitful than his first, and within a year his new wife had been brought to bed of a son, effectively removing Paul and his father from the succession. From this point on, the intercourse between the two families had dwindled to a sporadic correspondence. And even this had come to an end in recent years. When word of Paul's liaison with Lady de Lacey had reached Lord Wyland's ears, he had written his nephew a thundering letter full of warnings about the awful fate awaiting fornicators in the afterlife. When this letter had gone unanswered, Lord Wyland had written another, still more thundering letter to his nephew, informing him that henceforth he intended to wash his hands of him entirely.

The memory of those letters still made Paul wince when he thought of them. He looked uneasily at the new letter in his hand, wondering what possible circumstance could have motivated his uncle to renew his correspondence after having declared in such unequivocal terms his intention of breaking it off. A closer look at the letter's superscription gave him yet more matter for speculation. It had been seven years since he had seen his uncle's handwriting, but he remembered it as being crabbed and close, not firm and flowing as this writing was.

Perhaps the letter was not from his uncle at all, but from some other person at Wycliff—his new aunt, perhaps.

"There's only one way to find out," said Paul aloud. Inserting his thumb beneath the seal of the letter, he broke it open and unfolded the single, closely written sheet.

Smithson had continued to hover near at hand in his usual unobtrusive manner. As soon as Paul began to open the letter, however, he came quickly forward. "Allow me, sir," he said, deftly clearing away the pen, inkbottle, and sandshaker that were lying on the blotter so that Paul might spread the letter open in front of him. Lady de Lacey's letter was also lying on the blotter. Smithson made a move as though to clear it away, too, then pulled back his hand abruptly with a glance at his master.

Paul saw the movement. "It's all right, Smithson," he said, with a faint smile. "You might as well clear that away, too. Or no—stay—I must send it back to Lady de Lacey along with her other ones. She's given me my *congé,*" he added, with a forced attempt at lightness.

"I see," said Smithson. His voice conveyed nothing but a respectful sympathy, but Paul, glancing toward him, surprised a look of unmistakable satisfaction on Smithson's normally expressionless countenance. Paul felt vaguely that he ought to resent this. As he turned his attention to the letter once more, however, he soon forgot all else in a rising sense of astonishment.

The letter read:

Wycliff
March 1, 1814

Dear Sir,

I am writing at the request of my employer, Lord Wyland, to acquaint you with a distressing circumstance which has lately befallen him and his family. There has been an outbreak of smallpox in this area which has recently claimed the lives of his wife, Lady Wyland, and his son, Lord Wycliff. Lord Wyland himself now lies gravely ill of the same disease. Recognizing that the out-

come of this illness may probably prove fatal, and knowing that in such an eventuality you would be his legal
successor, he is most anxious that the estrangement which
has existed between you in recent years should be brought
to an end.

If at all possible, he would like you to come to Wycliff
and be reconciled to him in person. Realizing however
that the risk of disease may render this course of action
inadvisable, he requests me to convey herein his most
respectful compliments to you, along with his regrets that
relations between you have not conformed to the Christian ideal. He also beseeches you most earnestly to act
responsibly by the inheritance that will pass into your
hands in the event of his death.

If you feel at all equal to making the journey to Yorkshire, I beg you will send word as soon as possible
through the messenger who delivers this, whom I have
instructed to wait for a reply. Your uncle is very anxious
to see you, and I believe the sufferings of his illness have
been much aggravated by this anxiety. Anticipating your
reply, I am

Yours very sincerely,
M. Grant

For some minutes after Paul finished this letter, he sat stock-
still, staring dazedly down at the even lines of M. Grant's flowing handwriting. At last he looked up and found Smithson still
hovering near at hand, silently awaiting his orders.

"My uncle is very ill, Smithson," he said. "I must make
arrangements to leave for Yorkshire immediately."

Smithson received this news with his usual impassivity.
"Very good, sir. I'll see to packing your things. Will you be
traveling post?"

"I suppose I must. I've already missed this evening's Mail,
worse luck." Distractedly running his fingers through his hair,
Paul rose to his feet. "I'll go tell the messenger my intentions,

so he can carry word to my uncle that I'm coming," he told Smithson. "And I'll send Mrs. Clark's boy down to the Bull to make arrangements for the post-chaise."

The next hour passed swiftly, as Paul made preparations for his journey to Yorkshire. He was so busy that he had no time to reflect on the possible implications of M. Grant's letter in regard to his own position. Neither did he have time to reflect any more on Lady de Lacey's letter of rejection. Indeed, as he scrambled together his baggage and wrote notes to cancel his engagements for the coming week, he came close to forgetting all about it. When he did remember it, it was with a greatly diminished sense of pain. The idea of having a purpose, a set task to perform in a severely limited amount of time, had entirely dissipated his former mood of melancholy. It occurred to Paul once or twice, as he and Smithson went about the business of preparing for his journey, that one species of shock was a very effective cure for another.

In the event, however, his preparations were destined to be in vain. The post-chaise had just been brought around to his lodgings when a second express arrived from Yorkshire. Smithson brought it to him and stood silently waiting as he broke the seal. Even before Paul read the letter's opening address, he had a presentiment as to the news it must contain.

> Wycliff
> March 1, 1814

Dear Sir,

It is my melancholy duty to inform you that your uncle passed away shortly after the dispatch of my previous letter. I therefore write again, both to inform you of this event and in hopes of preventing your journey north, which must now be to no purpose. Owing to the contagious nature of the late Lord Wyland's illness, the local authorities have insisted upon an immediate interment of his remains, along with those of his wife and son. As there is no possibility of your attending the obsequies attached to this event, you may think it better to defer your visit here until some more convenient season. Accordingly, I have included herein the names of the late Lord Wyland's London men of business. His solicitor is Mr. Jacob King of Temple Bar, and he also has dealings with the firm of Everett and Taylor in Lombard Street.

Your uncle's final words before his demise were to beg you once more to act responsibly by the solemn charge that now passes into your hands. Trusting that by means of this letter I have discharged my duty by him and to you, I am

Yours sincerely,
M. Grant

As he had done after reading M. Grant's previous letter, Paul sat silent a minute or two, trying to absorb its contents. Smithson, hovering nearby, did his best to look solicitously disinterested. This disinterest was clearly feigned, however, as was shown by the circumstance of his addressing Paul without waiting for Paul to address him.

"I trust there has been no decline in your uncle's condition, sir?" he said.

Paul said nothing but merely handed the letter to Smithson. As he watched him peruse its contents, it occurred to him that he would never again hear his servitor address him with a simple "sir," as he had done just now. Henceforth it would be "my lord" or "your lordship," for Smithson's attention to such niceties was as well-developed as any dowager's. With a sense of awaiting some momentous and decisive event, Paul sat watching Smithson composedly read through the letter.

At last the valet finished the letter and, having refolded it neatly, returned it to Paul. "A very sad letter," he observed. "Allow me to express my condolences to you, my lord."

There was no undue emphasis on the last two words, but they fell on Paul's ears with the finality of a death-knell. Until then, the intelligence contained in M. Grant's letter had not seemed real to him. Now it seemed both real and overwhelming. Paul cleared his throat.

"Thank you, Smithson," he said. "I wonder—I wonder what I had better do now."

Smithson considered the question gravely. "I suppose you will not be needing the post-chaise," he ventured. "As this Grant person says in his letter, you could not possibly reach Yorkshire in time for the—ahem—burial."

"Yes, that's so," agreed Paul. "I suppose I had better go pay off the post-boys and tell them to take the chaise back to the Bull. Or do you think I had better go to Wycliff anyway, for the appearance of the thing?"

Again Smithson considered. "No, I think not, my lord," was his eventual decision. "Unless, of course, you have other family in that district whom you would wish to share your condolences with?"

"No, none. Lord Wycliff and his wife and son were all the family I had."

"Then I see no point in your going to Yorkshire at present. Eventually, of course, you will wish to visit your relations' resting place and see to the erection of a suitable monument, but that could better be attended to some months from now. It seems to me your best course at present would be to see your uncle's men of business, as this letter suggests." Smithson looked down at the letter which Paul was holding in his hand. "A very sensible letter, upon the whole. Would this Grant person be your uncle's steward?"

"I don't know. I don't remember the name from the last time I visited Wycliff. But that was more than ten years ago, of course, and I daresay there have been changes since then." Paul reopened the letter and scanned its finely written lines. "Yes, a sensible kind of letter. I suppose I had better do as it says. I'll send round to Temple Bar first thing in the morning."

"If I may interpose a suggestion, my lord, you ought also to send round to your lordship's tailor. There will be your mourning to be attended to, you know. . . ." Smithson let his voice trail off discreetly.

"Yes, of course," said Paul, with a nod. "I'll send a note to him, too, early tomorrow. For now, I'll see to the post-boys and send word to Mrs. Clark that I won't be leaving Town after all." Paul rose to his feet and cast a crooked smile at his valet. "And then I think I'll try to get some sleep. What with one thing and another, it's been an exhausting kind of day, Smithson."

Smithson bowed. "I can well imagine, my lord," he said with feeling.

Three

With the reception of M. Grant's second letter, Paul's whole existence underwent a sudden and dramatic change.

He continued to dwell in his old lodgings, to patronize his old club, and to be waited on by the faithful Smithson. But these were almost the only points in which his life remained constant. His landlady Mrs. Clark, who had formerly treated him with the insouciance typical of her species, now became embarrassingly servile, and the dinners which she sent up bore scant resemblance to the plain grilled steaks and chops that he had formerly been regaled with. Paul thought privately that he would have preferred plain steaks and chops to the often indifferent imitations of French cookery which now came up from Mrs. Clark's kitchen. But he bore with this trial patiently, as he bore with all the other major and minor irritations that were his at this changeful period.

The greatest change—and in some ways the greatest irritation—was the altered way he was treated by his acquaintance. Most of his former friends now appeared abashed and ill-at-ease in his company, while men to whom he had hardly spoken before became suddenly and pressingly civil. Letters of condolence poured in from all quarters, accompanied by invitations that would have astonished and gratified him at an earlier period. Astonished he was even now, but his astonishment was mixed with contempt rather than gratification. So evident was it that his newfound popularity was linked directly to his new wealth and title that he was in no danger of having his head turned by it.

Cynicism was indeed Paul's predominant state of mind at this period. His cynicism was heightened by a letter he received from Lady de Lacey shortly after his uncle's demise. She wrote ostensibly to condole him on his loss, but concluded her letter of condolence with a few lines which alluded delicately to the possibility of a reconciliation. After mature consideration, Paul elected to let this letter go unanswered. He had already returned Lady de Lacey's other letters to her in obedience to her last missive, and her bid to resume relations with him now only confirmed him in his resolve to have nothing more to do with her. It was a source of bitter amusement to him when he reflected that he was now wealthier and of higher estate than Lord Dunbury, the man who had supplanted him in her affections.

There could be no doubt as to the extent of his new wealth, as Paul discovered after meeting with his uncle's men of business. The late Lord Wyland's annual income had numbered in the tens of thousands and was derived not only from his several estates but from interests in mining, government stock, and various rental properties in and around London.

"I had no idea my uncle owned so much property in Town," exclaimed Paul, when the full extent of his uncle's holdings was made known to him. "I must say I am surprised. When I visited him as a boy, he often spoke of London as a den of iniquity and said that he would have been glad to dispose of his house there if the property had not been entailed. And this property here, around the Fleet—you can't mean to say that belonged to him? Why, it's common knowledge that that whole area is given up to taverns and bawdy houses!"

Mr. Everett, the attorney who was attending Paul at this meeting, coughed slightly and spoke in a repressive voice. "The late Lord Wyland was a shrewd man who did not allow his religious scruples to stand in the way of turning a profit," he said. "It is true that the property you mention is not in the most select quarter of Town, but I assure you it brings in its rents most regularly, my lord."

"I have no doubt that it does, but I would prefer not to derive my own income from the kind of businesses that reside there," said Paul frankly.

Mr. Everett settled his spectacles more firmly over his nose and regarded Paul with surprise. "Are you saying you wish to dispose of the Fleet property?" he asked.

"As to that, I could not say. Perhaps the more moral alternative would be to turn out the present tenants, clear out the area altogether, and build it up anew—in the form of inexpensive housing, perhaps, or something of that nature."

Mr. Everett advised most strongly against these measures, however. "Your lordship cannot have considered the cost that would be incurred by such a project," he said earnestly. "Why, I daresay it would dissipate some tens of thousands of pounds with no hope of return in your lordship's lifetime." Seeing that Paul was by no means deterred by this argument, Mr. Everett changed tacks swiftly. "And though I am not perfectly familiar with the area around the Fleet, I do know that it is occupied by many respectable businesses as well as the—ahem—more objectionable ones you mentioned. If you turn them all out wholesale, the dubious tenants will have no difficulty finding new quarters—they never do, alas—while the respectable ones may end by being permanently displaced. Indeed, I would advise your lordship to consider well before taking such measures as you propose."

"But what would you propose as an alternative?" demanded Paul in exasperation. "I've already said I would rather not derive my income from such a source."

"Of course, and I can quite understand your scruples, my lord," said Mr. Everett, in a voice that strongly implied the reverse. "Perhaps the best alternative would be for your lordship to dispose of the property altogether. I am sure I could find a buyer for it."

Having obtained Paul's reluctant consent to these measures,

Mr. Everett moved hastily on to other matters. "And then there is his late lordship's own house in London, which is at present untenanted. There is a small skeleton staff to keep it in order, however, and I have sent word to the caretaker in charge, notifying him of the change in ownership. I suppose, as your lordship resides in London, you will wish to have it opened for your own use?"

"I don't know," said Paul, frowning. "I hadn't thought so far ahead as that. I suppose I had better take a look at the place before I decide what to do about it. Can you give me the caretaker's name?"

Mr. Everett readily supplied Paul with the name of the caretaker, then bowed him ceremoniously off the premises with an air, Paul thought, of being relieved to be rid of so quixotic a client. Getting back in his curricle, Paul drove to Hanover Square, where the late Lord Wyland's townhouse was located. Here he made a minute tour of the house and inadvertently won the enmity of his uncle's caretaker by declaring that the rooms would have to be entirely new-furnished before he could consider living there.

"And what would ye be wanting new furnishings for?" demanded the caretaker, one Mr. Higgins, a small man with bushy white brows and a belligerent manner. "These was all bought new by his late lordship's first wife, and I'm sure I've kept 'em that careful, they're in as good shape now as when they was new. Forty-three years I was in his late lordship's service, and it's a matter of pride to me that never once in all that time did he raise a complaint against me."

"That's very commendable, I'm sure, but you know tastes in furnishings do differ, Mr. Higgins. I, for one, could not sleep in such a bed as that without experiencing nightmares." Paul gestured toward the funereal-looking bed that stood in the center of the gloomy chamber allotted to the master of the house. "Please have the dust covers removed and see that everything undergoes a thorough cleaning as soon as possible. I'll come back in a week or so to look it over and decide which of the furnishings I want to dispose of."

Mr. Higgins vouchsafed no reply to these instructions, but regarded Paul in glowering silence. When Paul took leave of him a few minutes later, he slammed the door behind him and barred it noisily from within, as though hurrying to shut out a malign influence.

Paul was slightly incensed by this treatment, but by the time he had driven a few blocks he was able to take a more equitable view of the situation. Resistance to change was a natural human trait, he reminded himself, and a certain amount of resentment on Mr. Higgins's part was also natural, given his status as an old family retainer. To one who had been long in the late Lord Wyland's employ, a mere nephew must appear as an outsider, even an interloper. Paul told himself that he must be prepared to encounter similar displays of resentment from other of the late Lord Wyland's servants when he got around to visiting Wyland Park and Wycliff. He resolved in advance that he would go slowly in making changes about those properties, and that he would be kind but firm in his dealings with his uncle's domestics.

He already felt he had been a little hasty in ordering Mr. Higgins to have the London house cleaned and made ready for occupancy. It would probably have been better to wait for a second interview to issue these orders, and to have contented himself during his first interview with merely seeing the house and establishing a rapport with the elderly caretaker.

The orders had already been given, however. That being the case, Paul felt it would do more harm than good to countermand them. He therefore looked forward to the time when the house might be clean and clear of dust covers, and he could start looking for new furnishings. But when he paid a visit to Hanover Square the following week, he found nothing had been done toward following his instructions. This proved also to be the case on the third and fourth visits he paid there. Mr. Higgins always had plausible excuses for his failures, but by the time Paul had been three times disappointed, he was beginning to be thoroughly exasperated with the caretaker. If he had not suddenly been called out of town about this time, he might have been tempted to dismiss Mr. Higgins from his service, even despite his long tenure with the late Lord Wyland.

The reason for Paul's leaving town was a letter which he had received from the steward at Wyland Park, inquiring civilly when he meant to come and see to some business matters pending there. Having already spent the best part of two months in London wrestling with the complexities of his uncle's business affairs and locking horns with Samuel Higgins, Paul was ready to turn his attention to something else. Wyland Park, his uncle's largest and most valuable property, seemed like a logical next step.

It was true that for a time he had debated whether it might not be his duty to go to Wycliff first. During the last two months he had received three more letters from M. Grant, urging him to make the trip to Yorkshire at his earliest convenience. But Paul easily found several reasons why this would not be convenient at present. He was most reluctant to revisit a place with so many unpleasant associations and which had now the additional unpleasant distinction of being the scene of his relatives' deaths. The idea of Wyland Park was much more appealing. And so, at the end of April, Paul gave permanent notice to his landlady, took leave of such of his acquaintance as he was still on close terms with, and set out for Wiltshire with Smithson.

At Wyland Park he found enough to keep him pleasantly occupied for several months. The steward there, a Mr. Baines, was as civil in person as he was in writing, and the rest of the staff were equally civil and accommodating. Paul found all this a refreshing change after his dealings with Mr. Higgins. And it was even more pleasant to find himself the owner of an elegant Palladian mansion set in the midst of a handsome park and surrounded by green and thriving fields and pastureland.

It had not been the late Lord Wyland's habit to spend much time at Wyland Park. Consequently, the house bore no stamp of his unyielding personality. It seemed on the contrary a

friendly and welcoming house, and it was gratifyingly apparent
from the attitude of the staff that they preferred their new master
to their old one. All this combined to put Paul at his ease at
Wyland Park. For the first time since his uncle's death, he felt
as though he were coming to terms with his new position. Under
Mr. Baines's kindly tutelage, he entered eagerly into the business of running the vast estate and found so much to interest
and occupy him that he elected to spend the whole of the summer there. It was not until early September that he began, reluctantly, to think of moving on once more.

He was, in fact, beginning to feel he could put off visiting
Wycliff no longer. He had not received any more letters from
M. Grant, but his conscience still reminded him now and then
that he had not visited his uncle's grave or arranged for a funerary monument. He supposed there must be other matters at
Wycliff that needed his attention as well. So after dashing off
a note to M. Grant, Paul ordered Smithson to pack his bags,
took a friendly leave of Mr. Baines, and set off on the long
journey to Yorkshire.

Being in no particular hurry to reach his destination, Paul
was three days on the road, reaching Wycliff late in the afternoon of the third day. But despite traveling in such easy stages,
he was feeling tired and jaded when at last the post-horses
turned between the gray stone gateposts that marked the beginning of the Wycliff property. Smithson, seated beside him in
the carriage, let out a smothered exclamation.

"I beg your pardon?" said Paul, turning to look at him.

"I beg *your* pardon, my lord," said Smithson, staring at the
house that loomed ahead of them at the end of the long sloping
drive. "I did not speak, but was merely expressing
astonishment, as it were. Is *that* Wycliff?"

"Yes, that's Wycliff," said Paul, surveying his property rather
grimly. The afternoon was fading to dusk, and in the half-light
the house appeared like some gigantic beast, crouched on its
rocky outcrop above the ocean as though driven there by some
still more gigantic pursuer. Its gray stone walls stood square

and uncompromising, even while the roof above them bristled with a fabulous collection of towers, cupolas, obelisks, spires, and columnar chimneys. Altogether it was an eccentric-looking structure, but there was nothing whimsical about its eccentricity. It had rather an air of keeping itself to itself, as though it did not seek or welcome outside interest in its affairs.

"Cheerful-looking place, isn't it?" said Paul, with a grimace. "Wait until you get a look at the inside, Smithson. I've often wondered if Mrs. Radcliffe didn't use it as a model for her Castle Udolpho."

The sweating horses at length brought the carriage to the top of the drive, which opened into a courtyard fronted by the house's entrance porch. Paul got out, followed by Smithson, who continued to stare up at the house's crazy roofline. "I don't see any lights, my lord," he said. "I trust your lordship's letter did not go astray. It doesn't look as though we were expected."

"No, it doesn't," agreed Paul, also looking up at the house. "However, you can't judge by that, Smithson. It's still pretty early, and the servants may not have lit the lamps yet. I'll go find out."

"It would be more fitting if I were to do that, my lord," began Smithson, but Paul was already halfway up the steps to the front door. Upon reaching it, he laid hold of the knocker, which was shaped like a griffin with a singularly unpleasant expression. Before he could ply the knocker, however, the door suddenly opened inward, so that Paul had to catch himself to keep from falling forward into the arms of the woman who had opened it.

She was a young woman of perhaps some five- or six-and-twenty years, though the manner in which she was dressed might have made her look older than she was. Her brown stuff gown was made high to the neck with no ribbon or lace to enliven its prim lines, and her dark hair was drawn straight back into a knot at the back of her head without a single wave or curl to soften its severity. Notwithstanding this, she was a handsome woman whose features were better able to withstand such treatment than many another. But it was her air of self-possession that chiefly distinguished her, even more than her smooth oval face, high cheekbones, and large dark eyes. As Paul righted himself in the doorway, she stood surveying him with a gaze that was at once interested and slightly critical.

"Good evening," she said.

"Good evening," returned Paul, smiling at her in a tentative manner. "My name is Paul Wyland. I'm the late Lord Wyland's heir, as you may probably know. Are you—did you—?" He halted, at a loss how to proceed. The woman appeared too young to be a housekeeper, but she was obviously not a housemaid, unless it were a housemaid of a very superior kind. The woman made no effort to help him in his difficulties. She merely stood regarding him with the same searching, slightly critical gaze.

"I sent a letter," Paul went on awkwardly, feeling rather intimidated by the woman's silent regard. "I have been in correspondence with one of my uncle's servants here, a gentleman named Grant. Perhaps you will be good enough to inform him that I have arrived?"

The woman regarded him in silence a moment longer, and then a faint smile appeared on her lips. "I am Mary Grant," she said. "Come in, my lord. We have been expecting you."

Four

As Paul followed Mary Grant into the house, his mind was whirling with startled speculations. It had never entered his head that the unknown M. Grant might be a woman. Looking at her slim, straight back in her brown stuff gown, he wondered again what position she had filled in the late Lord Wyland's household. It struck him that she was a very attractive woman, even in spite of her drab dress and severe hairstyle. He was just regarding her ankles with admiration when she turned around to address him.

"I will take you to the blue drawing room, my lord," she said. "It's the most comfortable of the reception rooms, and there's a fire burning there, which I daresay will be very welcome after your journey."

"Thank you," said Paul, smiling at her once again. She did not return his smile, but merely gave him another of her cool, critical stares before turning and leading the way toward the drawing room once more. Paul followed her, puzzled by her air of disapproval and not a little piqued.

If he had only known it, Mary's state of mind was not much different from his own. The new Lord Wyland's appearance had come as a shock to her. She had been unconsciously expecting him to resemble his uncle, a pale, stern-looking gentleman with a spare and rather stooping physique. In addition she had been expecting Paul to look like a libertine, for the late Lord Wyland had not been sparing in his criticisms of his nephew's character.

But the young giant whom she had just admitted to the house looked nothing like a libertine, and nothing like the late Lord Wyland, either. He was fair, to be sure, but it was a golden fairness compounded of dark blond hair, vivid blue eyes, and quite the handsomest face it had ever fallen to Mary's fortune to see.

Try as she might, she could see no signs of dissipation about that face. Indeed, as she had surveyed him there on the doorstep, she had been irresistibly reminded of a picture of Sir Galahad that had appeared in one of her childhood storybooks and which had always seemed to her the epitome of masculine beauty. Lord Wyland had the same strong nose, firm, sensitive mouth, and square jaw as Sir Galahad, and the same frank and intensely blue eyes, so different from his uncle's pallid orbs. He seemed moreover a pleasant and personable young man, not in the least like a libertine. As Mary was leading him toward the drawing room, she could not resist the urge to look back at him, under pretext of addressing to him a commonplace remark about the drawing room fire.

In doing so, however, her feelings had suffered a check. She had caught Sir Galahad looking at her ankles, and this had instantly destroyed the more favorable opinion that she had been forming of him. Clearly he was a libertine, just as his uncle had said. Mary told herself sternly that she would have to be very careful in all her dealings with him and not say or do anything that he might construe as encouragement. The remark about the fire was made in a voice of great coldness, therefore, and Mary would not allow herself to return the friendly smile that accompanied his reply. It cost her an effort not to do so, however. Really he did not seem like a libertine at all. If she had not had his uncle's warnings to put her on guard, she might have found herself succumbing to his charm, Mary told herself, as she opened the drawing room door.

"Here you are, my lord," she said formally. "Dinner will be ready shortly. Do you wish to see your room so you may change first, or would you prefer to dine as you are?"

"I should like to change, I think," he said, looking down at his dusty boots. "What room have you put me in? Not my uncle's, I hope and pray?"

This last question was spoken in such an apprehensive voice that Mary could hardly keep from smiling. "No, I thought you would probably prefer to occupy some other room until you have had a chance to go through your uncle's effects," she said. "I have put you in the south turret room for now, my lord. It's the last door on your left as you go along the gallery—"

"Yes, I know where it is," he said, looking pleased. "That's where I stayed last time I was here. It seems a very long time ago." He cast a look around the drawing room, his eyes lingering on its bright chintz-covered furnishings and the watercolor sketches that decorated its walls. "I must say, the place looks a deal cheerier than I remembered it."

"That would be your aunt's influence, I expect," said Mary, turning to quit the room. "She did quite a lot toward improving the house, I understand. If there is nothing else, my lord, I will take leave of you now and go see to dinner. I thought, as you dine alone, you would prefer to eat in the breakfast room rather than the formal dining room?"

Paul, remembering the vast dark vault of the formal dining room, agreed fervently. "But do not go yet, if you please, Miss Grant," he said, laying a hand on her arm to detain her. She gave him such a look of affront that he removed his hand immediately, but continued to address her in what he hoped was a winning manner. "I didn't get your title wrong, did I? The name is Miss Grant and not Mrs.?"

"That is correct," she said, looking at him suspiciously.

"I was wanting to ask you . . . who are you exactly? Or rather, as I should say, what position did you fill in my late uncle's household?"

"I was governess to his son, Lord Wycliff," she replied, and quit the room hastily, leaving Paul with as many unanswered questions as before. Supposing however that he would have an opportunity to question her further at dinner, he removed his hat and greatcoat, warmed himself briefly at the fire, then went upstairs to the south turret room, where Smithson was engaged in unpacking his baggage.

Twenty minutes later he presented himself in the breakfast room, freshly shaved, scrubbed, and brushed, and properly clad in black evening breeches and topcoat. Since his last visit, the breakfast room had undergone a transformation similar to the one he had noticed in the drawing room. Watercolor landscapes had replaced the lugubrious portraits he remembered so well, and the hard leather seats had been enlivened with bright needlework chair covers. With a feeling of surprise, however, he observed that only one place was laid at the round oaken table.

"Where's Miss Grant?" he inquired of a rosy-cheeked maidservant, who had just come into the room carrying a soup tureen. "Doesn't she mean to dine with me?"

"Miss Grant usually dines in the servants' hall with the rest of us, my lord," she replied, looking Paul up and down with an admiration that would have abashed him if he had not been intent upon Mary's nonappearance. "Though to be sure, she used to dine with the family when his lordship was alive—his late lordship, that is, your lordship's uncle."

"Then perhaps Miss Grant will condescend to dine with the present Lord Wyland, too," said Paul. "Please tell her I should regard it as a personal favor if she would do so."

With another admiring look at Paul's face and physique, the maidservant bobbed a curtsy of assent, deposited the tureen on the table, and departed with his message. She returned a minute later accompanied by Mary, whose face wore a forbidding frown. "You wished to see me, my lord?" she said.

"Well, yes, I do," said Paul. "Not to put too fine a point on it, I should like you to dine with me. There are some questions I would like to ask you over dinner."

She drew herself up and regarded him with the same suspicious expression she had worn during their previous conversation. "I hardly think it would be proper for me to dine with you, my lord," she said. "Besides, I am needed in the kitchen."

"Nonsense. You are a governess, not a cook. Why should you

be needed in the kitchen? And according to this girl here, you often dined with the family when my uncle was alive." Paul looked toward the maidservant, who spoke up helpfully.

"The name's Ellen, my lord," she said, bobbing another curtsy.

"Thank you, Ellen," said Paul with a smile, and turned again to Mary. "According to Ellen here, you were quite in the habit of dining with my uncle and his family, so you have no possible excuse for not dining with me now."

Mary looked obstinate. "But it happens that I *am* needed in the kitchen, my lord," she said. "You will think it a peculiar circumstance, but it happens that we are altogether rather peculiarly circumstanced here at Wycliff just at present—"

"Yes, I can see that you are, and I'm burning with curiosity to find out why," said Paul frankly. "And you're the only one who seems to know exactly what's going on, Miss Grant. Could not they manage without you in the kitchen for the space of one meal?"

"Sure we could, Miss Grant," put in Ellen, before Mary could answer his question. "You go on and eat with his lordship, and Alice and I'll help Hannah in the kitchen. Between the three of us, we'll manage all right."

Mary bit her lip. She felt she ought to continue to assert the need for her presence in the kitchen, but that was difficult in the face of Ellen's counter-assertion. And in truth, she was not so loath to accept Paul's invitation as she was striving to appear. He seemed so sincerely eager for her company, and so anxious to ask her advice—and then, too, he looked so staggeringly handsome in his black-and-white evening clothes! Altogether it was enough to shake the resolve she had made to stay out of his way. But the sight of him in evening clothes reminded her of another difficulty. How could she possibly sit down to dinner with this handsome, elegantly clad gentleman, when she was wearing her old brown stuff gown? "I am not dressed to dine in company, my lord," said Mary, with great finality.

"But you are not dining in company, Miss Grant. You are

dining with me, and I will not permit your dress to be an excuse. In any event, you appear to me finely enough dressed to attend any gathering, with the exception perhaps of one of the Queen's Drawing Rooms. They insist upon plumes and hoopskirts for the ladies there, you know," said Paul, with a solemnity that brought a reluctant smile to Mary's lips. "Don't you think she looks fine just as she is, Ellen?" he continued, appealing to his former ally for support.

Ellen giggled, but came willingly to his aid. "To be sure, my lord. Miss Grant's got such an elegant figure that she looks well in anything. We all say as much back in the kitchen."

"There you are, then. Have another cover laid, Miss Grant, and while we eat you can tell me all about the peculiar circumstances that prevail here at Wycliff."

"Very well," said Mary, feigning a look of resignation to hide the real pleasure this exchange gave her. "Ellen, never mind about laying me a cover. You'd much better go back to the kitchen and help Hannah with the fish."

Paul watched curiously as Mary fetched more plates and cutlery from the sideboard and set another place opposite him at the table. "Why are *you* doing that, Miss Grant?" he asked. "Surely that is not a governess's job, any more than cooking is. Why is not the butler here to attend to it?"

Mary gave him a faintly incredulous look as she seated herself at the table. "The butler is in Long Medford gaol, awaiting your decision on his fate," she said. "And I do hope you will find time to attend to that matter while you are in Yorkshire, my lord. Mr. Rundell, the magistrate for our district, has asked me so often if you were coming soon to Wycliff that I cross the street now when I see him coming rather than disappoint him with another negative."

"What?" In his astonishment, Paul nearly overset the soup tureen, which he had just drawn toward him in order to serve him and Mary with soup. "What did you say, Miss Grant? I cannot have heard you correctly."

With some belligerence, Mary repeated her statement. "A

few months after your uncle's death, Mr. Steadman, who was butler here, and his wife, who was cook, made an attempt to abscond with the silver," she explained. "Fortunately, we discovered the theft early on, and the local constable was able to capture the Steadmans with the silver still in their possession. They have been in gaol ever since, awaiting your decision. Surely you know all this, my lord? I have written you repeatedly about it in the last few months."

Paul shook his head, looking rather dazed. "I had heard nothing about it until now," he said. "You say you have written me, Miss Grant? I remember getting several letters from you this spring when I was still in London, but I am sure there was nothing in them concerning this matter. And since I have been staying at Wyland Park, I have got no letter from you at all."

"You have been at Wyland Park?" said Mary in surprise. "I had thought you were in London. Your uncle's man of business wrote me in April and mentioned you were setting Wyland House in order, so I made sure to address all my letters to you there after that. But you say now you were not in London?"

"No, although that doesn't explain why I didn't receive your letters. They should have been forwarded to me from Wyland House. Wait a minute, though: perhaps that does explain it!" With a kindling brow, Paul sat up straighter in his chair. "That old scoundrel, Samuel Higgins! He's the caretaker of the London house, and he has done everything he could to make difficulties for me ever since I took possession. I've borne with him up till now, out of respect for his age and the high opinion my uncle seems to have had of him. But this—this is the final straw. If I find he's been keeping my correspondence from me, I'll sack him on the spot, forty-three years of service or not."

Mary had listened in growing surprise to Paul's explanation. "So you did not get my letters?" she said. "You knew nothing about Mr. and Mrs. Steadman?"

"No, nothing. Good heavens! Do you mean to say you've been managing without a butler and cook all this time?"

"Yes, and without a housekeeper and footmen even longer."

"What?" Again Paul regarded Mary with astonishment. "You don't mean to say they're in gaol, too?"

"Oh, no, they left back when the first case of smallpox was diagnosed in the village," explained Mary. "I suppose one can hardly blame them. None of them had been inoculated, you see."

"But how odd! The vaccine has been available for years. I remember my mother inoculating me and my father and all our servants ages ago, when I was only a child. Why in heaven's name did not my uncle do the same for himself and his household? It has puzzled me to no end that he and my aunt and cousin should have died of a disease that could so easily have been prevented."

Mary smiled grimly. "You are not allowing for your uncle's religious convictions, my lord," she said. "The late Lord Wyland was of the opinion that all such matters were better left in the hands of Providence. If Providence chose that he and his family should escape infection, well and good. If not . . . ?" Mary spread her hands wide in an eloquent gesture. "If not, then it was clearly God's will that they should perish, and it would be sinful to do anything to try to avert that end."

"But Miss Grant, that is madness!" Paul's face was aghast as he stared at Mary. "Do you mean that he sacrificed his wife and son to such a scruple?"

Mary shook her head. "It was not a scruple to him, my lord, but a matter of principle. Perhaps you were not well enough acquainted with him to know how fanatical he was about such matters. I do not say his principles were always right, mind you. Indeed, in this case, I think they were dreadfully wrong, just as you do. But whether right or wrong, they *were* his principles, and he stood by them even when they demanded a sacrifice as enormous as the one you mention. The loss of his son, especially, was a great blow to him. For days afterwards he could hardly speak, but when he did, it was to compare himself to Abraham and Lord Wycliff to Isaac. He maintained the same attitude right up till the end. I never found much to admire about him when he was living, my lord, but I could not help but admire him in death."

Paul said nothing, but got out his handkerchief and blew his nose loudly. He had already been obliged to do this once or twice while Mary was speaking, and it was obvious now that he was deeply moved. Once again, almost in spite of herself, Mary found her opinion of him improving. He might be a godless libertine, as his uncle had claimed, but he appeared to be still capable of proper feeling. And if his previous speech was to be believed, he had been by no means so remiss in his duties as she had supposed. Instead of idling about Town, indulging in a veritable rake's progress, he had been living in the comparative quietude of Wyland Park. And even if his motives for going there had more to do with sport than seignorial duty, it was still commendable that he preferred country diversions to the more dissolute ones of London. On the whole, Mary felt he was perhaps not so black as he had been painted, and her voice was insensibly warmer as she continued her narrative.

"Indeed, my lord, you must not feel badly about what happened," she told Paul. "Your uncle was a man unshakable in his opinions, both for good and ill. I am sure there is nothing you or anyone else could have done to avert the catastrophe." In a more diffident voice, she added, "Perhaps you would like to see the place where he and your aunt and cousin are buried? It is a pretty place, I think, and not far from here: about halfway between the village and Long Medford."

Paul nodded. "I should like to see it," he said. "Indeed, that is the chief reason I came into Yorkshire, so that I might see to putting up a funerary monument for them all." Looking pensive, he continued, "It seems odd that such a task should have fallen to me. I had only met my uncle once, you know, and my aunt and cousin not at all. What were they like, Miss Grant? If you tell me a little about them, perhaps they will seem less strangers to me than they seem now."

"What were they like?" Mary considered the question at length before replying. "Lady Wyland was a good woman, I think, although her behavior toward her domestics was not always so considerate as might be desired. But of course I speak as one prejudiced in that regard. And then, too, there is no doubt that your uncle gave her much to try her. She was only seventeen when she married him, you know, while he was in his forties and already very set in his ways. Poor woman, I'm sure it's no wonder if she broke out publicly now and then in ill temper, considering what she was obliged to endure in her private life."

"She seems to have had good taste, if not a good temper," said Paul, looking around the breakfast room. "The house is vastly improved over what I remember it."

"Yes, I believe she did a great deal of redecorating in the early years of her marriage, when Lord Wyland was somewhat more indulgent toward her. He was much less so toward the end. Indeed, toward the end he seemed to regard any kind of indulgence as abhorrent, financial or emotional. If he had lived, I think he would have ended up a complete miser and probably a complete hermit as well. He was certainly headed in that direction."

Paul nodded. "It wouldn't surprise me," he said. "I am sure he must have led my aunt a sad life of it. Poor woman, one might almost consider her death a merciful release. But of course it is tragic that she should have died so young, and my cousin with her. What was *he* like, Miss Grant? I know even less of him than of my aunt, if that were possible."

Again Mary considered. "As far as looks are concerned, Lord Wycliff was a handsome child," she said, rather guardedly. "Your aunt was a pretty woman, you know, and your uncle not ill-looking." Although nothing like as handsome as you, my lord, she added silently, with a sideways glance at Paul's face.

Paul looked dissatisfied. "But what was he like?" he asked again. "What were his habits, his interests, his personality? I wish you would speak frankly, Miss Grant. As his governess, you must have known him better than anyone."

"Yes, I think I did." Mary hesitated a moment, then went on with an air of detachment. "Lord Wycliff was an intelligent child—the most intelligent child I have had the teaching of. But in his personality he was less fortunate than in his intellect. He was, I think, genuinely fond of me—fonder of me perhaps than of any other person. But that did not prevent him from making my life a misery six days out of the seven."

"Come, that's frank enough," said Paul, looking startled.

"It is the truth, my lord." Mary raised her chin and looked Paul squarely in the eye. "I do not say that I entirely blame him for his bad behavior, mind you. For that, his upbringing must be held in large part responsible. His father was, in my opinion, far too strict with him—and his mother far too indulgent. It would have been better, perhaps, if he could have gone away to school and been with other boys his age. But your uncle was of the opinion that public schools are hotbeds of vice and irreligion, and he was insistent that Lord Wycliff be schooled at home where he could keep him under his eye."

"Poor boy," said Paul feelingly.

Mary nodded. "You may well say so, my lord. His existence was a very trying one—and so, by extension, was mine. Indeed, I often found it almost impossible to discharge the duties I had been hired to perform. Lady Wyland would hear of my using no punishment but threats when Lord Wycliff misbehaved, but unfortunately the only threat that had any effect on him was to threaten to inform his father of his misbehavior. And since Lord Wyland punished every fault, great or small, by beating him severely, I naturally could not like to do that. Often he escaped punishment altogether when his conduct undoubtedly merited it. But what could I do? I do not hold with corporal punishment for children, unless it be as a last resort."

"Indeed, your position must have been very difficult," said Paul sympathetically. "I think governesses as a race must be the most overworked, undervalued mortals on earth." He surveyed Mary curiously. "What motivated you to take up such a demanding occupation in the first place, Miss Grant?"

"What usually motivates people to take up demanding occupations, my lord. Want of money, that is."

Mary's voice was bitter as she made this statement. Again

Paul surveyed her curiously. He had been intrigued by the account she had given him of his uncle's family, as much by her manner of delivering it as by the information itself. She had not minced words in delivering her opinion of his relations' characters. And though he had been rather shocked by her refusal to gloss over unpleasant facts, he had also found her honesty refreshing. She seemed altogether an unusual young woman, and he was curious to know more about her personal situation.

"I suppose want of money is a great motivator for us all," he said, in what he hoped was an easy voice. "Were your parents very badly off, Miss Grant?"

"No, not so very badly. My father was vicar of a small parish near Reading. As long as he was alive, we lived quite well, but unfortunately he was not a great man for saving. When he died, he left me with barely enough to live on until I was able to find a position. My mother had died some years before, you understand."

"But were there no relatives you could have gone to?" asked Paul. "It seems hard that a young woman should have to work for a living."

"In my case, I thought it preferable to living off the charity of relatives who did not really want me," responded Mary tartly.

"I see. I see. Yes, that is certainly understandable. But at the same time . . ." Paul gave Mary a smile that was slightly embarrassed. "You are, if you will forgive me for saying so, a very attractive young woman, Miss Grant. Was there no suitor to marry you and save you from such an unpleasant dilemma?"

"There was a suitor, but he died." Mary's voice was very short. "He contracted pneumonia only a few weeks before we were to be married."

Paul felt sorry for having revived what was obviously still a tender subject. "I am sorry, Miss Grant," he said awkwardly. "It sounds as though you have had a great deal to suffer." He knew he ought not to pursue the subject, but so strong was his curiosity that he could not resist the urge to question her further. "And so you were engaged to be married," he said. "This fiancé of yours—what sort of man was he, Miss Grant? What was his profession?"

"He was my father's curate. And he was an excellent man, the best man I have ever known." Mary's voice softened as she spoke these words. Paul observed that her expression, too, grew softer as she went on. "Francis was good, and kind, and generous—everything that was admirable. He was not very well-to-do, of course, being only a curate, but he had a little independence that would have been enough for us to live on in the beginning. And it had been arranged that he should have my father's living whenever Father should grow too old for it. But it all turned out quite differently than we had planned. First Francis caught pneumonia and died, and then Father died, too, only a few weeks later. After that, I had no choice but to take up governessing to support myself."

The finality with which Mary pronounced these words made it clear that she wanted no sympathy on the subject. Paul refrained from sympathizing, therefore, although he could not help being moved by the tale of tragedy she had recounted so matter-of-factly. But he contented himself with helping her to the joint of mutton which Ellen had just brought in, together with a couple of dishes of vegetables.

"Will you take some cauliflower, too, Miss Grant? I assume this is cauliflower, at any rate." Paul looked dubiously at the watery white gruel contained within one of the dishes.

"No, thank you, my lord, and I would advise you not to take any, either. Hannah is doing much better with her cooking lately, but I still cannot convince her that vegetables taste better when not boiled for an hour before coming to the table. Oh, dear, and she has overcooked the mutton, too. I told her most particularly to roast it only until the juices ran clear."

"I think she must have misunderstood you and roasted it until there were no juices at all," said Paul, swallowing with difficulty an extremely dry bite of mutton. "Hannah is the cook, I take it?"

"No, she is really only a maidservant, but since Mrs. Steadman is presently in gaol, we had to find someone to take her place. Hannah seemed to have more kitchen experience than any of the other maids, though not so much as I could wish."

Paul took up another bite of mutton on his fork, regarded it, then set it down again. "But why did you not simply hire a new cook, Miss Grant?" he asked. "I should think that would be easier than trying to train an inexperienced maidservant."

Mary gave him an exasperated look. "Undoubtedly it would have been easier, my lord, but unfortunately I had no authority to hire new servants. I did write you several times, asking for your permission—but it seems now my letters did not reach you. In any case, having received no word from you, I could only conclude you wished to maintain the *status quo.* For the past six months, we have been struggling on here at Wycliff with no cook, no butler, no footmen, and only half our proper allotment of maidservants."

"Good God," said Paul, regarding her with amazement. "Do you mean to say you've been enduring meals like this for the past six months? No wonder you detested the sight of me."

Mary felt a deep flush suffuse her cheeks. "Oh, it was not so bad as that, my lord," she said hastily. "Mrs. Steadman did not leave us until early in May, so we've only had to endure Hannah's cooking for the past four months or so. And I assure you, she has improved vastly in that time. This is princely fare compared with what we were served with in the beginning."

"If this is the improved version of Hannah's cooking, then I shudder to think what it must have been like at first," returned Paul, pushing away his plate. "I can see I shall have to look into hiring a new cook as soon as possible." Taking a small memorandum book from his pocket, he opened it and turned over its leaves until he found a blank one. " 'Cook,' " he wrote, repeating the word aloud for Mary's benefit. " 'Visit Long Medford Gaol' and 'Visit churchyard.' I shall have a full program tomorrow at this rate. In the meantime, perhaps we can have Ellen take away these things and bring on the dessert. I could use a glass of wine, too, to wash that mutton down my throat. It seems to have got stuck about halfway down."

Mary shook her head, a faint smile on her lips. "I am afraid you will have to be content with water to wash down your mutton, my lord," she said. "You will find nothing resembling a spirituous liquor in this house, not even small ale."

"My uncle was a teetotaller, I suppose?" said Paul, with a look of resignation. "I ought to have guessed it."

"Yes, he was quite fanatical on the subject of drink," said Mary. "He ended up breaking with the Nonconformist minister in the village, simply because Mr. Elfred once permitted a glass of wine to an ailing servant."

"Good God," said Paul again, and shook his head. "I don't understand that kind of fanaticism. But then, I never understood my uncle anyway. His behavior was always quite beyond me." He looked at Mary curiously. "Tell me this, Miss Grant. You say my uncle broke with the Nonconformists over the subject of drinking. Where then did he go of a Sunday? I know he broke with the Church of England years ago."

Mary smiled grimly. "For the past few years he was in the habit of conducting his own Sunday services, my lord," she said. "He held two three-hour services in the chapel, morning and evening, and all the staff and tenants were required to attend. And let me say that, with all due respect for your uncle's memory, we were none of us sorry to see them suspended!"

"Well, you needn't worry that I'll reinstitute the custom," rejoined Paul, picking up his memorandum book once again. "However, I do mean to reinstitute the more civilized custom of drinking wine at dinner. I'll have to drop by the village and order some in. I trust my uncle's fanaticism did not impel him to destroy the wine cellars along with the wine?"

"No, the cellars are quite intact, my lord. But I am afraid that any wine you find in the village is likely to be extremely *ordinaire*. You would do better to order some from a wine merchant in Long Medford."

"That's a good idea. Perhaps I can see to it tomorrow, after I call at the gaol." Paul made another note in his memorandum book and put it away, just as Ellen came into the room bearing a steaming pudding on a tray. Paul regarded it with favor.

"Well, hullo, this looks quite palatable," he said. "I trust appearances are not deceiving." Having served Mary and himself with generous portions, he sampled a bite and smiled across the table at Mary. "No, it is quite as delicious as it looks. I tell you what, Miss Grant: we ought to have skipped the rest of the meal and gone directly to dessert. Hannah obviously does better with puddings than with mutton and vegetables."

"No, as a matter of fact, she does not. *I* made the pudding, my lord," said Mary. She tried to speak matter-of-factly, but was inwardly conscious of a glow of pleasure as Paul regarded her with surprised admiration.

"Did you indeed?" he said. "You seem to be a remarkably accomplished young woman, Miss Grant. This is an excellent pudding, as good as any I've ever tasted. You wouldn't care to take over the job of cook from Hannah, by any chance?"

His voice was so hopeful that Mary could not help laughing. "No, I am a governess, not a cook, my lord, as you pointed out before," she said. "And I'm afraid my abilities in the kitchen don't extend much beyond pudding-making. But I thank you for the compliment all the same."

"You are very welcome, I assure you. Any time you care to step outside your profession and exercise your pudding-making abilities, I beg you won't hesitate." As Paul helped himself to a second serving of pudding, he shot a smiling look across the table at Mary. "Upon my word, you seem able to turn your hand to anything, Miss Grant. Cooking, governessing, housekeeping—and I daresay many other things as well." In a more serious voice, he added, "Would I be wrong if I guessed you nursed my uncle in his last illness?"

Once more Mary felt an inward flush of pleasure, though she endeavored to disguise it behind a brusque manner. "I did do a certain amount of nursing during his illness, but I beg you will not make too much of it, my lord. I had already been in-oculated for smallpox, so it is not as though I was taking any great risk in nursing him. And it was the least I could do for him, considering all he had done for me." Mary looked soberly across the table at Paul. "In his way, your uncle was very good to me, my lord. He paid me a decent salary for a governess, and when he required additional duties from me, as happened from time to time, he always paid me something for my time. He had so many business dealings that he was occasionally in need of a secretary, and I was glad to assist him in filing, and writing letters, and other such matters."

"I am sure my uncle found you an invaluable assistant," said Paul. The words were no empty compliment, for he had been much struck by Mary's air of competence during their interview thus far. She impressed him as being an extremely intelligent, level-headed young woman. And he could not help noticing that she was an extremely attractive one, too, in spite of her evident desire to disguise the fact. As Paul studied her slim figure and smooth oval face, he found himself wondering how she would look with a more fashionable dress and hairstyle.

Mary found his gaze disquieting. A few minutes before, when they had been laughing and talking in such a friendly manner, she had come close to forgetting that he was a dangerous libertine, but now she was reminded of the fact. It seemed to her best that their interview should be brought to an end. Pushing back her chair, she rose to her feet.

"I hope you will excuse me if I take leave of you now, my lord. I must go and assist the maids with their evening chores."

Paul looked disappointed at this speech—so disappointed that Mary felt a sense of gratification. She scolded herself for it roundly, however, as she curtsied slightly and moved toward the door. Paul got hurriedly to his feet and went to the door to open it for her. "But you will come back to the drawing room when you are done, won't you?" he asked, looking down at her hopefully. "There are still a great many things I need to ask you about, Miss Grant."

"I am afraid my duties will keep me busy the rest of the evening," said Mary mendaciously. "I hope you will find your

rooms to your liking, my lord. Do ring if you need anything we
have not provided you with." Having curtsied again and wished
him a good evening, she hurried out of the breakfast room with
the sensation of having narrowly escaped a situation of peril.

Five

Through the exercise of considerable ingenuity, Mary managed to stay out of Paul's way for the rest of the evening. She took care, however, to see he was provided with every comfort that Wycliff's rather comfortless household could provide, and when at last Ellen reported that he was safe in his room for the night, she went upstairs to her own small room on the house's uppermost floor.

This was a Spartan chamber, furnished only with an iron bedstead, a straight chair and deal table, and a battered chest of drawers. These furnishings Mary had supplemented with a framed pen and ink drawing of her father's vicarage and a small iron-bound trunk.

Following her usual custom, Mary washed, changed into her nightdress, and braided her hair for the night. Then she knelt down beside the trunk, unlocked it, and drew from one of its compartments a small painted miniature.

The miniature depicted a young man with a thin, earnest face, fine gray eyes, and a mane of unruly dark hair. As Mary looked down at it, she was visited once more by a familiar sense of loss.

"Oh, Francis," she said aloud, and shut her eyes, waiting for the wave of bitterness that invariably visited her at such moments. Tonight, however, the bitter feeling was not so strong as it usually was. Mary opened her eyes and again surveyed the young man's painted features. Almost she could fancy there was a smile on his lips, and a tremulous answering smile appeared on her own.

"Oh, Francis, I do miss you," she whispered, raising the miniature to her lips and kissing it. "But I have no doubt you are better where you are. You were always too good for this earth, Francis—and much too good for me."

As Mary laid the miniature back in the trunk, her fingers brushed against a bundle of letters that lay in a nearby compartment. She hesitated a moment, but in the end let them remain where they were. She was not in the mood tonight to indulge in her usual custom of taking them out and reading them over, weeping over the lover who was now lost to her and reviling the fate that had deprived her of him and her father in the space of a few short weeks. This double loss had not only deprived her of the two people she had held most dear in the world, but had left her to make her way alone in the world in a position of servitude.

It had never seemed to Mary that she had deserved such a fate. Yet as she considered it now, she realized that both her father and Francis would have condemned this attitude on her part. Even the late Lord Wyland, unorthodox churchman that he was, had endeavored to accept his loss with more of a Christian resignation than she had done. On an impulse, Mary gathered up both letters and miniature and put them in the trunk's lower compartment, beneath some old copybooks and her winter petticoats.

"And that's that," she said aloud. The moment had something of the finality of a funeral, and Mary remained with bowed head beside the trunk for several minutes more before rising to her feet. Having relocked the trunk and restored the key to its usual position on a ribbon around her neck, she blew out the candle and got into bed.

As Mary lay in the dark, waiting for sleep to come, she thought over the events of the day just past. It had been an unusually eventful day, thanks to the arrival of the new Lord Wyland. Mary reflected on how different he had been from what she had expected—more personable, more intelligent, and infinitely more attractive. Once more in her mind's eye she saw him as he had looked at dinner that night, his shoulders broad and square in his black broadcloth coat, his dark blond hair swept back from his handsome face, and his eyes, intensely blue, looking into her own. He was a regular Apollo, and it was no wonder if he had enjoyed great success among the ladies of London. With such assets as he possessed, it would have been a greater wonder if he had not.

At this thought, a warning bell sounded in Mary's mind. Was it possible that she, like those susceptible London ladies, was falling prey to Lord Wyland's practiced charms?

Mary's first impulse was to reject this idea with great energy. Yet when she forced herself to examine it dispassionately, she found to her dismay that even in spite of the brevity of their acquaintance and her certain knowledge of his bad character, she did indeed harbor a dangerous soft spot for the new Lord Wyland. This was perhaps most obvious in the way in which, after meeting him, she had immediately tried to convince herself that the bad reports she had heard of his character must be false or exaggerated. But it was obvious as well in the way she could perfectly recall every remark he had made to her, every compliment he had paid her, every smile he had bestowed on her— every separate thing he had said and done, in fact, throughout the whole course of the evening.

"Oh, but this won't do," said Mary aloud, opening her eyes and sitting up in bed in sudden alarm. "This won't do at all, Mary."

Now that her eyes were open to the situation, she was fully alive to the dangers it held for her. Indeed, she had had some acquaintance with such situations before. The household she had lived in prior to coming to Wycliff had contained a young gentleman in his late teens, elder brother to the small boy and girl who had been Mary's charges. Soon after joining the household, it had been her misfortune to attract the eye of this gentleman, who had thereafter found frequent excuse to visit the

schoolroom and to bestow upon her several inarticulate, but
perfectly honorable testimonies of his regard. He had been discovered in the midst of one of these testimonies by his mother,
who had promptly flown into a fit of hysterics and had de-
nounced Mary as an unscrupulous adventuress intent on entrap-
ping her offspring into an unequal marriage.

If it had been left to this lady's discretion, Mary would have
been turned out of the house that instant without a penny of the
salary that was owing her or a shred of character left to her name.
Fortunately for her, the lady's fairer-minded spouse had inter-
ceded in her behalf. He had not only paid her her full salary for
the quarter, but had written a decent recommendation that had
enabled her to obtain her position with the late Lord Wyland.
Without such a recommendation, it would have been nearly impossible for her to find work, for the faintest breath of impropriety was enough to permanently taint a governess's name.

"And heaven knows I never felt the least *tendre* for Freddy
Templeton, poor boy," she told herself. "But Lord Wyland is
something different altogether. I do feel something for him, even
in spite of my scarcely knowing him—and in spite of my knowing
his reputation too well. Very well, then, Mary: what are you going
to do about it? It's obvious you can't remain in the same house
with him. I suppose the best thing to do would be to give notice
and start looking for a new position right away. Since Lord Wyland has no children, he can have no possible use for a governess,
and my leaving will seem quite natural to him, I daresay."

Mary was surprised to find that the idea of leaving Wycliff
made her feel a little blue. She had toyed with the idea of leaving
it often enough during the past five years, but now that she knew
she must go, she found herself strangely reluctant to do so. This
reluctance had nothing to do with Wycliff's new owner, she assured herself. It was not possible that she could have formed a
serious attachment to a man she had only known a few hours.
And even if she had, it would have only been an additional reason
why she ought to leave Wycliff as soon as possible. Making a
resolve to give notice to the new Lord Wyland first thing in the

morning, Mary shut her eyes determinedly, pulled the covers up
to her chin, and endeavored to sleep.

Sleep she did eventually, but it was a light and troubled sleep
from which she awoke at the first cockcrow. She had dreamed
that the late Lord Wyland was berating her for shirking her
duties. Then somehow, imperceptibly, the dream had changed
into another dream involving the present Lord Wyland: a dream
which made Mary blush to remember it.

"I *am* susceptible, and no mistake," she told herself, as she
splashed cold water on her face and twisted her hair hastily into
its customary severe knot. It took her several minutes to decide
which dress to wear. She found herself strongly leaning toward
her black silk, normally reserved for Sunday wear, but after she
had examined her motives for wishing to wear her finest dress,
she took out her oldest serge working frock and put that on
instead. She then spent several minutes packing away the few
trifles of clothing and personal effects that were scattered
around the room. Finally she put on her pelisse and her glazed
straw round bonnet. This bonnet was a piece of headgear so
aggressively unattractive that it effectively counteracted even
the modest beauties of her best black silk, and Mary felt it might
be counted on to render her a complete dowd when combined
with the nonexistent beauty of her present garb. A glance in the
hall mirror as she went downstairs fully justified her in this
opinion. Having ascertained from one of the maids that Lord
Wyland was in the breakfast room, Mary squared her shoulders,
took a deep breath, and pushed open the breakfast room door.

Paul was seated at the table, surveying with a dubious eye a
dish of eggs that was lying in front of him. He looked up in
surprise at Mary's entrance, but his look of surprise immediately
gave way to a smile of pleased recognition.

"Why, good morning, Miss Grant," he said. "I was just wondering when you would put in an appearance."

"Good morning," said Mary, feeling suddenly shy. Since taking leave of him the evening before, she had been trying to
convince herself that she must have been mistaken in her first

impression and that he could not possibly be as handsome as she remembered. As she surveyed him now, however, she saw that she had, if anything, been too modest in her original appraisal. He was unquestionably the best-looking man she had ever seen, and the sight of him sitting there smiling at her was enough to make her forget why she had come into the breakfast room in the first place.

It was Paul himself who assisted her in remembering her errand. "You are up and about early this morning, Miss Grant," he said. "I see you are dressed to go out." His eyes rested on her bonnet for a moment with a look of pained distaste before returning to her face. "Or is it possible that you have already been out and are just returning?"

"No, I am getting ready to go out now," said Mary, steeling herself reluctantly to her purpose. "But I was wanting to speak with you for a few minutes before I left, my lord."

"Certainly, certainly," said Paul heartily. "This works out very conveniently, Miss Grant, for I was wanting to speak to you, too. Why don't you sit down and have some breakfast with me while we talk over our business?"

"I am afraid that is impossible, my lord. It is necessary that I leave Wycliff immediately," said Mary. She dropped her gaze as she spoke, for she found it impossible to hold true to her purpose while those brilliant blue eyes were looking into her own.

"Oh, yes?" said Paul. His voice was concerned, but his next words made it clear he failed to grasp the import of her speech. "Your business must be very urgent to take you out so early. But surely it cannot be so urgent that you must go without breakfast, Miss Grant? It wouldn't take ten minutes to have a roll and a cup of coffee with me—"

"Oh, no," said Mary in great haste. Collecting herself, she went on more composedly. "I have no urgent business, my lord. It is merely that, as my services can no longer be needed here at Wycliff, I think it is time I gave you my notice."

She paused. Paul was looking so dumbfounded that it was clearly unrealistic to expect any immediate reply. Mary went on, in a not quite steady voice. "I realize that you are not in a position to speak for my character and accomplishments, my lord, but if you could see fit to provide me with some sort of recommendation, it would be very helpful in enabling me to find a new position. Your uncle's bailiff would vouch for me, I think, and the vicar of the local church—"

"But what is this?" demanded Paul, finding his voice at last. "You say you are leaving, Miss Grant? But that is impossible. I only just got here yesterday, and I was depending on you to help me in finding my feet here at Wycliff. And surely it is not necessary that you leave now, before breakfast?"

"Yes, I'm afraid it is, my lord. It is not proper that I should remain in a bachelor's household, you know." Mary spoke primly, her eyes still downcast, for she did not dare meet Paul's gaze in making this speech. "And though I have no wish to inconvenience you, my lord, I cannot see that my presence here is at all necessary. You can have no possible need for a governess."

"Not for any governess, perhaps, but I do have need of you. Why, you're the only thing that's been holding the house together since my uncle died, as far as I can see. If you leave now, I am quite sure it will all fall to pieces." Paul was silent a moment, raking his fingers through his hair and regarding Mary with an air of perplexity. "Look here, Miss Grant," he said at last. "There must be some way to keep you here. I'll do whatever it takes, upon my word. I'll double your salary, to begin with: how will that be?"

"Oh, but my salary is not an issue, my lord. An increase would be very welcome, I don't deny, but—"

"Then consider it increased, Miss Grant. I'm sure you're not being paid half what you deserve, considering the extent of your duties. And if you're concerned about the impropriety of staying in a bachelor's establishment, I'll be happy to hire you a chaperone. There must be some decent woman hereabouts who would come and stay with you. Name your own terms, only say you will stay on at Wycliff for at least a few more weeks. If you still feel you must go at the end of that time, then of course I will accept your notice. But you must see what difficulties it would involve me in if you left now. You seem to be the only one here who had any acquaintance with my uncle's affairs."

Mary knew she ought to give a firm and decisive refusal to this petition. The longer she delayed, the greater the likelihood that she would weaken in her resolve and give way to the temptation which Paul's offer represented. If the late Lord Wyland had been there, he would certainly have counseled her to reject a temptation so manifestly infernal in its origin. He would have urged her to take the narrow and uphill path of duty instead of the broad, downhill thoroughfare that beckoned so enticingly.

But even in reminding herself of all this, Mary recognized that it was too late to take that uphill path. Such strength of mind as she had originally possessed had all melted away beneath the new Lord Wyland's beseeching blue gaze. As a sop to her conscience, Mary told herself that it was really her duty to stay on when he had such evident need of her assistance. It could not be Christian to abandon a person in need, even if that person was a libertine. And the presence of a chaperone would of course go a long way toward mitigating the impropriety of the situation.

"Well, I don't know," she said hesitantly. "If you really need me, my lord. . . ."

"I do need you," said Paul, with such ringing sincerity that Mary forgot her qualms and felt only a glow of gratification.

"If you really need me, then I suppose I could get Miss Eaton to come and stay with me for a few weeks," she said. "Miss Eaton is one of my best friends in the village, a retired schoolteacher and a very good, decent woman. I am sure you would like her, my lord."

"And I am sure I should, too, if she is a friend of yours, Miss Grant. Have your Miss Eaton by all means, or anyone else you like. Could she come today, do you think?"

"I don't know, but I doubt there's anything to stop her. I'll drive into the village and ask her, right away."

"But surely there is not so much hurry as that," protested Paul with a smile. "Now that we have settled that you are not

to leave, there's no reason why you may not join me for breakfast before you go dashing off to the village." He gestured toward the chair opposite him. "Take off your bonnet, Miss Grant,
and I'll pour you a cup of coffee."

Mary was no more proof against this offer than his last one
and accepted it with a smile. "Thank you, my lord," she said,
as she untied the strings of her bonnet. "As you insist, I must
confess that a little breakfast would not come amiss."

Paul helped Mary to coffee, rolls, and eggs, then watched as
she removed her bonnet and placed it carefully on a side table.
She looked to his eyes infinitely better without it. He wondered
once again why such an attractive young woman would go to
such lengths to make herself unattractive. Before he realized
what he was doing, he found himself asking the question aloud.

"Why is it that you are so determined to disfigure yourself,
Miss Grant?" he said, then mentally kicked himself as he realized how impertinent his words sounded. Mary paused in seating herself at the table and regarded him with raised eyebrows.

"Disfigure myself?" she repeated. "Whatever do you mean,
my lord?"

Paul, more embarrassed than ever, gestured helplessly toward
her bonnet. "Why would you voluntarily choose to put such a
thing as that on your head?" he said. "I don't pretend to be a
judge of ladies' bonnets, but it seems to me no bonnet at all
would be better than that one."

"As it happens, I had little choice in the matter, my lord," said
Mary, stung by Paul's words. Even though she had gone out of
her way that morning to make herself look unattractive, it still
hurt to have him disparage her appearance. Struggling to keep
her voice level and matter-of-fact, she continued, "I had a different bonnet when I first came to Wycliff, but my pupil, Lord
Wycliff, destroyed it in a fit of mischief a few weeks after my
arrival. Lord Wyland punished him most severely and then
bought me the one I wear now as restitution. As it was a gift from
my employer, I could hardly refuse to wear it, you know, my lord.
And indeed, it was quite a generous gesture on your uncle's part.

You will observe there are several expensive plumes on this bonnet, and a silk lining. I will admit that it is not a bonnet I would have chosen if left to myself, but it does very well for me. Most employers prefer their governesses not to look too fine."

"I suppose not," said Paul. He was greatly intrigued by this glimpse into the private life of a governess. Since Mary had not seemed to resent his first question, he decided to risk asking her another one. "Is that why you wear the kind of dresses you wear, too?" he said, indicating her gray serge dress. So closely did it resemble the one she had worn the day before that he had at first been deluded into thinking it the same dress, until a closer look had revealed that this one was drab gray in color instead of drab brown.

Mary knew she ought to snub Paul for asking such a personal question, but his motive seemed to be nothing worse than curiosity. In the same matter-of-fact tone she had used before, she replied, "That is one of the reasons, my lord. This style of dress has also the advantage of utility, and the still greater advantage of warmth. Perhaps you are unaware that your uncle forbade the lighting of fires in the schoolroom before the first of November or after the last of February. If I had worn anything resembling a fashionable dress, I should certainly have frozen."

"Good God," said Paul, taken aback. "Did my uncle think *everything* pleasant must necessarily be sinful as well?"

"I think in this instance he was actuated more by motives of economy, my lord. And seeing that you benefit so greatly by his economy, you can have nothing to cavil at in that."

Mary could not resist adding this last barb, in retribution for his criticism of her dress and bonnet. Paul did not look embarrassed, however, but merely ran his fingers through his hair in his characteristic gesture of bewilderment.

"I suppose not," he said. "But economical or not, that's another one of my uncle's practices that I intend to discontinue. Feel free to light all the fires you like, Miss Grant, whenever and wherever you want them. In fact, I think you'd better tell the maids to light fires in all the rooms until further notice. I hate a cold, dark house, and this one's as cold and dark as they come."

"Indeed," said Mary with feeling. "The maids shall hear your decision with rejoicing, my lord." Finishing the last of her coffee, she pushed back her chair from the table. "I suppose I should be off to the village now and see Miss Eaton."

"And I must be off to Long Medford and see my fugitive butler and cook," said Paul, watching with disapprobation as she resumed her bonnet. "Do you need a ride into the village, Miss Grant? I would be happy to take you in my carriage."

"No, I can take the gig, my lord. That is, I can with your permission. I assure you, I am quite capable of driving it. When your uncle was alive, he was always used to let me take out the gig when I had errands in the village."

"To be sure you may use the gig, Miss Grant. Go see your friend, and if your errand prospers I will hope to see you both at dinner tonight. And if you should happen to find any stray cooks running loose in the village, I beg you will bring one of them back, too—by force if need be." With a grimace, Paul pushed away the remains of his breakfast. "I never thought I was very nice in my requirements, but I find Hannah's cooking insupportable. For the good of my digestion, I would have her replaced by an experienced cook as soon as possible."

Mary laughed. "Very well, my lord," she said. "I won't make any promises, but I'll see what I can do."

Six

Mary was smiling when she left Paul, but her smile had faded somewhat by the time she got to the stables. By the time the gig was harnessed and brought around to her, it had vanished from her face completely. As she mounted the gig, touched the whip to the old horse's flanks, and started the gig down the steep and winding drive, she found herself brooding over the conversation she had just had with Paul in the breakfast room.

It still nettled her that he should have presumed to criticize her appearance. It was no less nettling because his criticisms had been so fully justified. With one hand, Mary reached up to touch her bonnet, then let it drop again with a sigh.

"Perhaps I ought to get a new bonnet," she told herself ruefully. "Now that old Lord Wyland's gone, I suppose I need not make a guy of myself any longer by wearing this one. Adcock's in the village had several pretty hats and bonnets in their shop the last time I was there. And I can certainly afford a new bonnet, since my new employer has been good enough to double my salary."

But this reflection, far from easing Mary's mind, caused new doubts to spring up there. It was, no doubt, very generous of the new Lord Wyland to pay her so lavishly for duties that were no more onerous than her former duties as governess. But was it not possible that he hoped to obtain more with his money than mere assistance in running the house?

This unwelcome idea caused Mary to nearly unseat herself

from the gig. "No!" she said aloud, clutching the reins convulsively and causing the old horse to break into a momentary canter. Mary automatically slowed him to a trot again while she reviewed in her mind all the conversation that had passed between her and Paul that morning. Most particularly did she dwell on that conversation which had followed his offer to double her salary. But she could find nothing suggestive in any of it, barring his remarks about her dress and bonnet, and she still felt these had been actuated by no worse motive than curiosity. Indeed, his willingness to provide her with a chaperone seemed to acquit him of any dishonorable intention.

Nevertheless, Mary felt that it would be as well to err on the side of caution. If she were to suddenly appear in a new, more becoming mode of dress, it was quite possible that Lord Wyland would take it as a compliment to himself and consider it encouragement to pursue her on a less professional level. And as Mary admitted frankly to herself, he would be quite justified in doing so, at least insofar as supposing that the compliment would be intended for him. Ever since he had arrived, she had been conscious of a desire to look well on his account. It was with difficulty that she had prevented herself from primping for him only that very morning. Mary told herself sternly that this was a desire she would have to repress if she wished to continue in his employment. And it followed by the same token that she should continue to wear the bonnet and dresses she had and to preserve at all costs a proper decorum between her and her employer.

"Though I must say, he does not *seem* like a libertine," she told herself wistfully once again. "But then, I have never known any libertines before, and I would not know what they normally behave like. Perhaps he behaves as he does in order to throw his victims off their guard. But really, that seems like unnecessary trouble on his part. With his looks, I would suppose he had women enough throwing themselves at him without going to the bother of seducing them."

Mary continued to ponder this enigma as she piloted the gig along the winding coast road toward the village of Cliffside.

Cliffside was a small hamlet located a few miles south of Wycliff and situated like it on the rocky Yorkshire coast. With such a location it was natural that the principal occupation of most of its residents should be fishing. This was so much the case that Cliffside partook largely of the character of a seaport, with shipping offices, wharves, and warehouses clustered around a natural harbor. Further inland, however, Cliffside lost much of its nautical character and became simply an ordinary provincial village with a scattering of shops, businesses, and residences ranged along its narrow cobbled streets.

Along one of the narrowest and most precipitous of these streets Mary drove the gig, until she came to a large, slightly down-at-heels clapboard house tucked between a tailor's shop and a disreputable-looking establishment professing itself to be an alehouse. There were several gentlemen with pipes and tankards lounging on the front steps of this establishment. They whistled, stamped their feet, and let out loud catcalls at the sight of Mary, but she steadfastly ignored them. Dismounting from the gig, she tethered the horse to the railing and hurried up the steps of the clapboard house.

In the front window of the house was a fly-blown sign with the words "Rooms to Let" emblazoned upon it. Mary knocked, but there was such a tremendous noise of children screaming inside the house that she was doubtful of being heard. Accordingly, after she had knocked once again without receiving any response, she opened the door and stepped into the house's rather dingy front hall.

She was immediately hailed by a stout, slatternly maidservant, who had just come hastening down the corridor from the kitchen regions. "Oh, it's you, Miss Grant. I was just coming to the door, only it took me a minute to get my pastry where I could leave it," said the maidservant, wiping her hands on her apron. "Miss Eaton's in the parlor with those two young devils of Mrs. Mason's. They've been at it hammer and togs all morning, till you can't hardly hear yourself think."

"Thank you, Huldah," said Mary, and directed her steps toward the parlor. The noise grew markedly louder as she approached it. Above a child's infuriated roaring, Mary could hear Miss Eaton's voice patiently remonstrating.

"If you hit her, she will only hit you back, and what will that serve? Much better you should simply ignore her, Betsy. You know she only makes those faces because she knows it annoys you. If you ignored her, or simply laughed at her, she would soon stop of her own accord, and then we could all be comfortable. Why don't you just sit down in the corner with this nice book and—"

Here followed the unmistakable sound of a slap, accompanied by redoubled roars on the part of Betsy and an outraged shriek from her presumable victim. "Now, children," said Miss Eaton wearily. "Children!"

Mary opened the parlor door. Before her, on the faded drugget covering the floor, two small girls wrestled and rolled and roared out threats, only too obviously intent on killing each other. Above them hovered Miss Eaton, wringing her hands in the classic posture of despair.

Mary took in the situation at a glance. "I should think the thing to do would be to douse them with a bucket of water, as if they were a pair of quarreling dogs," she told Miss Eaton, raising her voice to be heard above the racket the two girls were making.

This advice proved unnecessary, however. The sound of her voice had already caused the two girls to suspend their conflict. Releasing their grip on each other's throats, they scrambled to their feet and retreated to the far end of the room, regarding Mary with wide eyes and open mouths.

"I thought someone must be skinning the two of you alive, at the very least," she told them, before turning again to Miss Eaton. "Good morning, Charlotte. I take it Mrs. Mason is away again?"

"Yes, she has gone to visit her mother in Birmingham for a few days," said Miss Eaton, rubbing her forehead wearily. "I am keeping an eye on Betsy and Lettie while she is away."

"I'm hungry," piped up one of the girls opportunely. "I want something to eat."

"I'm hungry, too," said the other immediately. "Can I have something to eat, too?"

"Go and ask Huldah for something," said Miss Eaton. The two girls at once made a mad dash toward the parlor door. "And whatever she gives you, mind you eat it in the kitchen," she called after them. "You know your mother wouldn't want you getting crumbs all over the house, as you did with those biscuits yesterday."

A distant shout was her only answer. Miss Eaton sighed and smiled wanly at Mary. "Children," she said.

"Mrs. Mason's children," corrected Mary. "I refuse to let two bad specimens color my opinion of the whole species. There are good, obedient, well-mannered children in the world somewhere, I'm sure. It simply has not fallen to my lot to encounter any of them in recent years."

"I have known a few," said Miss Eaton, sinking down upon an upholstered armchair. "In the main, however, I must say that most of my pupils more nearly resembled Betsy and Lettie than the cherubs you describe. But there, I don't mean to dwell on my difficulties, Mary. I've been so busy with the girls that I haven't even greeted you. Do take a seat and make yourself comfortable—as comfortable as you can, at any rate, on these abominable chairs. I think Mrs. Mason must have all her furniture stuffed with iron so as to make it wear better."

"I don't understand why you stay on here, Charlotte," said Mary, seating herself gingerly on a singularly unyielding chair. "It cannot be comfortable for you, and it is infamous the way Mrs. Mason expects you to take charge of her dreadful children whenever she is away."

"Yes, but she takes three shillings off my rent for doing so," said Miss Eaton frankly. "And I am not in a position to turn up my nose at three shillings, Mary. Indeed, as boarding houses go, I assure you this is quite a superior one. Betsy and Lettie are a heavy cross, of course, and I could wish Huldah's cooking was better, but in the main I have nothing to complain about."

"Then perhaps you will not be interested in changing your

place," said Mary. "I came here with the intention of luring you away to a new and better one, you see. Or perhaps I should say rather a new and somewhat less faulty one. There will be no Betsy and Lettie to trouble you at Wycliff, which is some improvement at least, but I must warn you that you will find the cooking there no better than it is here. If anything, you will likely find it a good deal worse!"

"At Wycliff?" said Miss Eaton, looking intrigued but mystified. "What place could there possibly be for me there, Mary?"

Mary explained about Paul's arrival, and her need for a respectable woman to bear her company. To her relief, Miss Eaton accepted the story at face value and seemed to find nothing out of the way about the situation.

"And so the new Lord Wyland is here at last," she marveled. "That will put the whole neighborhood in a taking, I have no doubt. Particularly the neighborhood girls! You must remember what a fuss they made over Reverend Biddle when he first came here, simply because he was a bachelor and tolerably good-looking. Why, even now the poor man can hardly walk down the aisle at church without one of them dropping her handkerchief or prayerbook in front of him. It's perfectly shameless the way they pursue him, and they'll be twice as bad with an eligible earl to chase after. Is Lord Wyland as good-looking as Reverend Biddle?"

In Mary's mind rose a clear picture of Paul's handsome face and form. "Better," she said fervently. "Much, much better. About a hundred times better, I should say."

Miss Eaton shook her head. "That will set the cat among the pigeons," she predicted fatalistically. "I expect he's very charming, too? You must watch yourself, Mary, or you'll be succumbing to him yourself."

"He *is* very charming, but I have no intention of succumbing to his charm, Charlotte. I would be a fool if I did, for I happen to know that his reputation is not of the best. His uncle was used to speak of him very severely as a libertine and profligate."

"Oh, well, his uncle was used to speak severely about nearly everyone," said Miss Eaton leniently. "I daresay the stories about this young man have been exaggerated, like most of the stories one hears." As though something in her friend's manner had just struck her, she looked sharply at Mary. "He has not behaved improperly toward you in any way, has he, Mary?"

"Oh, no," Mary made haste to assure her. "It is only that I thought it better to take precautions, Charlotte. You know how dreadfully people talk, and I cannot afford to compromise my reputation if I am ever to get another position after this one. I don't know how long Lord Wyland wants me to stay on, but it can hardly be less than a month. That would give you an opportunity to earn a little extra money and to get away from Betsy and Lettie for a while. Although, as I mentioned, it may not be an improvement so far as the cooking is concerned. Lord Wyland has certainly not been much impressed by Hannah's efforts. When I left today, he told me that if I ran across a good cook in the village, I was to use force if necessary, to bring her back to Wycliff."

Miss Eaton laughed heartily at this speech, but an instant later her expression grew thoughtful. "I wonder," she said. "I just heard today that Sally Fisher's sister was looking for a new place. And she is a very good cook, by all accounts. You ought to go and speak with her, Mary. The Fishers' place is just around the corner from here, you know."

"Yes, I know where it is. That's an excellent notion, Charlotte. I'll go and speak to her as soon as I leave here. But I can't do that until you tell me whether you will come and play chaperone for me." Mary clasped her hands and regarded her friend with an imploring expression that was only half feigned. "Will you, Charlotte? I do wish you would. I am fully decided not to stay on at Wycliff myself unless I can persuade you to stay there with me."

Miss Eaton shook her head with a tolerant smile. "Oh, my dear, you must not speak like that," she said. "If Lord Wyland has offered you such a generous salary as you say, then you would be foolish not to stay on. And really, I see no reason why I may not come and stay with you, as you propose. The only difficulty is that I would not be able to come immediately. I promised Mrs. Mason that I would look after the girls while she was gone, and we do not expect her back until tomorrow."

"I suppose one day will not matter," said Mary. "After all, I've already spent one night in the same house with Lord Wyland and escaped with my virtue intact. I daresay I will be safe enough for another."

She spoke lightly, but Miss Eaton gave her a shocked look. "Oh, my dear, you don't really think there is any chance of his forcing himself on you?" she said in a scandalized voice. "Why, if I thought such a thing, I would find someone else to take charge of Betsy and Lettie and come back with you this instant!"

"You would never find anyone to take charge of those demonic children, and I don't believe it is necessary in any case, Charlotte. Lord Wyland may be a rake, but I am sure he uses charm rather than brute force to make his conquests. And as I said before, I am quite proof against his charm."

Mary made this statement with great firmness, notwithstanding certain inner misgivings that came to mind when she remembered the losing battle she had fought against temptation that morning. Miss Eaton seemed convinced by her show of strength, however, and looked relieved.

"Well, I am glad to hear you say so, Mary. And indeed, it may be that the reports we have had of him are greatly exaggerated. You know it would be unfair to condemn him on his uncle's word alone."

"I am sure old Lord Wyland's word was quite reliable on this point, Charlotte. He told me enough details about his nephew's conduct to convince me of that. But of course his nephew is my employer now, and it will not do for me to gossip about him." With a rather forced smile, Mary rose to her feet. "I shall have to be running along now if I wish to interview Sally Fisher's sister," she told Miss Eaton. "But I'll look forward to seeing you tomorrow, Charlotte. Will it be satisfactory if I send the carriage for you and your baggage sometime in the afternoon—say, around three o'clock?"

"Yes, that should do very well. I'm sure Mrs. Mason will be back by then." Miss Eaton also rose to her feet and extended her hand to Mary. "I must thank you for bringing me this windfall, my dear," she said, squeezing Mary's hand. "I am sure it sounds a very easy and agreeable position, and the extra income will be very welcome, too, I don't deny. And I can't tell you how excited I am at the prospect of coming to Wycliff. You've told me so much about the place that I am quite eager to see it for myself."

As she was speaking, Betsy and Lettie came racing back into the parlor, their faces decorated with smears of jam and honey and their voices upraised in demands that Miss Eaton play with them. Mary thought it best to take leave of her friend while her charges were still in this amicable mood. With a last farewell to Miss Eaton, she went back out to the gig, once again ignoring the whistles and catcalls from the gentlemen next door. A short drive took her to Sally Fisher's house around the corner, where she met with that lady's sister, a Mrs. Bloomfield, who had been employed as cook in a gentleman's house for the past twelve years.

Mrs. Bloomfield seemed a quiet, capable, sober-looking woman, and the references she brought forth for Mary's inspection were irreproachable. After looking them over, Mary had no hesitation about engaging her on the spot, subject to Lord Wyland's approval. Unlike Miss Eaton, Mrs. Bloomfield made no difficulty about taking up her new employment immediately. As soon as she had packed up her modest belongings, Mary helped her load them in the gig and drove her back along the road toward Wycliff.

It was mid-afternoon by this time. The road wound its way high along the rocky cliffs, giving occasional glimpses of the sea below, sparkling in the afternoon sunlight. A stiff breeze ruffled the ribbons of Mrs. Bloomfield's hat and the plumes of Mary's bonnet. As the old horse picked his way carefully along the rough surface of the roadway, Mary reflected that she had accomplished her business in the village with a high degree of success. She wondered if Lord Wyland had fared as well with his business in Long Medford.

Seven

Paul did not arrive back at Wycliff until nearly dinner-time. On entering the house, his first act even before removing his hat and greatcoat was to seek out Mary in the housekeeper's room. This was a matter of intense gratification to Mary, though she strove to hide it behind a businesslike manner as she rose and greeted him.

"I just this minute got back from Long Medford," he told her, pulling off his hat and running his fingers through his hair. "And I had quite the adventures there, as you shall hear during dinner, Miss Grant. But before I went up to change, I wanted to ask you if your errand in the village was successful. Did you speak with your friend? And is she willing to come?"

He sounded so anxious as he asked these questions that Mary experienced another rush of gratification. "Yes, indeed she is willing, my lord. She could not come today, owing to a previous engagement, but I am to send the carriage for her tomorrow afternoon." With a smile, she added, "You will be happy to hear I was also successful in finding you a new cook, my lord. She is in the kitchen cooking even as we speak, and from what I have seen of her work, I believe you will find it more satisfactory than Hannah's."

Here Mary paused. Paul was regarding her with such a singular expression that she felt a sudden qualm about what she had done. "I hope I did not presume too much, my lord?" she asked uncertainly. "Perhaps I should have consulted with you before hiring anyone."

Paul's response to this was to seize Mary's hand in his own and squeeze it fervently. "No, indeed, Miss Grant," he said, with a smile that finished the work which his handclasp had begun. "I am quite willing to abide by your decision in the matter. If I looked surprised just now, it was only because I did not expect you to accomplish so much in such a short time. But there, I don't know why I should be surprised. I could tell from the moment I first laid eyes on you that you were an exceptional young woman. If this new cook proves half as satisfactory as you, she will be a veritable treasure."

Having half crushed Mary's hand in another fervent squeeze, Paul released it and turned to go. "I suppose I'd better run up and change now, or I'll be late for dinner," he told Mary over his shoulder. "It wouldn't do to antagonize my new cook on her first day here!"

After he had gone, Mary gingerly flexed the fingers of her right hand. Nothing appeared to be broken, but she decided it would be as well if she avoided any future expressions of young Lord Wyland's gratitude. The decision was not prompted solely out of concern for her physical welfare. When she recalled the praises he had heaped upon her, she felt such a glow of pleasure as to assure her that she was by no means so impervious to his charms as she had boasted to Miss Eaton.

"Indeed, this won't do," said Mary aloud, shutting the account book she had been working on and rising determinedly from her desk. "I'd better go dress for dinner and try to put all this nonsense out of my mind."

Dinner that evening was altogether a more successful meal than on the evening before. Since Mrs. Bloomfield had only been at Wycliff a few hours, she had had no time to prepare a very extensive menu, but the few dishes she sent to the table were a vast improvement on Hannah's amateur efforts. The service, too, was of a higher caliber than on the evening before, for Smithson had undertaken to fill the role of butler. He handed round the dishes with quiet efficiency and served forth the beverages as though he had been born to the task. There was wine as well as water to serve this evening, for Paul had brought back a few bottles of claret with him from Long Medford.

"Most of what I bought will be delivered by the merchant later this week, but I thought it would be nice if we could have something decent to drink with tonight's dinner. I had supposed, you know, that I would be subjected to another round of Hannah's cooking, and that a little wine would serve to remove the sting, as it were. But it will serve equally well to enhance this delightful meal which Mrs. Bloomfield has prepared for us. May I give you a glass, Miss Grant? You know I hold with my Biblical namesake's opinion that a little wine is good for the stomach."

"Very well, my lord," said Mary, rather surprised to hear him quote St. Paul. For a moment she was reminded of the familiar maxim concerning the devil's willingness to quote scripture to serve his ends. But that was ridiculous, as she quickly assured herself. She had never shared her late employer's prejudice against wine-drinking. Her father, during his lifetime, had regularly taken his glass of port after dinner, and she herself had occasionally drunk wine or champagne punch at parties in younger, happier days. Since coming to Wycliff, however, she had drunk nothing stronger than tea or coffee, and she was conscious now of a faintly guilty sensation as she accepted the glass of wine from Paul. After two or three sips, however, the sense of guilt faded and was replaced by an agreeable sensation of warmth and well-being.

"Indeed, the wine is excellent, my lord," said Mary, finishing off the contents of her glass and permitting Smithson to replenish it with half a glass more. "And the dinner is excellent, too. These cutlets are delicious."

"Yes, Mrs. Bloomfield appears to be an exemplary cook," agreed Paul, helping himself to a third cutlet. "I doubt, however, that she can make a pudding any better than you can, Miss Grant."

He smiled across the table as he spoke. Mary smiled back and took another sip of wine, feeling the glow of pleasure that his compliments always aroused in her. Tonight, owing to the wine perhaps, the sensation was much stronger than usual. Mary felt all at once a little light-headed and set down her glass rather hastily.

"No more wine, thank you," she told Smithson, who was hovering close at hand with the decanter. Having taken a long draught of water as an antidote, she arranged her features into a look of businesslike efficiency and turned again to Paul. "You said you would tell me at dinner about your business in Long Medford," she reminded him. "Was it successful? Clearly you were successful in your visit to the wine merchant."

"Yes, I did attend to that, but that was only a side issue, as you know. My chief business was seeing to this affair of my uncle's fugitive butler and cook. I talked to the magistrate first, then went over to the gaol and had an interview with Mr. and Mrs. Steadman."

For a moment Paul sat silent, looking down at his plate. At last he glanced up at Mary with a rather embarrassed smile. "I must confess I could not help feeling sorry for the Steadmans after I had spoken to them. You know that under the terms of my late uncle's will, they received no legacy, but were merely recommended to the generosity of his successor. Of course, at the time the will was made, my uncle expected that his successor would be his son, Lord Wycliff. And I daresay he never imagined that clause would be called into play in any case, since Lord Wycliff was not likely to succeed to the title until after Mr. and Mrs. Steadman were retired from service. But as you know, the event proved otherwise."

"Yes," said Mary, as he seemed to expect some answer. "I remember the Steadmans being quite upset when the terms of the will were made known to us all."

"Really, I don't know that I blame them. Even assuming his

son was to be his successor, my uncle seems to have managed the business in a rather haphazard manner. The Steadmans had both been in his service for over twenty years, you know."

"Yes, I know," said Mary. "They had been at Wycliff longer than any of the servants except your uncle's bailiff."

"That's right. And when they found they were dependent on my generosity for their legacy, it was a great blow to them. They had somehow gotten the idea that I was a heartless wastrel who was unlikely to give away anything I wasn't absolutely obliged to under the terms of the will. I suppose my lack of response to your letters must have confirmed them in the idea." Paul smiled ruefully at Mary across the table. "So after waiting a few months, they decided to take matters into their own hands and make off with the silver."

Mary nodded. "Yes, it was I who discovered it was missing," she said. "They did not take all the silver, you know, but only a few of the larger pieces."

"So I understood from the Steadmans. They explained at great length that they had only taken enough to equal the legacy they felt they ought to have received. I was altogether impressed by the modesty of their claims. And when you consider that they have already spent four months in gaol as punishment for their crime and might be further punished by transportation or even hanging if the matter came to trial—really, the whole situation borders almost on tragedy. I wish heartily I had come here immediately after my uncle died, as was my first intention."

"So what did you decide to do in the end?" asked Mary curiously. "What is to be the Steadmans' fate?"

"Ah, that was no easy matter to decide, Miss Grant, I do assure you. Sorry as I was for what had happened, I felt I had to draw the line at taking them back into service. Theft is theft, after all, even if theirs was in a measure justified. So I ordered them released, gave them twenty pounds apiece, and advised them to seek their fortunes somewhere other than Yorkshire." Paul stopped and looked at Mary, who was regarding him with astonishment. "You look surprised, Miss Grant. Do you think I should have done more for them?"

So humble was his voice in asking this question that Mary was both touched and a little amused. "Oh, no," she said. "If anything, I should say you did too much, my lord. The Steadmans did commit a crime, after all. I quite agree that they should not have been punished further after spending so many months in gaol, but to give them money in addition seems almost like rewarding criminal behavior."

Paul ran his fingers through his hair. "I see what you mean," he admitted. "Still, forty pounds is less than the legacy they would have received if they had behaved honestly. And they are neither of them hardened criminals, after all. I had hoped that by giving them the money, I was enabling them to put this whole ugly business behind them and make a fresh start elsewhere."

He looked at Mary so wistfully as he made this statement that she felt compelled to reassure him. "Indeed, your behavior was very generous, my lord," she said warmly. "And it's true that the Steadmans never showed any signs of dishonesty up till now. Let us hope they have learned from their experience and will keep to the right side of the law after this."

"Yes, let us hope," said Paul, brightening somewhat. He picked up his wineglass and held it aloft with an air of mock solemnity. "Let us have a toast, Miss Grant: a toast to the Steadmans' rehabilitation. And we must also drink to Mrs. Bloomfield's fine cooking, and to the enterprise of Miss Grant, who was instrumental in bringing her here." He drank off the wine in his glass, then turned to Smithson. "Smithson, please carry my compliments to Mrs. Bloomfield. An excellent meal, and your service was excellently rendered as well." Turning to Mary again, he added, "Shall we adjourn to the drawing room, Miss Grant?"

Mary, still in a glow from wine and compliments, readily agreed. "For we do need to go over the household accounts together," she told him, striving to be conscientious in spite of her exalted mood. "This evening will be as good a time as any.

Please excuse me, my lord, if you please. It won't take me a minute to fetch my ledgers from the housekeeper's room."

Paul pulled a face at this proposal, but made no demur. "You intend to keep my nose to the grindstone, I see," he said, pushing back his chair from the table. "Very well, Miss Grant. I'll meet you in the drawing room in a few minutes."

He was already seated on the drawing room sofa when Mary came in, bearing a stack of ledgers in her arms. A cheerful fire crackled and burned in the fireplace, and several branches of candles had been lit, bathing the room in a golden light. "Do take a seat, Miss Grant," he said, rising at her entrance and indicating with a smiling bow that she was to seat herself on the sofa beside him.

Somewhat self-consciously, Mary did so, clutching her ledgers to her chest. She felt suddenly shy in Paul's company. Although she tried to tell herself that this was only a business consultation and he was only her employer, still she could not help being aware that he was a man as well as her employer, and a singularly attractive man at that. The candlelight gleamed off his dark blond head and touched his features with a subtle glow, making him look, if possible, even more staggeringly handsome than before. Mary thought he looked magnificent, and it was with an effort that she wrenched her eyes away from him and opened the first ledger.

"If you will just verify these numbers, my lord," she said. "All this was done some months ago by the former housekeeper, but I can probably explain anything you have a question about."

Paul took the ledger and bent over it. Mary tried to keep her eyes on the ledger, too, but in spite of herself they kept straying to her companion's face. He read with concentration, his brows drawn together and his expression deeply absorbed. "He really is tremendously handsome," Mary thought, before she caught herself and made herself look away again. Folding her hands in her lap, she fixed her gaze on the fireplace. Beside her, she could hear Paul's measured breathing and an occasional rustle as he turned over a page in the ledger. They were the only sounds in the room besides the crackle of the fire in the grate. As Mary sat regarding the dancing flames, she was conscious of a growing tension inside her. When Paul spoke suddenly, her heart gave such a galvanic start that it was all she could do to keep from jumping.

"This number here," said Paul, pointing to a figure in the ledger. "Does this represent the whole amount of coal and firewood ordered for the quarter, do you think, or only for the month?"

Composing herself as well as she could, Mary bent down to look at the ledger. "The quarter, my lord," she said in a slightly breathless voice. "I am sure she means it for the quarter."

"But see what she has written here," said Paul, pointing to another line in the ledger. Mary bent down to read the line he indicated. Paul shifted the ledger to his other knee to allow her to see it more clearly, and in doing so his arm brushed against hers. Its touch affected Mary like an electric shock. She drew back sharply, conscious that her heart was beating fast and that there were little frissons of alarm and excitement running up and down her spine.

"I do not think . . . I am quite sure she means it for the quarter, my lord," said Mary, running her tongue over lips that had suddenly become dry. "She has merely written 'month' in error."

"Do you think so? I am not so sure, Miss Grant. See how she has arrived at this figure here—and here. I think she does mean month, though heaven knows it's an extravagant sum for a month's worth of coal and firewood. Especially considering how miserly my uncle was about lighting fires. One wonders if someone, somewhere, wasn't lining their pockets with the excess."

With a feeling that was half reluctance and half something else, Mary bent down to look at the ledger once more. As she read through the figures, she could feel Paul's breath warm on her cheek. This sensation affected her even more powerfully than the touch of his arm had done a moment before. She had always been aware of him in a physical sense, but now that awareness was heightened to a nearly unbearable degree. She was acutely conscious of his arm resting behind her on the back of the sofa; and of his leg, sheathed in fawn-colored stockinette, brushing the skirt of her dress. Even as she noted this, he shifted slightly on the sofa, so that his leg touched hers for a brief instant. Brief as it was, that touch seemed to set Mary's whole body trembling.

"Yes, I think you are right, my lord," she said, in a voice noticeably weaker than the one she had used before. "As you say, it is an extravagant figure, but she quite clearly means it for the quarter."

"For the month, you mean," said Paul, glancing at her curiously.

"Yes, of course," said Mary. "Here, you had better look at these later accounts, my lord. I can answer much better for them, as they were done by myself. I am sure we have had no such expenses for fuel since I have taken over the housekeeping. But of course that might simply be attributable to the milder weather this spring and summer, and to the reduced number of persons living in the house."

She presented Paul with the second of the ledgers, contriving at the same time to draw away from him slightly on the sofa. He opened the ledger and bent over it, running his fingers through his hair with an absorbed frown. As Mary watched him, she found herself imagining what his hair must feel like to the touch. It looked thick and lustrous and fine as silk. Indeed, with the candlelight gleaming off it, it strongly resembled silk, or some even finer substance: spun gold, perhaps. Mary felt a sudden impulsive urge to reach out and run her own fingers through it. She wondered what Paul would do if she did. If he were the rake his uncle had described him, he might well respond by making an assault on her virtue. And it was a question whether she could withstand such an assault in her present state of susceptibility. If he were to suddenly sweep her into his arms and lower his lips to hers—

"Well, all seems to be in order here," said Paul, shutting the ledger and smiling at Mary. "You seem to keep accounts as admirably as you do everything else, Miss Grant. Have you anything more to show me?"

Mutely, Mary picked up the last of the ledgers and handed it to him. Opening it, he lay it on his lap and began to read through its entries as he had the other two. Mary, conscious of her danger, felt she ought not to watch him, but she watched him nevertheless, admiring his profile as he bent over the ledger. A lock of hair hung over his forehead, accenting its noble form. Beneath the fine arch of his brows, his vivid blue eyes were narrowed in concentration as he studied the columns of numbers.

Mary's gaze dwelt caressingly on these details, then went on to admire the clean, strong lines of his nose and jaw. Lastly, her eyes came to rest upon his mouth, that same mouth which a moment before she had been visualizing in the act of ravishing hers. It was in all respects a handsome mouth, possessing both strength and sensitivity in its modeling. There was about it none of the overtly sensual quality Mary would have expected in a libertine. Yet its effect on her was far more devastating than a mouth overtly sensual could have been. As she gazed at it, she found herself imagining again, in greater detail, what it would feel like to be kissed by that mouth. She could imagine Paul's arms around her, crushing her close against him; she could imagine his eyes looking deeply into her own; she could imagine her whole body aflame with excitement as he slowly lowered his lips to hers. . . .

And suddenly Mary found she was not merely imagining but longing for such an embrace. Her skin tingled in anticipation of Paul's touch, and she felt as though a touch would be sufficient to ensure her surrender. Already there was a hungry ache inside of her that forcibly reminded her of her dream the night before. As she stared fixedly at Paul, he suddenly turned his head and looked directly at her.

"Well, Miss Grant, I don't see—," he began, then stopped short as his eyes met hers. For a long moment he looked at her without speaking. Mary looked back at him, also without speaking. She felt as though a spell had been cast over her, making it equally impossible for her to speak or look away.

At last, and seemingly with an effort, Paul withdrew his gaze from hers. "I don't see any difficulty here, either, Miss Grant," he said, glancing down at the ledger again. "Your accounts are admirably clear, and everything seems to be in order."

He spoke in quite a natural voice, but Mary observed that a faint flush had appeared on the back of his neck. "That's good," she said, hardly knowing what she said.

"Oh, yes," agreed Paul, in a voice slightly less natural than before. "Very good indeed." With great care he shut the ledger, placed it meticulously atop the other two on the table, and leaned back. "Well," he said, looking briefly at Mary and then away again. "Well. . . ."

"Well," began Mary, then could think of nothing more to say. They sat in silence for what seemed a very long time. When a log in the fireplace suddenly collapsed, sending out a shower of sparks, both of them jumped at the sound. Paul cleared his throat.

"Well," he said again.

But by this time Mary was beginning to be mistress of herself once more. The shower of sparks had reminded her of one of the late Lord Wyland's Sunday harangues, in which he had described the fiery fate that awaited sinners in hell. A particularly warm spot had been reserved for those unfortunates who succumbed to the temptations of the flesh. And Mary knew she was being tempted in this regard: tempted so that it was a question whether she possessed the necessary strength of will to flee.

Summoning up all that remained of her resolution, she rose shakily to her feet. "I must go," she said, in a voice as tremulous as her legs. "Please excuse me, my lord. It is necessary that I go now."

"Must you?" asked Paul. Mary did not dare look at him. Even the sound of his voice—and more particularly, the disappointed note in it—made it difficult to keep her resolution.

"Yes," said Mary, keeping her face averted. "Good evening, my lord." Picking up the ledgers, she left the drawing room as fast as her shaky legs would carry her.

Eight

After Mary had gone, Paul remained sitting where he was on the drawing room sofa. He could not have explained what had just taken place between the two of them a moment before, but he felt rather dazed by it. It gave him a strange thrill when he remembered that instant when he and Mary had looked into each other's eyes. She had beautiful eyes, intensely dark and deep, yet possessing a spark of fire in their depths.

Nor were her eyes her only beauty. It was difficult to see it with her hair scraped back and her figure swathed in a shapeless sack of gray serge, but she was really an attractive woman altogether. With her hair arranged differently, and her figure set off by a more becoming style of dress—

Here Paul caught himself, with a sensation of guilt. It was none of his business to imagine Mary Grant in another style of dress, becoming or otherwise. She might be an attractive woman, but she was also his employee, and it was unconscionable of him to think of her in any other capacity. He reminded himself that she had been within an amesace of quitting his service that morning only because she fancied it improper to work for a bachelor employer. She would think it a thousand times more improper if she knew the kind of thoughts he had just been entertaining about her. Paul could not quite rid himself of the conviction that he had felt *something* between them, there on the sofa a few minutes ago, but he told himself firmly that it had been only his imagination.

Mary herself was under no such delusion. After leaving Paul, she had gone up to her bedchamber, which like the other servants' rooms lacked any source of heat and thus possessed a distinctly frigid atmosphere at that season of the year. But even after she had stripped to her chemise and splashed cold water on her face, arms, and neck, she still felt as though she were in a fever. Distractedly she began to walk back and forth across the room, endeavoring to calm herself by this exercise. But the room was too small to allow her to take more than a few steps in either direction, and at last she ceased pacing and seated herself on the edge of the bed.

"Whatever am I to do?" she said aloud.

She felt she could never forget the scene that had just taken place between her and Paul. Every detail was seared into her memory, and the remembrance of those details made her burn with a higher fever than before. It had been intolerable sitting there on the sofa with Paul's arm brushing hers and his breath warm on her neck: intolerable and intolerably arousing. Mary burned and blushed and burned again as she lived through it all once more. And then there had been that heart-stopping moment when he had looked up and caught her staring at him. How he had looked at her then—silently and searchingly, almost as though he were reading her thoughts. Mary suspected that he *had* been reading her thoughts. If he had been ignorant of her feelings previous to that moment, she felt grimly certain that he could not be ignorant now.

Nor could she be ignorant of the nature of those feelings. Never in her life had she felt such a powerful physical attraction for a man, not even for her former fiancé. She had admired and respected Francis, and had loved him with a tender, almost maternal affection, but the few mild attempts at lovemaking he had essayed during their engagement had not affected her half so much as the mere act of sharing a sofa with Paul. This was a mortifying reflection to Mary, but she could not deny that it was so. With a sensation of mingled shame and guilt, she folded her arms over her chest and told herself once more that she had never been worthy of Francis.

"To be attracted to a man, merely because he has a handsome face and charming manners. And that man an out-and-out libertine, not fit to tie the laces of poor Francis's shoes. You *should* be ashamed, Mary," she berated herself. "You know very well that what you are feeling is nothing more or less than—oh, I can't say it. Yes, I can, though. Lust," she said aloud, speaking the word resolutely. "What you are feeling is lust, Mary, just like old Lord Wyland used to thunder about during his Sunday sermons. Lust . . . what an ugly word it is, heavy and lumpish and ending in a hiss. But I suppose the word is no uglier than the thing itself. In any case, I don't intend to give way to it. Whenever I see Lord Wyland, I must simply remind myself that he is a libertine and profligate and endeavor to keep my distance from him until I come to my senses."

Yet even as she made this resolution, Mary feared she was being simplistic in attributing the whole of her attraction for Paul to merely physical causes. This was clear enough from the way her heart sprang to defend him when she tried to dismiss him as a libertine. After all, she had only his uncle's word for it that he deserved such a title, and Lord Wyland had been highly accomplished at picking motes out of the eyes of his fellow men while ignoring much larger obstructions in his own. In his blindness, might he not have exaggerated the depths of his nephew's depravity?

Mary wanted to believe it, and there were several circumstances which gave her hope. For one thing, if the new Lord Wyland had been as immoral a man as his uncle had claimed, he would never have behaved so generously by the Steadmans. And she could not forget the way he had repeated the Steadmans' unfavorable view of his character when he had been describing his day's activities to Mary during dinner. "They had the idea I was a heartless wastrel," he had said. There had been no self-consciousness in his voice, but rather a note of hurt, as though he could not imagine anyone holding such a mistaken opinion of him.

Surely if a man was a heartless wastrel, he would be aware of the fact and would be amused rather than hurt by other people's criticisms, Mary told herself hopefully. But on second consideration, she was forced to acknowledge the fallacy of such reasoning. People were notably poor judges of their own characters. The late Lord Wyland, for instance, had considered himself a model of Christian rectitude, and his son had often boastingly referred to himself as a good boy, even when his behavior had done nothing to support such a claim.

It was all too likely that the new Lord Wyland, in common with most of humanity, kept a blind eye to his own failings and perceived himself to be a very good sort of fellow. Or—even worse possibility—it might be that his act of innocence was merely that: an act designed to inspire in Mary the very doubts she was struggling with right now.

This idea made Mary wince as though she had been struck. But when she had considered it carefully, she was thankful to find several points that argued against it. In the first place, why would Lord Wyland go to so much trouble to deceive a mere governess? In order to seduce her? But he had made no attempt to seduce her that evening. Indeed, if the truth were admitted, his behavior had been more restrained than Mary's own.

And though his manner had become less restrained toward the end, Mary acknowledged to herself that her own forward conduct had probably been responsible for that. Altogether it seemed most likely that he had never intended to seduce her at all, and that his reasons for keeping her at Wycliff were exactly what he had told her in the first place: namely, a desire to retain her services until he had his household running smoothly.

This thought ought to have been a comfort to Mary. In actual fact, however, she found it profoundly depressing. This, more than anything, served to enlighten her as to the state of her own feelings.

"You are a fool," she told herself severely, as she got into bed and tried to settle herself to sleep. "It's insufferable vanity on your part, Mary. Why would he waste time trying to seduce a mere governess, when he could probably have his pick of the most beautiful women in London? In all likelihood, this whole business has been a figment of your overheated imagination. Until he gives you more reason than he has to suppose he has designs on your virtue, you'd better just do your job and not indulge in any more flights of fancy. Thank heaven Charlotte is coming tomorrow. Having her around will help me to keep my feet on the ground—and more importantly, it will keep me from having any more dangerous *tête-à-têtes* with Lord Wyland. Poor man! I begin to think Charlotte's main business will be to protect him from me, rather than the other way around!"

Miss Eaton arrived at Wycliff the following afternoon, accompanied by half a dozen shabby bags and boxes and bursting with eagerness to take up her new position. Her belongings were carried to the room that had been prepared for her, while butler pro tem Smithson ushered her into the housekeeper's room where Mary was working.

"Here I am, you see, my dear," Miss Eaton told Mary buoyantly. Having thanked Smithson and waited for him to take himself off, she turned again to her friend with a joyous air.

"Oh, Mary, I feel as though I had just escaped from prison. You can't imagine how happy I am to be here. This is quite the house, isn't it? All twists and turns—a regular labyrinth. I am sure I lost myself at least three times when your butler was taking me through it just now. If I had known what I was getting into, I would have borrowed Theseus's trick and come armed with a ball of string!"

"At least we have no Minotaur in this labyrinth," said Mary, extending her hand affectionately to her friend. "Our only resident monster is Lord Wyland, and you will find him a tractable enough creature on the whole."

Miss Eaton looked sober. "I hope so," she said. Lowering

her voice to a whisper, she added, "I trust you had no difficulties last night, my dear?"

"None at all," said Mary, forcing a light laugh. "Such a dashing beau as Lord Wyland would have no use for a dowdy creature like me, you know, even as an object of seduction."

Miss Eaton looked her over critically. "Well, I don't know," she said. "You're a handsome woman, Mary, though it's true you don't make much of your advantages. Is it necessary to pull your hair back so very tight? And that dress, my dear! I'm all for economy myself, but it looks to me as though it ought to have been consigned to the rag basket long ago."

Mary, who from various motives had chosen to wear her gray serge again that day, looked down at herself self-consciously. "Perhaps this dress is a little worn, but you know I have no taste for finery, Charlotte," she said. "If Lord Wyland wants his employees to look like fashion plates, he will have to be content with you!"

Miss Eaton, who was clad at the moment in a serviceable dark wool pelisse, stout boots, and a plain bonnet, laughed and shook her head. "Stuff and nonsense," she said. "I'm no fashion plate, as you well know, my dear. However, I don't know but I shall outshine *you,* seeing you make so little show of yourself! You'd better take me to my room, so I can decide which of my dazzling dresses I'm going to appear in this evening."

The dress she chose was a black bombazine, slightly shiny about the seams but still comparing favorably to Mary's gray serge. "Are you not going to change, my dear?" she asked Mary, who had stayed in the room with her friend to help her unpack and dress.

"No," said Mary, who had already fought and won a personal battle on this subject. "I'll just fetch my shawl from my room, and then we can go down."

Miss Eaton accompanied Mary to her room on the top floor while she fetched her shawl. "Oh, my dear, is this your room?" she exclaimed, looking around the tiny chamber in dismay. "And you have given me all that lovely set of rooms downstairs!

Don't say Lord Wyland will not allow you better accommodation than this?"

"I have no idea whether he would or not," said Mary, removing her shawl from the battered chest of drawers and shaking it out briskly. "He has never troubled himself to ask about my accommodations."

"No, and very queer it would look if he did! However, I daresay he would allow you to change rooms if you asked him, Mary. You said he was quite a tractable gentleman. And there must be at least a dozen bedchambers in this house—real bedchambers, I mean, not chilly little cells like this."

"Actually there are closer to two dozen, Charlotte. But I assure you, I have no wish to change my quarters. It's only fitting that you should have one of the best bedchambers since you are in the way of being a guest here, but I have had this room ever since coming to Wycliff, and it suits me very well."

Miss Eaton shook her head dubiously. "You seem determined to be uncomfortable as well as unattractive," she observed, as they went down the stairs together. "I do not understand you, Mary. If I didn't know better, I'd say some of old Lord Wyland's odd religious scruples must have rubbed off on you." Not giving Mary any chance to respond to this statement, she went on in a confidential voice. "Upon my word, I find myself a little nervous about meeting the new Lord Wyland. I feel like one of those unfortunate girls in the fairy tales, when they are about to encounter the ogre of the castle!"

Mary laughed. "Whatever else Lord Wyland may be, I don't think he is an ogre, Charlotte," she said, leading her friend across the drafty hall toward the drawing room. "But you can judge for yourself in a moment. I suspect we will find him waiting for us in the drawing room."

As Mary had predicted, Paul was already in the drawing room, stretched out on the sofa with a newspaper. He put the paper aside, however, and stood up as the two ladies entered the room. "This must be Miss Eaton," he said, advancing toward that lady with a smile. "It is very good of you to come to us like this, ma'am—very good indeed. I trust Miss Grant has made you comfortable?"

"Yes, very," said Miss Eaton, regarding him with fascination. "And so *you* are Lord Wyland?"

"So they tell me," he replied, with a bow. "I still find it rather hard to believe myself, ma'am, truth to tell. But I can't see that I have any alternative. If it's a dream, it's been going on longer than any dream I've ever had before! You seem real enough at any rate," he continued, looking the ex-schoolmistress over with approval. "Miss Grant, I congratulate you once again on having admirably filled the bill. Your friend looks as though she will be a valuable addition to our household."

"To *your* household, you mean," said Mary, far too loudly. Fortunately, neither of the others heard her, for Paul was addressing Miss Eaton with an air at once smiling and deferential.

"I am very pleased to make your acquaintance, ma'am," he said, taking her hand and bowing over it. "Miss Grant has spoken of you very highly, and I do appreciate your coming to us this way, on such short notice. Has she explained about your duties?"

"Why, yes, I think so," said Miss Eaton, still regarding him with fascination. "As Mary described them, I cannot think they will tax me overmuch, my lord! But I expect I can also help a bit about the house and so justify my keep."

"That would certainly be very kind of you. A place this size must necessarily be a great deal of work to run, and though Miss Grant makes no complaint, I am sure she would appreciate your assistance. Of course, we must take that into account when settling your salary. I had thought—" Paul lowered his voice still further and spoke for several minutes, while Miss Eaton listened in absorbed silence. "I trust that will be satisfactory?"

"Oh, yes," said Miss Eaton in a failing voice. "Entirely satisfactory, my lord!"

Smithson appeared in the drawing room doorway just then, with the announcement that dinner was ready. Paul offered Miss Eaton his arm, then turned to Mary. "Unfortunately we have no suitable escort to take you in, Miss Grant. But my other arm is at your service if you would condescend to accept it," he told her with a smile.

"That is not at all necessary, my lord," said Mary, drawing herself apart and wrapping her shawl more closely around her. "I thank you, but I can go in by myself."

"Just as you like, of course," said Paul pleasantly. Miss Eaton threw Mary an exasperated look, which Mary pretended not to see. Silently she followed the other two into the dining room and seated herself at the table while Paul was assisting Miss Eaton into her seat. She continued silent throughout dinner, but her silence went largely unnoticed, for Miss Eaton was busy giving Paul a description of the neighborhood and of the families he was likely to meet during his stay at Wycliff.

"The Foleys are pleasant people whom you are certain to encounter if you go out socially. And then, of course, there is our local magistrate, Mr. Rundell. He has a very considerable property not far from here, just on the other side of the village."

"Yes, I have already made the acquaintance of Mr. Rundell," said Paul, helping her and Mary to a ragout of lobster. "I met him yesterday when I was in Long Medford. He seems a very pleasant, courteous old gentleman."

"Oh, he is, my lord. I often see him in Cliffside, and he never fails to bow to me, although our acquaintance is of the slightest. I believe his wife is very pleasant, too, although I am not personally acquainted with her. I do know his daughters, however: Fanny, Sophy, and Gussy. I believe everyone in Cliffside knows them, for they often come into the village to do their shopping. Most people hold Fanny, the eldest, to be the prettiest girl in the neighborhood, though to my mind, Miss Gussy, the youngest, is much more appealing. However, I expect Mr. Rundell will be inviting you to dinner at the Manor one of these days, my lord, and then you can judge for yourself."

"Indeed," said Paul pleasantly. "He did speak of inviting me to dinner the other day when we were talking over some legal matters in which I find myself concerned. Are dinner parties the usual form of entertainment hereabouts?"

"They are the most common, I would say, although we do have the occasional ball or rout-party to liven us up. And then, of course, there are monthly assemblies over at Long Medford. Since they're public assemblies, they naturally attract a rather mixed crowd, but even people of very high standing do not scruple to attend them. The Misses Rundell go regularly, I believe, and so do Sir Stanley Summerville's daughters when they are staying at Summerville Place."

"I am sure they must be very enjoyable parties. Have you ever attended them, Miss Grant?" asked Paul, turning to Mary.

Mary gave him a brief look, then returned her attention to her plate of ragout. "Never," she said shortly. "Obviously you are unaware of your uncle's views on dancing, my lord. He considered the assemblies at Long Medford little better than orgies and would certainly have discharged me from his service if I had ever shown any inclination to attend one."

"Of course, I ought to have guessed as much," said Paul easily. Miss Eaton, however, threw Mary a reproachful look, and when dinner was over and the two ladies were alone in the drawing room, she wasted no time in taking her young friend to task for her conduct.

"You were rather short with Lord Wyland during dinner, were you not, my dear? You know he could not be expected to know all his uncle's odd quirks as well as you do. And I thought you were rather short with him earlier, too, when he offered to take you into the dining room. Why do you dislike him so much? He seems to me quite a charming young man."

"He's a libertine," said Mary shortly. "It's his business to be charming."

Miss Eaton shook her head doubtfully. "Indeed, I find it hard to believe his character is as bad as you say," she said. "He seems such a pleasant young man—though at the same time, I can easily see that he would be very attractive to women. I don't think I ever saw a better-looking man, and he seems quite intelligent, too. So many good-looking men are quite dull, you know, able to talk about nothing but sport and such trifles. Yes,

I can easily see why Lord Wyland would be popular with women, but I daresay, if the truth were known, they do more pursuing of him than he does of them. I don't like to speak ill of my own sex, but really, it is disgusting the way women will throw themselves at a good-looking man."

"Indeed," said Mary, to whom this was a home thrust. "I do not pretend to know the details of all Lord Wyland's affairs, but I heard enough from his uncle to convince me that his past conduct will not bear close scrutiny."

Miss Eaton smiled. "Upon my word, my dear, I don't think any of our past conduct could bear close scrutiny if old Lord Wyland was doing the scrutinizing," she said. "That man could have found fault with the behavior of a saint."

Mary grudgingly admitted this. "But you know, Charlotte, there is more to it than that," she added. "If old Lord Wyland had only criticized his nephew's conduct in general terms, I would be tempted to believe as you do. But it happens that he was quite specific in his criticisms. He mentioned dates and names—one name, at any rate, and I have no doubt he could have named many more if he had wanted to. That you cannot discount so easily, Charlotte."

Miss Eaton made no answer, but drew a sigh that seemed to acknowledge the truth of Mary's statement. "At any rate, this young man does have charming manners," she said, with an air of giving the devil his due. "And he is certainly very generous. My dear, he is paying me fifteen pounds a quarter, and that is without taking into account my room and board! I nearly fell over when he told me."

"That *was* very generous of him," Mary admitted.

"Yes, it's twice as much as I ever received for teaching. It is very wicked of me to say so, no doubt, but for such a princely salary I think I can overlook a few indiscretions in my employer's past. And I would advise you to do the same, my dear. If he were to behave indiscreetly now, of course, with the two of us in the house, that would be a different matter. But I don't think we need worry about that. He appears intent on behaving well now, whatever his behavior in the past may have been. I am sure he will never do anything to put us to the blush."

Mary was not called on to reply to this statement, for Paul came into the drawing room just then, prompting a general change of subject. Miss Eaton's remarks had made a strong impression on her, however, and she thought about them often that evening, as well as in the days that followed.

She had plenty of time for thinking, for the presence of Miss Eaton had done a great deal to make her daily tasks less numerous as well as less onerous. Before many days had passed, Mary found that nearly all of her household duties had been usurped by her friend and that she was left with little more than bookkeeping.

Now, instead of Mary, it was Miss Eaton who issued the maids' daily orders and saw to it that they were carried out. It was she who arranged the day's menus with Mrs. Bloomfield, and she who found a couple of sturdy young men to replace the footmen who had fled at the first diagnosis of smallpox in the area. The same air of calm authority that had enabled her to successfully impart the rudiments of education to several generations of reluctant pupils served her equally well now in this capacity, as did her warm smile and unfailingly sunny disposition.

"Why should I not be cheerful?" she asked, when Mary expressed surprise at her seeming contentment. "I never had such an easy job in my life, or one that put me in such pleasant surroundings. You can't think what a relief it is to escape from boarding house life, my dear. What with Betsy and Lettie's constant wrangling, and Huldah's sour bread and stringy beef—but there, I ought not to complain. Mrs. Mason's house may have been no paradise, but it was far better than some of the boarding places I've had over the years. However, it doesn't begin to compare to this place. I thank heaven every night that I had the opportunity to come here, Mary. Not only has it enabled me to put away a little more money for later on, but it has allowed me to feel myself useful again. When one grows older, people are rather apt to treat one as though one were merely so much superfluous clutter, I find."

"I suppose they do," said Mary, feeling a pang of guilt. She supposed she ought to feel grateful that the difficulties facing her were so much less than the ones that faced Miss Eaton. At the very least she ought to share her friend's gratitude in being gainfully employed. But in spite of her comparative good fortune, she could not quite share Miss Eaton's contented state of mind.

Perhaps part of the trouble was that she had so little to do. Now that the house was more or less fully staffed again, with Miss Eaton doing most of the housekeeping duties, she found herself with altogether too much time for reflection. And the subject for her reflection, more often than not, was Paul.

It was not that she wanted to think about him. She did her conscientious best to push him out of her thoughts whenever he appeared there, but the feelings she had acknowledged after that momentous *tête-à-tête* in the drawing room would not be so easily denied. The awareness lurked beneath the surface of her thoughts like a constant physical ache. The ache was a hundred times worse when she was actually in Paul's company, yet she often found herself inventing excuses to go where he was, merely for the painful pleasure of seeing him and perhaps exchanging a few words with him. It was a constant struggle to deny herself these unhappy indulgences, but for the most part she did deny herself and took care to keep out of his way during the morning and early afternoon.

In the evenings, of course, it was a different matter. Mary could not avoid seeing Paul then, for if she had sought to excuse herself from the dinner table, he and Miss Eaton would have joined forces to argue her back. At all events, this was Mary's excuse for appearing punctually in the dining room night after night, though she sometimes suspected that it was only another instance of self-indulgent weakness on her part. But it was an indulgence she could not deny herself, even though it brought her more pain than pleasure.

Paul was always very kind to her on these occasions. He often made efforts to draw her into conversation, but though Mary could not resist the opportunity to see and listen to him, she could and did refuse to converse with him more than was necessary for civility's sake. She sat silently at the table, picking over her food, while he and Miss Eaton argued cheerfully about politics and foreign policy.

When dinner was over, as soon as she possibly could, Mary would excuse herself from the drawing room and go up to her own room.

As time went on, however, these stratagems became less necessary. It began to be a regular thing for Paul to be away from home at least one or two evenings a week. In the course of his activities about the neighborhood, he had made the acquaintance of several local families and often received invitations to dine and spend the evening at their homes. His absence ought to have been a relief to Mary, and in a way it was a relief not to eat her dinner with that sick ache of longing in the pit of her stomach. But she found, often as not, that the ache of longing was replaced by an ache of jealousy. She was jealous of the Sir Stanleys and Mr. Rundells that took him away from her, and she felt physically ill when she envisioned the Misses Summerville and Rundell clustering around him, smiling their sweetest and doing their best to make him fall in love with them.

"This won't do," Mary told herself over and over, as she grappled nightly with the twin demons of longing and jealousy. "I can't go on like this or I'll lose my health, if I don't lose my mind first. And I can't afford to lose either one when I have my living to earn. I don't see any way around it. I'm going to have to leave Wycliff, and the sooner, the better."

Yet the thought of leaving Wycliff was so painful to Mary as to make her other sufferings seem negligible. She feared she lacked the self-discipline to make such an enormous sacrifice. "I should have left in the beginning, as soon as I knew my weakness," she reproached herself unhappily. "What am I to do now? What will become of me?"

Mary had no answer to these questions. She could only resolve to go on as she was and hope that somehow, in some way, a merciful providence would provide an escape from her increasingly intolerable situation.

Nine

Paul's days at Wycliff were very busy ones, as he set about acquainting himself with his new property and the tenants who farmed it. As Mary had observed, his evenings were beginning to be busy, too, for as he had become better acquainted with his neighbors, he found himself the recipient of frequent invitations to dine, dance, and otherwise divert himself at their homes.

His first social engagement in the area had come about through the agency of the local magistrate, Mr. Rundell, who had early fulfilled his promise to invite Paul to dinner. Paul had accepted the invitation with pleasure, and on the evening in question he had driven himself to Mr. Rundell's manor house, a large and imposing residence located some miles inland on the south side of the village. There he had made the acquaintance of the magistrate's wife, Mrs. Rundell, a lady as large and imposing as the home she presided over, and of the three Miss Rundells, known familiarly as Fanny, Sophy, and Gussy.

All three sisters united in having hair that was red or reddish in color, but apart from this similarity they were of strikingly different types. Fanny, the eldest, was the prettiest as far as form and feature was concerned. She was tall and slender with reddish-blonde hair and an air of consequence that probably came from having heard herself described as the prettiest girl in the neighborhood for the past six or seven years. Paul thought her very pretty, but he had spent no more than five minutes in her company before reaching the conclusion that she was very conceited as well.

Sophy, the middle sister, was somewhat shorter than Fanny, but her figure made up in curves what it lacked in inches. She had auburn hair, full, rather pouting lips, and a trick of glancing upward through her lashes that was clearly meant to be seductive. Paul, conversing with her and her sisters before dinner, was at first rather amused by her obvious efforts to allure, but after a while he wearied of her constant innuendoes and significant smiles and was glad to turn from her to Gussy, the youngest sister, a young lady just turned sixteen and recently emancipated from the schoolroom.

Gussy was neither tall like Fanny nor curvaceous like Sophy. Her figure unhappily combined the worst aspects of both her sisters', being both short and perfectly devoid of curves. Her hair was also less attractive than her sisters', being a plain carroty red that did not admit of such poetic euphemisms as auburn or strawberry blonde. Notwithstanding this, Paul agreed with Miss Eaton in finding her the most attractive of the three Miss Rundells. Gussy did not seek to impress him with her consequence or entice him with her charms, as Fanny and Sophy did, but merely chattered away to him in an unaffected way about her friends, her family, and her horse, of whom she seemed to be inordinately fond.

If Paul could have spent the whole evening conversing with Gussy and Mr. Rundell, he would have counted his time well spent, but Mrs. Rundell was insistent that he should be made to admire her elder daughters, particularly Fanny, whom she hinted would make an excellent wife for a gentleman of high estate. Fanny seemed quite to concur in this viewpoint. In the drawing room after dinner, she entertained Paul with an interminable series of songs on harp and pianoforte while Mrs. Rundell quizzed him in a none-too-subtle way about his matrimonial prospects.

Paul bore the ordeal as politely as he could, but inwardly he was seething with resentment. It was not merely the impertinence of Mrs. Rundell's conversation that he resented, or the fact that it masqueraded behind the guise of motherly advice. That would only have amused him under other circumstances, but he could take no amusement in his present situation. He felt rather as though he had been lured to the Manor by the promise of a friendly dinner, only to find that he was to serve as the main course.

It was clear that Mrs. Rundell hoped to marry him off to one of her daughters. It was equally clear that her daughters shared her hopes, save perhaps for Gussy, whom he adjudged innocent of her mother's schemes. Even Mr. Rundell he could not acquit of a share in the plot, for it was evident the kindly magistrate was pretty well under his wife's domination. Paul could imagine exactly how Mrs. Rundell had addressed him. "Albert, you must invite Lord Wyland to dinner. It would be a wonderful thing if he were to marry one of the girls." "A wonderful thing"—that was all he was to them, and so long as he retained his title and fortune he would have been equally wonderful if he had been eighty and toothless, or a confirmed idiot.

If he had still been plain Paul Wycliff, an untitled gentleman of modest fortune, would they have been so eager for his company? Paul felt quite certain they would not. Watching Fanny flaunting her skill at the harp, he wondered bitterly if all women were mercenary creatures, willing like Lady de Lacey to sell themselves to the highest bidder.

The rest of the evening passed off uneventfully, though with little enjoyment for Paul. When Fanny was done playing, he had to listen to Sophy and Gussy take their turn at the harp and pianoforte, and at the conclusion of their performance, Mrs. Rundell invited him to attend a rout party she was giving the following month, wording her invitation in such a way that it was virtually impossible for him to refuse. As soon as he decently could, he excused himself to the Rundells and left the Manor with a sense of relief mingled with indignation.

He could not help seeing a great deal more of the Rundells in the weeks that followed, however. When he attended church in the village on Sunday, they were all there, the girls resplendent in furs, fine pelisses, and their best bonnets. When he drove through the village, it was an even chance that he would see at least one of them and be forced to stop and exchange a few words. They were present at one or two other parties he attended in the neighborhood, though here Mrs. Rundell's efforts to secure him for her daughters were foiled by the other neighborhood ladies, who were equally determined to secure him for their own. Paul soon began to feel hunted whenever he went abroad, and to dread the sight of a bonnet. He was not even safe at Wycliff, for twice Mrs. Rundell had come to call upon him there accompanied by one or more of her daughters. Once the intrepid Fanny even came by herself, under pretext of delivering an invitation to the Rundell's upcoming rout party.

Mary was a witness to this visit. She had just returned from an errand in the village when Fanny came rattling up the drive in her little pony phaeton. Having brought the ponies to a halt, she stepped gracefully from the phaeton and turned her whip and the ponies' reins over to the small boy who was serving as her groom.

Mary, who had been returning the gig to the stables, stood in the stable door and watched as Fanny ran up the steps. She was admitted to the house by Smithson and reappeared a moment later, accompanied by Paul. Mary felt a jealous pang at the sight of them together. Fanny looked entrancingly lovely in a lilac sprig muslin carriage dress, a velvet spencer, and a dashing French bonnet trimmed with plumes and flowers.

"That's a new bonnet," Mary told herself. "Fanny and Sophy must be keeping the milliners in the village busy. They both had new hats at church last Sunday, too."

Having noted that Fanny's dress and spencer also appeared to be new, and that she was wearing her hair in a new and very becoming style, Mary continued to watch as Paul helped Fanny back into the pony phaeton. His back was to her, so that she could not see his face, but she could see Fanny's coquettish smile as she accepted his hand to step inside. The sight gave Mary another jealous pang, but she could not make herself look away. She watched Fanny settle herself inside the phaeton and accept the whip and the ponies' reins from the small groom. As she flicked her whip over the ponies' backs, her parting words came clearly to Mary's ears.

"We shall look to see you on the eighth then, my lord. And remember, you are pledged to dance the first dance with me!"

Mary remained in the stable until Paul had gone back inside the house. She then went to the house's side entrance, let herself in, and went up the backstairs to her room.

Once there, she removed her bonnet and pelisse, then went to the small looking glass over the wash basin to smooth her hair. After she had done so, she remained looking at her reflection for some time.

"I am twenty-four years old," she said aloud. "An old maid, Fanny would say, yet I can't be more than a year or two older than she is. And I am quite as handsome as she is, too, or would be if I had the same advantages."

Once more Mary felt a wave of bitterness toward the fate that condemned her to wear plain dresses and toil about the countryside in a gig while other girls went dashing about in velvet spencers and pony phaetons. The bitterness was made worse by the new jealousy that stabbed her when she thought of Fanny and Paul together. Gradually, however, her emotional turmoil began to give way to a more rational state of mind.

"Your dresses may not be as fine as Fanny Rundell's, but you know perfectly well that Charlotte would be happy to help you make up some new ones, if only you would ask her," Mary reminded herself. "And only this morning Lord Wyland offered you his carriage to go to the village, and you told him you would *rather* take the gig! The fact is, Mary, that you're like a spoiled child who rejects all his playthings simply because he can't have the one he wants. And that is foolish, Mary: foolish, foolish, foolish. You ought to thank heaven for the advantages you have, instead of sighing for the moon."

Yet even as she scolded herself for her foolishness, Mary knew she would continue to wear plain dresses and drive herself about in the gig as long as she remained in Paul's employ. It had become a matter of pride with her not to descend to the level of the girls who chased after him so wantonly. That such pride was foolish she well knew, but if her heart were doomed to be broken she hoped she might at least escape with her self-respect intact. It seemed likely that little else would remain to her in such a case. With a resolution that would have won her late employer's approval, Mary vowed to keep struggling along the rocky and upward path on which her feet were set.

Ten

By the time Paul had been at Wycliff a month, his days had settled down into a regular routine of duties. During the mornings and afternoons he consulted with his bailiff, visited tenants, and attended to other business about the estate, while his evenings were generally given up to dinner, dancing, or card parties at some neighbor's house. But full as his days were, he was not too busy to notice Mary's evident distaste for his company.

He had expected that with Miss Eaton in the house she would feel more comfortable in his company and that in time her manner would become less reserved. But in fact, the opposite appeared to be true. Since Miss Eaton's arrival, she seemed to have frozen up completely. Paul liked Miss Eaton and enjoyed talking politics with her at the dinner table, but it bothered him that Mary never joined in the conversation. If he attempted to draw her out by asking her some question about her day's activities, she answered him as shortly as possible and lapsed into silence once more.

Paul was both puzzled and hurt by her behavior. That she had been stiff with him in the beginning he could understand, for they had been strangers then. But surely after four weeks in the same house they ought to have developed some kind of rapport! And in fact they had seemed to be developing a very nice rapport during their first two evenings together. It was only after they had gone into the drawing room to review the accounts on that second evening that their relations seemed to have taken a turn for the worse.

Paul went over everything that had passed between Mary and him that evening, trying to think if he could have said or done something to offend her. But he could think of nothing, unless it were simply that he had betrayed too much admiration in his looks to suit her sense of propriety. This explanation did not satisfy him, however, and whenever he saw Mary going quietly about her household duties or sitting mute across from him at the dinner table, he was filled with a sense of frustration.

On the evening of the Rundells' rout party, Paul's frustration was running particularly high. He had spent the afternoon in Wycliff's library, looking over some legal papers. When he had come out, he had seen Mary coming down the hall in his direction. Paul had waited in the doorway, intending to exchange a few words with her and if possible break through the shell of her reserve. But no sooner had Mary caught sight of him standing in the doorway than she had turned abruptly and hurried back the way she had come.

There had been no mistaking the deliberateness of the action. Paul could not decide if he were most hurt or angered by it.

"One would think I was some kind of vicious wild beast," he muttered to himself, and repeated the words later that evening as he was knotting his neckcloth and shrugging himself into his black broadcloth topcoat in preparation for the Rundells' party. The incident stayed with him, so that he was in a mood ill-suited for festivity when he finally accepted his hat and gloves from Smithson and set off for the Manor.

His arrival there had been eagerly anticipated. "Lord Wyland! We are delighted to see you in our humble abode once more, my lord," said Mrs. Rundell, in a voice calculated to reach the ears of everyone in the room. "Fanny, only see who is here, my love. Did you not say you were engaged to Lord Wyland for the first set?"

"Indeed, yes, Mama," said Fanny, hurriedly breaking off a flirtation with a red-coated grenadier to join her mother and

Paul. She was most magnificently attired in a dress of white lace over a silver lamé slip, and she smiled and curtsied as she greeted Paul. "Good evening, my lord. I hope I find you well this evening?"

"Very well," said Paul, and made the conventional inquiries after her own health and that of the other Rundells. While Fanny replied to these inquiries at some length, their group was joined by Sophy, who with less of obvious haste but no less alacrity than her sister had broken off a conversation with an inferior beau to attach herself to Paul.

"Good evening, Lord Wyland," she said, curtsying deeply and incidentally giving him a fine view of an impressive décolletage. Once she was fully upright again, she gave him one of her sultry looks from beneath her lashes. "It is delightful to see you *again,* my lord. I hope you are prepared to do your *duty* on the dance floor tonight? You must know that every young lady in the room will count the evening a complete *failure* unless she dances at least *once* with the great Lord Wyland. I do not exclude *myself* from the number, you understand."

"Of course I would be honored to dance with you, Miss Sophia," said Paul, bowing politely. Inwardly, however, he was deeply offended by the calculating manner in which Sophy had angled for this invitation. Indeed, he saw calculation everywhere he looked: in Sophy's blandishments, in the triumphant looks Mrs. Rundell was casting at her neighbors; in Fanny's proprietary grasp on his arm; even in the mere fact of the party itself, which he could not help suspecting had been given solely to further Mrs. Rundell's matrimonial schemes.

Of course there was nothing uncommon about such schemes. Most parents were anxious that their sons and daughters should contract eligible alliances, and nine out of ten parties given during the Season were inspired by this very natural anxiety. But Paul felt suddenly a distaste for the whole business. It was one thing to attend such parties as a disinterested onlooker; quite another to find one's self in the thick of the action, with a matchmaking mama bearing down on one in full cry. If he could have excused himself then and there he would have done so, and shaken the dust of the Manor from his feet forever.

But retreat at this juncture was impossible, as Paul was very soon brought to realize. Fanny was not about to lose the distinction of being the first girl in the room to stand up with Lord Wyland.

"You will have to dance with his lordship later, Sophy. He and I are already engaged for the first set," she informed her sister with ill-concealed triumph. "And I do believe it's time we were taking our places, my lord. The dancing is to begin at nine sharp."

"Very well," said Paul, and accompanied her onto the floor. The clock struck nine as they took their places in the set, and when the other dancers had ranged themselves longways down the room, the musicians struck up a lively country dance. Conscious of his duty, Paul forced himself to address a few words to his partner, though he would rather have remained silent.

"Your mother seems to have put a great deal of effort into her party, Miss Rundell," he said, glancing around the elaborately decorated room. "This is worthy of a London assembly."

"Oh, yes, to be sure," said Fanny, in a voice that made it clear she felt such praise no more than was due a Rundell *soirée*. "Of course, we do give several parties each Season when we are in London, so we ought to know what is *au fait*. But it is very amusing to see the efforts of those who do not, is it not, my lord? Look at poor little Miss Foster over there, for instance. I daresay she made that dress herself, and only see what a fright it is."

With a pitying smile, Fanny glanced toward a young lady in an awkwardly cut pink satin dress who was sitting forlornly among the chaperones, trying to look as though she did not mind this state of affairs. "But there, I daresay half the difficulty is her figure. She's such a dumpy little thing. It really takes someone tall like me to carry off these modern fashions, you know."

Paul nodded noncommittally, but resolved on the spot to ask Miss Foster to dance with him at the earliest opportunity. "I

suppose your family will be going to London again in the
spring, Miss Rundell?" he asked.

"Yes, we go every year for the Season. Of course, whether I
accompany them or not next spring depends a good deal on
circumstances. I trust I shall get to London one way or another,
however." She gave Paul a smile both arch and significant. "I
suppose *you* will be going to Town for the Season, my lord?"

"Perhaps," said Paul, with reserve. "My plans are not decided
as yet. It may be that I will simply remain at Wycliff this spring.
I have a great deal yet to do about the property, and I wouldn't
mind staying on a little longer. This is a very pretty neighborhood."

"Thank you, my lord," said Fanny, casting down her eyes.
Paul looked at her in wonder, but said nothing. As she seemed
determined to take his every remark as a compliment to herself,
he decided it would be in the interests of self-preservation to
maintain a strict silence throughout the remainder of the dance.

This he did, merely smiling briefly at Fanny whenever the
movements of the dance brought them together. But he soon
found he had other pitfalls to avoid as well. Sophy was standing
in the set next to her sister and insisted on giving him a sultry
smile every time he happened to catch her eye. This proceeding
obviously displeased her partner, a sturdy young man with dark
hair and the appearance of a prosperous country squire. As Paul
endeavored to get through the dance while simultaneously
avoiding conversation with Fanny, eye contact with Sophy, and
the dagger-looks the young man was shooting at him, he began
to wonder why he had ever accepted Mrs. Rundell's invitation
in the first place.

He was successful in his triple endeavor as long as the dance
lasted, but when it was over there was no escape from at least
one of his persecutors. "What a delightful dance," said Fanny,
possessing herself of his arm once more and smiling up at him.
"We are a well-matched couple, are we not, my lord? Of course
I am referring to our dancing, though you have my permission

to take the words any way you choose. Shall we dance the next set, too?"

"I am afraid I am already engaged to your sister for the next set," replied Paul. This was not the strict truth, and in fact the prospect of dancing with Sophy was no more appealing than dancing a second time with Fanny. But he was eager to discharge his obligation toward both sisters, so that he might be free to choose more congenial partners throughout the rest of the evening. He was still determined to dance with the forlorn Miss Foster, and he had also observed Gussy going doggedly through the set with a gangling young guardsman. So after delivering Fanny back to her mother, he went in search of Sophy, whom he had last seen headed for the refreshment room in company with her late partner.

He found the two of them drinking punch in one corner of the refreshment room. "Ah, *there* you are, my lord," said Sophy, fluttering her lashes at him as she took a sip of punch. "Is it time for our dance?"

"Yes, if you please, Miss Sophia," said Paul, bowing.

The dark-haired young man, who had listened to this exchange with a scowl, now turned to Sophy with a look of indignation. "Here now, Sophy! I thought you promised to dance the next set with me," he said.

"No, I never *promised,* George," she told him sweetly. "You merely took it for granted that I *would.* However, I would be happy to dance the set after that with you, if you promise to show yourself *properly grateful* for the favor." Having bestowed a seductive smile on him, and another on Paul, she rose from her seat, took Paul's arm, and accompanied him into the drawing room.

The dancers were already forming into a double line down the center of the room. "Oh, another *country* dance," said Sophy, making a *moue* of disappointment. "I don't think I care to jog through another tiresome country dance, my lord. Would you mind very much if we sat the dance out instead?"

"No, not at all," said Paul, not averse to being spared the

ordeal of another dance like the last one. "May I get you something to eat or drink, Miss Sophia?"

"No, I am not at all hungry or thirsty, my lord. But as you are so *obliging,* I'll admit I could use a little fresh air. It's dreadfully *warm* in here, isn't it? Indeed, I feel almost *faint."* With a wan air, Sophy laid a hand to her forehead.

"Oh, yes?" said Paul, taking all this quite seriously and regarding her in some alarm. "Perhaps I ought to fetch your mother, Miss Sophia. If you are feeling indisposed——"

"Oh, I don't feel so indisposed as all *that,"* said Sophy, hastily removing the hand from her forehead and straightening her drooping posture. "I think if we go out to the garden for a minute, I will do *very well,* my lord." Not waiting for any more argument on Paul's part, she took him by the arm and led him out of the drawing room.

All unsuspecting, Paul accompanied her through the rooms until they reached a set of double doors that opened into the garden. "Ah, *fresh air,"* said Sophy, drawing a deep breath as she swung open the door. "I feel much better *already.* Why do you not accompany me, my lord?" she added pointedly, as Paul hesitated in the doorway. "It would be as well if you were near at hand, just in case I should come over faint *again,* you know."

Reluctantly, Paul left the doorway and joined her in the garden. He was beginning to feel a sense of unease. It was really not at all the thing for a gentleman to walk alone with a young lady at night: certainly not without a chaperone within hailing distance. If Mr. or Mrs. Rundell were to come upon him alone with their daughter, he might very well find himself in a compromising situation. Indeed, he had begun to suspect that this had been Sophy's reason for bringing him there in the first place.

In this, he did Sophy an injustice. She would have been perfectly willing to encourage Paul if he had shown any inclination to seriously pursue her, but of such an event she had no real expectation. She was a sensible, level-headed girl with a clear idea of her own value on the marriage market, and common sense told her that her value was probably not high enough to win her the hand of a young, handsome, highly eligible earl. If Paul were to marry any Rundell, it would undoubtedly be Fanny, the acknowledged beauty of the family.

Sophy had faced this fact philosophically, but though she had given up all idea of marrying Paul, she saw no reason why she still could not turn him to account. George Reeves had been a regular suitor of hers for almost two years now. Of all her suitors, he was by far the most eligible, being reasonably well-off, of a decent family, and quite handsome in the bargain. Sophy had long ago made up her mind that he was as good as she was likely to get. But though she was quite willing to marry George whenever he might say the word, he was being unaccountably slow about saying that word. Only last week he had shown an alarming tendency to admire the youngest Miss Foley when they had gone together to the parish wakes festival.

Reflecting on this incident, Sophy had decided that it was time to force George's hand a bit. She had made her preparations for the party that evening fully determined to extract a proposal from George by some means or other, and as soon as she had caught sight of Paul, she had recognized him as the ideal instrument for her purposes. The sight of her on close terms with an eligible earl ought to be enough to spur George into action, she reasoned, especially when that earl was staggeringly handsome and had the reputation of being a dangerous rake. Sure enough, George had immediately shown his hackles when Lord Wyland had appeared on the scene, and when she and Lord Wyland had left the drawing room just now, she had observed George furtively following them. It now remained only to do something to galvanize him into action.

It was a still, cloudless, moonlit night. As Sophy strolled through the garden with Paul, she stole frequent glances at his profile. Her best strategy, she decided, would be to get him to kiss her or otherwise molest her, so that George might have the opportunity to rescue her from his dangerous embrace. This would entail no disagreeable labor on her part, for she felt she would quite enjoy being kissed by Lord Wyland, even if there was no possibility of his marrying her afterwards. It surprised her a little that he had made no attempt upon her person as yet. Here they were, in a perfectly good moonlit garden, with no one around but themselves—to all appearances, at least, although her ears had caught the creak of the terrace door a moment before. But still Lord Wyland did nothing but walk tamely by her side. Sophy decided to give him a little encouragement.

"What a lovely night," she said, moving a little closer and daringly resting her head upon his shoulder. "Is there not something romantic about moonlight, my lord?"

"I suppose so," he said, drawing away from her as though he had been scalded. "Have you had enough fresh air now, Miss Sophia? It's time we were getting back to the party."

Sophy began to think that for a dangerous rake, Lord Wyland was really very slow. "Surely we needn't go in yet," she said, tilting her face up to his and pouting invitingly. "You are not very gallant, my lord."

"No," he agreed baldly. Sophy was exasperated. Out of the corner of her eye, she had caught a glimpse of a shadowy figure stealing from tree to tree. This was George, of course, spying on her and Lord Wyland's actions, and if her plan were to work, it was vital that he be given something dramatic to witness.

With determination, Sophy turned to Lord Wyland and threw herself into his arms. "Kiss me, my lord," she demanded in a passionate whisper. When he merely gaped at her, she was forced to take matters into her own hands and kiss him instead.

This strategy served as well as any, however. "Unhand her, sirrah," shouted George, springing from his place of concealment and striding toward them. Sophy let out a little cry, pulled herself away from Paul, and ran to George, burying her face in his waistcoat. "There, there," he said, putting his arms around her and patting her awkwardly on the back. "There, there, little girl, there's no need to take on now. You're safe enough with me. It's a good thing I was here, though," he added, glaring at Paul. "By God, my lord, I'll have satisfaction for this, if it's the last thing I do."

Paul would have laughed, if he had not been so furious at being duped. "My good man, don't be an ass," he retorted. *"She* kissed *me."*

"How *dare* you!" gasped Sophy, raising her face from George's waistcoat to glare at Paul. "How dare you say such a thing? You, my lord, are no gentleman!"

"No, by God," agreed George, also glaring at Paul. "He's an out-and-out bounder, that's what he is. You run on into the house, Sophy, and I'll settle with his lordship, here."

Sophy, however, felt that further communication between the two gentlemen would not be to her advantage. "No, George, never mind about *him,"* she said, shooting a look of loathing at Paul. "He is not worth the *trouble* of calling out, upon my word. Just take me into the house and get me something to drink. I feel quite *shaken* by this whole experience."

"Of course you do," said George, patting her on the back once more. Having thrown a last menacing look at Paul, he began to steer Sophy toward the house, murmuring to her comfortingly all the while.

Paul, watching them go, was filled with a mixture of anger, amusement, and bitter cynicism. The evening which had been disagreeable before had now been elevated to the level of a positive disaster. Yet he felt he must go back to the party, if only to show Sophy and her rustic beau that their treatment had not daunted him. He deeply resented being cast as the villain of the piece, however, and as he walked slowly back to the house, he reflected once again on the duplicitous nature of the female sex.

Back in the house, he encountered Gussy coming out of the drawing room just as he was entering it. "Good evening, my lord," she said, dropping a curtsy and smiling at him with unaffected friendliness. Paul found her manner a relief after her sisters' and politely begged her to stand up with him for the next dance.

Gussy looked pleased but dubious. "Well, I don't know," she said, glancing back toward the drawing room. "The thing is that the next dance is an ecossaise, my lord, and I'm not much good at ecossaises. I daresay I would bungle it dreadfully. No, I think you had better ask someone else to dance with you, my lord. You know you needn't feel obliged to dance with me only because I am a daughter of the house."

"I do not ask because I am obliged to, but rather because I would like to," said Paul, smiling. "And if you would prefer to sit this dance out rather than dance it, I am perfectly willing to do that, too, Miss Augusta. Shall I fetch us something to drink?"

"Please," said Gussy fervently. "I am positively perishing with thirst, my lord. And if you wouldn't mind getting me something to eat, too, I would greatly appreciate it. I don't usually get to stay up this late, you see, and what with that and all the dancing, I find I am perfectly ravenous."

Paul laughed and obligingly fetched her a glass of punch and a generous plateful of cakes and sandwiches. He chose wine rather than punch for himself, feeling that he deserved it after the events of the past hour.

"This has been an exciting evening," said Gussy, munching happily on her sandwiches. "First Will Harris was sick in the men's cloakroom, and now my sister Sophy has got herself engaged to George Reeves. They announced it a few minutes ago, just before you came in, my lord. Of course, George has been dangling after Sophy forever, but still it was a surprise. Fanny was mad as fire about it," added Gussy with a reminiscent smile. "She has the idea she ought to be the first of us to get engaged because she is the oldest, but I think that's nonsense, don't you?"

Paul said nothing, but smiled cynically to himself. Since Gussy clearly regarded the question as a rhetorical one, his silence went unnoticed as she went on between bites of sandwich.

"After all, why should poor Sophy and George have to wait, just because Fanny isn't engaged yet? But Fanny is rather unreasonable sometimes. She told Mama she was expecting to get engaged herself any day now, and that Sophy should have waited until after her engagement was announced. *I* didn't know Fanny was expecting to get engaged, although Mama seemed to know what she was talking about. However, Mama said a bird in the hand was worth two in the bush, and that it would be better to go ahead and announce Sophy's engagement now, seeing that it might take longer than Fanny thought to bring Lord W. up to scratch. She didn't mean you, did she, my lord? You're the only Lord W. I know, but I hadn't heard you were going to marry Fanny."

"I'm not," said Paul, smiling grimly at this naive exposé of the Rundells' ambitions. "Your mother must have been talking about some other Lord W."

"Yes, that's what I thought," said Gussy, nodding with a satisfied air. On thinking it over, however, she must have judged this remark rather harsh toward her sister, for she made haste to qualify it. "Although I'm sure it would be no wonder if you did want to marry Fanny, my lord. She is very pretty, of course, and she plays and sings very well. I do think myself that Miss Grant plays better, but then I am no judge of music, as Fanny is always telling me."

"Miss Grant?" said Paul, looking at her in surprise. "Are you talking about my Miss Grant? The Miss Grant who lives at Wycliff, I mean, and who used to be my cousin's governess," he corrected in some haste.

Gussy nodded vigorously. "Oh, yes. I used to take lessons of her on the pianoforte. Not regular lessons, you understand, but she was good enough to help me last summer when my regular master was away. I wish they *had* been regular lessons. I'm sure I would play much better if I had studied with her rather than old Signor Vietti."

"I see," said Paul. The mention of Mary's name had brought her image before his eyes: calm, cool, Quakerish in dress, and unshakably reserved in manner. It also reminded him of the way she had run away from him that afternoon, and he frowned. "I did not even know Miss Grant played the pianoforte," he said shortly.

"Didn't you? But how odd, when she lives in the same house with you. She plays very well, I assure you, my lord. I wish she could have come with you to the party tonight, but when I suggested inviting her, Mama said it would not be proper."

"I suppose not," said Paul. He wondered if Mary would have come if she had been invited. On the whole he thought not, for she must have felt out of place among the glittering crowd in the Rundells' drawing room. Her plain dress and pulled-back hair would have made her look like a raven among peacocks. For the hundredth time he wondered why she felt compelled to disfigure herself so, and it occurred to him suddenly that the subject was becoming something of an obsession with him. Only the day before, when he had followed her into the dining room, he had felt the most uncontrollable urge to reach out and pull the pins from her hair. This was not, as Paul told himself firmly, a lustful urge so much as an aesthetic one. He would have felt the same desire to straighten a picture hanging crooked on the wall, or a statue askew on a pedestal.

Aesthetic or not, however, it was an urge that was improper to cherish in regard to a female employee, and Paul sought conscientiously to banish it from his mind. "I do not suppose Miss Grant would have attended your party even if she had been invited," he said, rather morosely. "She seems opposed to amusement of any kind. I have invited her to go out driving or walking with me any number of times, but she is always too busy."

Gussy nodded sympathetically. "Yes, she does work very hard. I often think how lucky I am not to have to earn my living as she does. I am sure I should not do it half so well, for I have not half her talents."

Gussy left Paul soon after this to stand up with a stout young man with whom she had previously promised to dance. Paul let her go with a smile, but her words haunted him for the rest of the time he was at the Manor. That time was not of long duration, for he was eager to quit the Rundells' party, but he did remain long enough to seek out and dance with the slighted Miss Foster, who was quite overwhelmed by the honor and whose popularity on the dance floor took a rapid upturn as a result.

Paul did not stay to witness the results of his philanthropy, however. Taking leave of the disappointed Mrs. Rundell, who had counted on his staying at least through supper, he ordered round his carriage and was soon embarked on the drive back to Wycliff.

Eleven

At Wycliff that evening, Mary had been unable to apply herself to any settled employment.

While Miss Eaton sat placidly knitting on the drawing room sofa, Mary had tried first to interest herself in a book; then in some needlework; then in the pianoforte, which she had somewhat neglected of late.

"You're as restless as a caged tiger this evening," observed Miss Eaton, as Mary broke off in the midst of a sonata and began to rummage through the music stand in a futile search for something new and interesting to play. "You ought to have gone for a walk with me earlier, and then you would not be so fidgety."

"Perhaps," said Mary. Abandoning her search of the music stand, she rose, went to the window, and drew aside the curtain to look out into the night. There was a full moon overhead, she noted, and not a wisp of cloud in the sky. The Rundells' guests would have no difficulty in making their way home when the rout party was over. Mary supposed the festivities must be nearing their height about now. She envisioned the party-goers laughing and dancing, the rooms ablaze with candlelight and decked with flowers. Most of all she envisioned Paul, the center of attention from all eyes and the object of the Misses Rundells' most concentrated efforts at flirtation.

As always when she indulged in such imaginings, Mary was assailed by a wrenching pang of jealousy. She knew she ought to put the idea from her thoughts, but instead she found herself enlarging upon it morbidly. She imagined Fanny and Sophy in their new dresses (of course they would have new dresses for such an important occasion as this), while Paul danced with them, admired them, perhaps even fell in love with one of them. If he did, most likely it would be with Fanny, the acknowledged belle of the neighborhood. Mary's hands clenched into involuntary fists at the thought.

"This is ridiculous," she told herself impatiently. "What does it matter whom he falls in love with? Better with Fanny than with some other girl who might not be able to take care of herself so well. Fanny would see he took no liberties, at least none for which he didn't render up full payment beforehand. Why, I daresay that between her and her mother, they might even coax an offer of marriage out of him. And why should he not marry Fanny? She would be quite a good enough wife for him, considering his character and past conduct."

Yet in spite of Paul's character and past conduct, Mary could not be happy with the idea of him married to Fanny Rundell. She was staring morosely out the window, trying to envision life at Wycliff with Fanny as mistress, when Miss Eaton spoke out suddenly.

"That's enough," she said.

Mary, who naturally applied the words to herself, gave a guilty start and shot a quick look of alarm at Miss Eaton. She wondered if her friend had somehow been able to read her thoughts. But Miss Eaton was folding up her knitting, quite unconscious of Mary's guilty expression.

"That's enough for this evening," she said, putting the knitting in her workbox and rising to her feet with a yawn. "It's eleven o'clock, and I think I shall go to bed now. Are you coming, too, Mary?"

"No, I'm not tired yet," said Mary, turning back to the window. "I think I shall stay up a little longer. Good night, Charlotte. I'll see you in the morning."

As soon as Miss Eaton had gone upstairs, Mary left the drawing room and began to prowl restlessly through the other rooms on the main floor. She met no one in her wanderings, nor did she expect to, for the servants had already retired for the night. As for Paul, she knew that he would probably not return until the early hours of the morning.

Mary passed through the formal saloon with its crimson and gilt furnishings, pausing to straighten one of the row of plush-upholstered chairs that stood against the wall. From there she passed through several small dark parlors and withdrawing rooms which were never used nowadays but which past generations of Lord and Lady Wylands had judged necessary to their consequence.

Making her circuitous way through these rooms, Mary came at last to the entrance hall, a room equally dark, but very much larger and draftier than the cramped apartments she had just left. Having paused to inspect the grotesque carvings on the screen that separated the hall from the passage, she made a mental note to remind Ellen to be more careful in her dusting, then moved on to the dining room on the other side of the hall. As she reached the dining room door, however, she heard the front door open and close and the sound of footsteps coming down the passage. With a start Mary turned, just in time to see Paul's hatted and greatcoated figure entering the hall.

For a moment Mary stood frozen with her hand upon the door. She had not expected him for several hours yet, and the shock of seeing him now, when she had imagined him still *en fête* at the Rundells', held her transfixed for what seemed an eon. At last, gathering her wits about her, she sought to retreat noiselessly into the dining room. But the door let out a grating squeak as she opened it, and Paul turned sharply at the noise.

"Who's there?" he called.

Abandoning stealth, Mary pulled open the door, ducked into the dining room, and slammed the door shut behind her. She had no more than done this, however, than she heard Paul's footsteps approaching the dining room, moving much faster than they had before. Mary made a desperate dash for the door at the other end of the room, only to be brought up short by the sound of Paul's voice.

"Oh, it's you, is it, Miss Grant?" he said, sounding at once vexed and relieved. "You're lucky I hadn't my pistols with me, or you might have found yourself a victim of manslaughter. Or would it be womanslaughter? In any event, the slaughter would have been justified, for I thought you were a burglar."

"No, my lord," said Mary. She stood rigidly a moment; then, keeping her back to him, she reached a cautious hand for the doorknob, hoping to escape without further parley. Before she opened the door, however, Paul spoke again in a tone that made his words a command, not a request.

"Just a moment, Miss Grant," he said. "I would like to talk to you for a minute or two, if you please."

Reluctantly Mary turned to look at him. As always, the sight of him affected her powerfully, in spite of her efforts to view him solely in the light of an employer. His greatcoat was open and thrown back over his shoulders, revealing the austere black-and-white evening clothes beneath. The sobriety of this attire threw his golden coloring into high relief, and Mary admired the gloss of his fair hair and the symmetry of his form and features even while her heart despaired.

"Yes?" she said, in a voice that was scarcely more than a whisper. "What did you want to talk to me about, my lord?"

Paul looked at her a long moment without speaking. His brow, shadowed by his hat-brim, was drawn into a frown. It made him look at once older and more forbidding than usual. Mary was sure he meant to address her in some excessively stern and serious vein, and was thus quite surprised by his next words. "I wonder if you would be willing to play for me on the pianoforte for a half-hour or so, Miss Grant. I was talking with Miss Augusta Rundell this evening, and she said you were quite proficient at the instrument."

"Oh," said Mary, taken off-guard by this unexpected request. "I'm afraid Miss Augusta rather exaggerated my talents, my lord. Certainly I play a little—and I would be happy to play for you if you like. But it is growing rather late, is it not?"

"Yes, it is. And I've the deuce of a headache," said Paul, removing his hat and driving his fingers through his hair as though trying to unseat some invisible burden weighing there.

"Well, then, surely it would be better for you to go up to your room, my lord," said Mary, grasping feverishly at this excuse. "I am afraid it would only make your headache worse to sit and listen to me play."

"No, I don't think it would, Miss Grant. I have always found music peculiarly soothing when I am feeling not quite the thing. I can remember my mother playing for me by the hour when I was a boy and laid up with some childish ailment."

"I see," said Mary, twisting her hands together nervously. "I am sorry to hear you are feeling unwell, my lord, and of course I would be happy to do anything that might make you feel better. But you know it *is* growing very late. The clock struck eleven some time ago, and Miss Eaton has already gone upstairs. I don't think—I am afraid that under the circumstances, it would be improper for me to sit alone with you in the drawing room."

The frown on Paul's voice grew deeper at these words. "If you are playing the pianoforte all the while, I fail to see how anyone could suppose we are indulging in improprieties," he said with asperity. "Will you play for me or not, Miss Grant?"

Mary, having exhausted all her arguments, said meekly, "Yes, my lord," and followed Paul into the drawing room. He took off his coat, threw it and his hat upon a chair, and stretched himself at full length upon the drawing room sofa. "What shall I play, my lord?" said Mary, averting her eyes hastily from his recumbent figure.

"Anything," he said, shutting his eyes and folding his hands behind his head. "If you will indulge me in the performance, Miss Grant, I will leave the choice of repertoire to you."

Mary hesitated a moment, then began to play Bach's *Aria with Thirty Variations*. Paul listened in silence, his eyes closed and his figure motionless on the sofa. Mary glanced at him from time to time, her eyes roving hungrily and unhappily over his chiseled features, the golden gloss of his hair, and the lean solid length of his body. She finished the first nine of the thirty variations and embarked upon the tenth. Paul lay so still throughout that she began to wonder if he were asleep, and it was a shock when he spoke out suddenly.

"There's nothing like Bach, is there? I know it's not the fashion to admire him nowadays, but he has always been one of my favorite composers. There is something so satisfying about his music. No matter how high it soars, one always senses that the foundation is solid, and that the most perfect logic and order reign throughout. And you capture those qualities beautifully in your playing, Miss Grant. Listening to you play Bach is almost enough to reaffirm my faith in the order of the universe."

Mary was so surprised by this speech that she let her hands drop from the keyboard and turned to regard Paul in astonishment. "But that's exactly how I have always felt," she exclaimed. "I have always enjoyed the logic and order of Bach's music, though as you say, it is not the fashion to admire him nowadays. How is it that you come to be so well acquainted with him, my lord? I would not have supposed you—that's to say, I did not realize you were interested in music," she finished, rather lamely.

Paul had opened his eyes and was surveying her quizzically. "Yes, I have always enjoyed music," he said. "As I mentioned, my mother used to play for me when I was a boy—not just when I was ailing, you understand, but at other times, too. It was she who introduced me to Bach, though of course I would have been bound to make his acquaintance anyway when I was studying for the church."

This speech caused Mary even more surprise than his last one. "Studying for the *church?*" she exclaimed, in a voice of rising disbelief. "You do not mean to say you ever studied to be a *clergyman,* my lord?"

Again he regarded her thoughtfully before replying. "Oh, yes, Miss Grant," he said. "Growing up, it was an understood thing that I was destined for the pulpit. If my father had lived a few months longer, I have no doubt that I would have fulfilled that destiny. But unfortunately he died just as I was on the verge of taking orders, and what with one thing and another, my life took a different turn after that."

There was a hint of emotion in his voice as he spoke these last words. Mary could not decide if the emotion were pain, or amusement, or merely irony, but she was in any case too astonished by the words themselves to dwell upon the tone in which they were spoken.

"And so you studied to be a clergyman," she marveled, surveying him in wonderment. "I must say I am surprised to hear it, my lord." She spoke no more than the truth, for the idea that Paul had once studied for the church upset all her preconceived ideas about him. There were, of course, worldly clergymen: wolves in sheep's clothing, as the late Lord Wyland had been wont to call them with a note of loathing in his voice. It was quite possible that his nephew would have been one of this number if he had gone on to take orders. Yet Mary was bound to admit that the gentleman before her did not in the least resemble the stereotypically bluff, hard-drinking, fox-hunting type of churchman that had been the late Lord Wyland's especial bane.

Turning back to the pianoforte, Mary began to play once more, hardly aware that she was doing so. As her fingers moved precisely and mechanically over the keys, her mind sought to arrange the new facts she had just learned about Paul into some kind of order. But it was impossible to do anything with facts so contradictory. All she could think, foolishly, was of what a sensation he must have made in the pulpit if he had actually become a clergyman.

"Heaven knows the girls make enough fuss over Reverend Biddle," thought Mary, stealing another look at Paul upon the sofa. "They would have positively mobbed Lord Wyland if he had ever appeared among them in a cassock."

For some twenty minutes more, Mary continued to play while casting frequent glances at Paul upon the sofa. The sight of him lying there with closed eyes did strange things to her heart, and to various other indeterminate regions within her as well. She finished the *Variations* and embarked upon another Bach piece, the *Italian Concerto.* Paul remained motionless on the sofa with his eyes closed, He was so still that Mary began to wonder once again if he had fallen asleep. The idea sent a little shiver down her spine. She tried to write it off as a shiver of cold, but her conscience knew better.

"I ought to go," Mary told herself. "If our situation was dubious before, it is doubly dubious now. I ought to go." And by dint of repeating the words half a hundred times, she finally brought herself to stop playing at the conclusion of the concerto's first movement instead of going on to its end.

Paul did not stir with the cessation of the music. "He really is asleep," Mary told herself, and knew not whether she was relieved or disappointed. Shutting the pianoforte carefully, she rose from the bench and began to tiptoe toward the door.

"Don't go," said Paul.

His voice shattered the stillness of the quiet room. Mary caught her breath in a gasp and spun around. Paul was still lying on the sofa with his eyes closed as before. Even as she watched, however, his eyes opened, and he regarded her for a moment, steadily and silently.

"Don't go," he said again, softly.

With an effort, Mary wrenched her gaze away from his and turned again toward the door. "I must go, my lord," she said distractedly. "I must!"

"Why?" he asked. Almost against her will, Mary turned again to look at him. He was sitting up now on the sofa, regarding her somberly. "Why must you go? What is it about me that you dislike so much, Miss Grant?" he asked.

"I don't dislike you," said Mary. The words came out sounding far too much like a cry from the heart, and she sought desperately to erase this impression. "I don't dislike you, my lord," she repeated, in a more level tone. "I don't dislike you at all. I merely . . . disapprove of you."

"But that's almost the same thing, isn't it?" said Paul. Mary thought to herself that it was a very different thing, but made no attempt to dispute his words. "Why do you disapprove of me, Miss Grant?" was his next question, unwelcome but not unexpected. "What is it I have done to offend you?"

"Indeed, you have done nothing to offend me personally, my lord," Mary hastened to assure him. This done, however, she could find no words to go on and merely stood regarding him dumbly.

"What is it, then?" he asked, sounding more curious than offended. "What have I done to earn your disapproval?"

Mary turned away, unable to bear his scrutiny any longer. "Indeed, you must know that without my telling you, my lord," she said.

"But I do not know, and I am asking you to tell me, Miss Grant. I can think of nothing I have done that is so dreadful it cannot be spoken of without blushes and evasions."

Stung, Mary turned to face him once more. "I had thought to spare your feelings, my lord," she said with spirit. "But since you insist—very well, I will tell you. You must know that your uncle made me his confidante in some measure, not only about business but about his personal affairs as well. He was used to speak quite openly about your—vices."

"I am sure he was," said Paul, looking grimly amused. "Speaking about other people's vices was one of his favorite pastimes. Do go on, Miss Grant. Which of my vices did he mention particularly during your discussions?"

Now that she was fairly launched, Mary wished desperately she had never embarked on such a perilous course. "Your intemperance, to begin with," she said, beginning with the least objectionable of the late Lord Wyland's charges. "He spoke of your frequenting White's and Watier's clubs in London—"

"Where I was known as an uncommonly staid and sober fellow," interrupted Paul impatiently. "Good God, Miss Grant, you must be aware that my uncle had a regular bee in his bonnet on the subject of drinking. I don't deny I take a glass of wine now and then, but I fail to see the crime in that—or the sin, either. After all, Jesus Himself drank wine. If He had really wanted to, I can't see that there was anything to stop Him from turning those jars of water at Cana into lemonade or green tea or something equally abstemious!"

In spite of her discomfort, Mary could not help smiling. "No, I suppose not," she said. "Still, I am sure your uncle would have found some ingenious way to reconcile that fact with his beliefs!"

"I daresay he would. But he would have been deceiving himself, just as he deceived himself about my supposed intemperant behavior. I assure you, Miss Grant, I haven't been the worse for liquor since my undergraduate days at Oxford. Even then it wasn't a regular thing with me. After one or two trials, I decided that the pleasures of intoxication were dearly bought at the price of the after-effects and made a point thereafter of limiting myself to strictly moderate potations!"

He spoke so drolly that Mary could not help smiling once more. Paul returned her smile, but his voice was serious as he continued. "Of course in my last year, when I was preparing to take orders, I abstained from motives of conscience. I could not feel it proper for a future clergyman to be seen in an intoxicated state. I assure you, Miss Grant, that my uncle was wholly mistaken in naming intemperance as one of my vices. You yourself ought to be able to vouch for that, for you have lived in the same house with me for over a month, and you have never once seen me even moderately drunk. Have you, now?"

"No," admitted Mary.

Paul smiled. "Very well, then," he said. "My character stands cleared of that charge, at least. Go on, Miss Grant. What other vices did my uncle charge me with?"

"Well . . . he said you were a gamester," said Mary reluctantly. "And indeed, you have already admitted that you used to frequent White's and Watier's, my lord. Even in Yorkshire, we hear reports of those places, and of how many fortunes have changed hands at their gaming tables."

"Yes, but I dare swear you've never heard a report of *my* fortune changing hands through such a means," responded Paul instantly. "If you have, it was a false report, for I've never lost more than a few pounds at the gaming table at any one sitting. Until recently my fortune was too moderate to allow me to indulge in deep gaming, and now that I've come into a larger one, I fear it's too late for me to acquire the taste. Having been bred up to frugality, I find it painful to see good, hard-earned money slip away at the roll of the dice or the turn of a card. No, Miss Grant: unless taking a hand of whist at shilling points now and then makes me a gamester, I'm afraid you must acquit me of that charge, too."

Mary nodded reluctantly. "Yes, although I fear your uncle would not have done so," she said. "His views on gaming were as extreme and inflexible as on the subject of drinking, you know."

"I didn't know, but I'm not surprised," said Paul with a grimace. "Very well, let us pass on to the next charge, Miss Grant. What else do I stand accused of?"

Mary had been dreading this question, and she found herself stammering now as she attempted to answer it. "Your uncle said—there was talk of your having formed a—an irregular alliance with a lady in London," she said, dropping her eyes as she spoke. "A Lady de Lacey was the name he mentioned."

Paul was silent a long time. Mary, stealing a glance at him, saw he was looking straight ahead of him with a grim expression. At last he sighed and turned his head to look at her. His brow was still a trifle furrowed, but his eyes met hers squarely and candidly.

"Yes, that is true," he said. "My uncle was quite right on that point, Miss Grant. I won't attempt to justify my conduct in that regard, for I am quite aware that from a moral standpoint it was and remains indefensible. But you must not be thinking too badly of me for all that. I assure you that I would have been glad to have regularized my relations with the lady you mention and did in fact ask her to marry me a number of times. It was she who would not countenance a more regular alliance. I know that still does not justify my own part in the business, but I hope it excuses it a little. I would hate to appear a villain in your eyes, Miss Grant."

It was Mary's turn to be silent. Paul looked at her searchingly. "Perhaps I am deluding myself, but it seems to me that I have not been such a blackguard as my uncle would have me. However, I would be glad to hear your opinion on the subject, Miss Grant. Do you not think the fact that I loved the lady and wanted to marry her makes my behavior less culpable?"

Still Mary was silent. She felt she ought to rejoice that the instincts of her heart had been right and that Paul was proved not to be the heartless rake his uncle had described him. In truth, however, the disclosures he had made about his relationship with Lady de Lacey had made her feel infinitely worse. Mary was appalled to find that in her heart of hearts, she would have preferred his relations with Lady de Lacey to have been a mere physical coupling rather than the loving and enduring union he had described. As miserable as it made her to think of him with another woman, it made her more miserable still to think he had loved that other woman and wanted to make her his wife.

The realization brought such a wave of pain to Mary that she knew she must either retire from the drawing room on the instant or disgrace herself by bursting into tears. She turned away abruptly.

"I must go," she said in a stifled voice. "Please excuse me, my lord." Blindly she moved toward the door, but before she could reach it, Paul rose from the sofa and moved swiftly to place himself in front of it.

"Don't go," he said again, in the same soft voice he had used before. Mary looked away, fighting to keep down the tears that she felt were ominously close to the surface.

"Indeed, indeed, you must let me go, my lord," she said passionately. "I cannot stay here any longer. Not in this room—and not in this house."

These last words were spoken without Mary's conscious volition. As soon as they were out of her mouth, however, she recognized their truth and clung to them even in spite of the pain they cost her. "It is time I found a new situation, my lord," she continued, endeavoring to speak more calmly. "Already I have been here longer than I intended. Your household is fully staffed and running smoothly now, and there is no need for me to stay any longer. If you desire a housekeeper, Miss Eaton can fill that position far better than I can. Why, for these past few weeks I have done nothing that could not be done equally well by an untrained maidservant. You can have no possible need for my services at Wycliff."

"But I should like you to stay on for all that," said Paul. He spoke calmly, but his calmness was only on the surface, for he had just experienced a moment of epiphany. Looking down at Mary's pale, resolute face, it had suddenly dawned upon him that here was a woman capable of speaking the truth even when the truth was downright painful. She had been too honest to feign approval of his behavior merely to conciliate him. The fact of his being her employer had not dissuaded her; neither had his title and fortune, or any other worldly consideration that might have inspired a lesser woman to hold her tongue.

After all that he had endured that evening from the two elder Miss Rundells, Paul found such honesty very attractive. Nor was this the only thing that attracted him to Mary, though he would have been hard-pressed to explain the exact nature of that attraction. All he knew was that she was about to slip away from him, and that he was resolved at all costs to prevent her from doing so.

"I want you to stay, Mary," he said, using her first name deliberately for the first time in their acquaintance. She gave him a startled look and shrank back slightly, her hand pressed to her breast.

"Indeed, I cannot stay, my lord," she.said, in a breathless voice. "You do not need the services of a governess, and I never intended to be a housekeeper forever, you know."

"Yes, I know, but it was not as housekeeper that I wished

you to stay on, or as governess either." Paul took a deep breath. "To put it bluntly, I had hoped you might consider staying on in the position of—my wife."

"Your wife?" Mary's lips formed the words, but no sound came out. She stared at Paul, wondering if she could possibly have heard him correctly. "What—what did you say, my lord?" she asked faintly.

"I asked if you would do me the honor of becoming my wife," said Paul, with some trepidation. It struck him suddenly that most people would think him mad for proposing to a woman whom he had known only a few weeks and who a moment before had been condemning his character in the strongest terms. If Mary had answered his proposal with a resounding "no," he would have been as much relieved as disappointed.

No resounding "no" was forthcoming, however. Having had the magical words confirmed by Paul's own lips, Mary felt a surge of joy so strong as to make her feel downright giddy.

She had just received a proposal of marriage from the man she had been longing for with all her heart and soul for the past four weeks. The idea that her longing was not, after all, to go unrequited seemed too wonderful to be true. And when her first rush of joy had subsided, she realized that it probably was.

"Marry you," she repeated, giving a disillusioned little laugh. "A marriage of convenience, I suppose you mean. I thank you for the honor, my lord, but in my eyes such a union would be no marriage at all. I have no opinion of marriages of convenience."

"Neither have I," said Paul, looking into her eyes. "It is a real marriage I mean, Mary." In a softer voice, he continued, "You must know that from the very beginning of our acquaintance I have had the greatest possible admiration and respect for you. I do not know how you feel about my company, but I have always enjoyed yours, and we seem to have a number of tastes in common. I think we might go on very well together as husband and wife. On my honor, Mary, I do esteem you most truly."

Paul had originally intended to say "love" rather than "esteem," but at the last moment he substituted the weaker word, fearing that any talk of love at this juncture might make Mary doubt his sincerity. In truth, he was not altogether sure of his feelings for her. He only knew that he could not bear to see her go and that he was willing to take any means necessary to insure her continuing presence at Wycliff.

Mary hardly noticed the substitution, however. She was too much overcome by the mere fact of Paul's proposal to pay its individual words much heed. It appeared that he was sincere after all in wanting to marry her. There was, indeed, no mistaking his sincerity: it was apparent in his eyes, his voice, even in the nervous way he raked his fingers through his hair. Mary smiled to see this characteristic gesture. She would have had trouble believing a passionate avowal of devotion, but the sentiments Paul expressed seemed no more than were credible under the circumstances.

And she was satisfied by those sentiments, or told herself that she was. In the back of her mind did linger a faint, wistful desire for something more. Mary pushed it aside resolutely, however. She told herself she ought to feel fortunate enough that Paul was proposing without finding fault in the manner of his proposal. And indeed, she did feel supremely fortunate. She contemplated Paul with glowing eyes, the smile still trembling on her lips.

Paul saw her smile and was encouraged by it. "I do hope you will accept my offer, Mary," he said, coming a step nearer and putting his hands on her shoulders. A tremor ran through her body at his touch. Paul noticed it, but attributed it to timidity on her part. "Being my wife may not be the kind of employment you are used to, but I think you will find it a better position than housekeeper," he told her with an encouraging smile. "Better even than governess. Only think of the perquisites! You can sit in the best pew at church, and take the carriage when you go out instead of being forced to drive yourself about in the gig—"

"I like driving myself in the gig," protested Mary foolishly. She hardly knew what she was saying, for the touch of Paul's hands on her shoulders was having a most disturbing effect on her thoughts. "I was always used to drive my father's gig at home," she went on, trying to ignore the little chills that were chasing each other up and down her spine.

"Were you indeed? Then I shall buy you your own phaeton and pair, so you may drive yourself in style."

"Oh, my lord, how can you?" said Mary, half laughing and half crying. "To bribe me with offers of phaetons and pairs—"

"Yes, it's a low tactic, but I will stoop to any means to win my end," said Paul, with mock solemnity. "I truly want you to marry me, you see." In a more serious voice, he continued, "Of course, I don't mean to persuade you into anything you're not comfortable with, Mary. If you find me—well, physically distasteful, or anything like that, then of course there is nothing more to be said." He looked down at her searchingly.

"I don't find you physically distasteful," said Mary, in what she felt to be one of the world's great understatements.

Paul contemplated her silently a moment, his hands still resting on her shoulders. Mary, looking back at him, felt suddenly as though the air around them was charged with electricity. At last, with a tentative air, he bent down and touched his lips to hers.

Mary shut her eyes. She could feel the warmth of his body close to hers and smell the faint masculine scent of him, a scent compounded of soap, starch, and clean linen. His lips were firm, yet gentle. Mary found their touch incredibly arousing. Without any conscious thought, she moved closer to him, twining her arms around his neck and running her fingers through his hair. It was as fine and silky as she had imagined, and this, too, she found arousing. She made a small noise like a sigh deep in her throat.

Paul made an answering noise and let his hands slip to her waist, pulling her even closer. He had meant only to kiss her briefly, a chaste and decorous kiss that would not frighten her. Now he found himself caught up in an embrace that was neither brief nor decorous nor in the slightest degree chaste. He was astounded by the passion of Mary's response, and by his own immediate and instinctive reaction to it. He wanted nothing so much as to forget he was a gentleman and ravish her on the spot. With an effort, he forced himself to let go of her and take a step backwards. She made another small noise that sounded like frustration and opened her eyes. For a moment they stood looking at each other, his hands still resting on her waist and hers still twined about his neck.

"Well, that settles it. You cannot kiss me like that and then refuse to make an honest man of me, you know," said Paul. He was smiling as he spoke, but there was an underlying seriousness in his voice as he continued. "Not that I mean to take your consent for granted, Mary, but if that wasn't a 'yes' kiss, then I'm a Dutchman! You will marry me, won't you?"

Mary had the idea that a young woman ought to display a maidenly coyness in accepting a proposal of marriage, but it was beyond her abilities at that moment to act either maidenly or coy. "Oh, *yes,* my lord," she said fervently.

Paul laughed and gathered her into his arms again. Mary shut her eyes and yielded blissfully to his kiss a second time. "Paul," he corrected, between kisses. "You must call me Paul now that we are engaged."

"Yes, Paul," she said submissively. He laughed again and kissed her twice more, once on her lips and once on the tip of her nose.

"We have so many things to discuss," he said, looking down at her. "Announcements, and wedding dates, and all manner of other minutiae—and yet, at this moment, I can think of none of it. All I can think about is kissing you. And it really will not do, my lady: indeed, it will not do. I think we had better postpone all further discussion until tomorrow, when there will be someone about to make sure we keep the line. I can see *you're* not going to be much help in that direction!"

Mary laughed and buried her face against his shoulder. She felt all at once young and light-hearted and full of an unaccustomed daring. "You did not mention that was one of my duties, my lord," she whispered, deliberately running her fingers through his hair once more. He promptly captured the offending hand between his and raised it to his lips.

"Witch," he said. "Do that again, and you'll suffer the consequences." After kissing her hand, he retained it in his own for a moment, looking down at her with a thoughtful expression. Mary, stealing a shy look at him, thought he had the air of wishing to say something but being too embarrassed to speak.

"What is it, Paul?" she asked. "Is something wrong?"

His air of embarrassment grew deeper. "No, not wrong, exactly," he said. "It's nothing important, but I was rather wanting to ask you something. About your hair," he added, with a still greater display of embarrassment.

"My hair?" Mary's hand went self-consciously to her head. "What's wrong with it?"

"Nothing's wrong with it, but I was wondering if you couldn't—er—arrange it a bit differently. Not that it looks bad the way it is, mind you," he added with great haste. "But now that we're engaged, I thought you might—er—loosen it up a little. What I mean to say is, you don't need to look like a governess anymore, and I have always thought it would look nicer if you wore it differently. Not pulled back so tightly, you know."

Paul was actually blushing by the time he was done with this speech. Mary felt she must be blushing, too, but she was entertained by her lover's diffidence and touched by his evident desire to spare her feelings. "I know perfectly well that I look a fright with my hair scraped back like this, so you need not mince words, Paul," she told him with a smile. "I'll see if I can't find some different way to wear it tomorrow."

A glowing smile lit up his face. "That will give me something else to look forward to," he said. "Something besides the prospect of kissing you again, that is. Good night, Mary."

"Good night," said Mary. She accepted a final brief kiss from him and left the drawing room with the sensation of walking on air.

Twelve

Mary's happiness continued intact for some hours after leaving Paul. She was in such an exalted state of mind that she went through the familiar motions of preparing for bed without being at all aware of what she was doing and was quite surprised, some little while later, to find herself seated on the edge of the bed in her nightdress with her hair brushed and braided for the night. Even after she had gotten into bed, her happiness did not desert her. She lay basking in its glow, finding it altogether a more potent source of warmth than the threadbare blanket and shabby quilt that served as her bedclothes.

For a long time Mary put off examining the source of her happiness. This was partly because it was enough merely to enjoy it, but mostly because she feared that if she scrutinized it too closely she would find a flaw in it somewhere. At last the temptation grew too great, however. Mary began to relive in her mind, word by word, the scene that had just taken place between her and Paul in the drawing room. And surely enough, as soon as she had begun to really analyze Paul's words and actions, she found the flaw she had been dreading.

There could be no doubt that Paul had proposed to her, and certainly he had kissed her with all the ardor she could desire. But he had said nothing about loving her. He had told her he respected, admired, and esteemed her, but that was all. Was it enough? For a while, Mary tried valiantly to assure herself that it was. But her mind would not allow her to shirk facts, however

painful or unpleasant they might be, and she was obliged at last
to admit that the emotion Paul felt for her probably did not
equal that which she felt for him, or that which he had felt for
his former love, Lady de Lacey.

The thought of Lady de Lacey was intensely painful to Mary.
She remembered what Paul had said about his former mistress;
how he had spoken of his feelings for her, and of his desire to
marry her. Was it likely that he had the same feelings and desire
for her? Mary bleakly acknowledged that it was not. He might
wish to marry her, as he said, but his proposal had been more
in the nature of a business proposal than a passionate outpouring
of emotion.

To be sure, the kiss that had followed had been passionate
enough. But without any declaration of love to accompany it,
Mary could not take much comfort in a mere kiss. He was a
man, after all, and everyone knew that men attached less sig-
nificance to such things than women did. He had probably
kissed dozens of women for whom he cared nothing with quite
as much enjoyment as he had just kissed her.

This idea was painful enough to Mary, but a worse one was
soon to follow. For it occurred to her suddenly that the whole
business that evening might have been a ruse on Paul's part,
intended to trick her into receiving his attentions. How likely
was it, after all, that a gentleman of his rank and fortune would
choose to marry a penniless governess? As Earl of Wyland, he
might have his pick of the most beautiful and accomplished
women in the kingdom. It was more likely that he merely had
designs on her virtue and had settled on this method as the
simplest to achieve his ends. There had been no witness to his
proposal, after all. He could freely deny it at any time, and Mary
would have no means of proving there had ever been an engagement between them.

This dreadful idea made Mary sit straight up in bed. "Oh,
God, could it be? Have I made a fool of myself?" she whispered,
clutching the bedclothes in an agony of fear and self-doubt. But
her momentary panic was almost immediately dissipated by a

cooling blast of common sense. If Paul's intention had really been seduction, he might perfectly well have seduced her right there in the drawing room, and she would never have been able to resist him. Instead, he had shown quite a gentlemanly restraint, contenting himself merely with kissing her a few times before sending her upstairs to bed.

Mary lay back in bed again, greatly relieved. "He must have been sincere about wanting to marry me," she told herself. "Heaven knows why, but he must have been. However, that's not to say he will still feel the same about it tomorrow." It made Mary slightly sick to think Paul might recant his proposal, but this idea, too, she sternly forced herself to face.

"Perhaps he had been drinking and did not realize what he was doing. To be sure, he did not seem drunk, but I don't have much acquaintance with gentlemen who drink, and I daresay he might have been intoxicated without my knowing it. In any case, I must go slowly and not presume too much on what he said tonight. The thing to do, I suppose, would be to act as though nothing has happened when I go downstairs tomorrow morning. I will let him be the one to speak of our engagement first—if indeed he does mean to speak of it. And if he doesn't, I will simply have to put the whole business out of my head and try to go on as before."

With such thoughts to keep her company, it was a long time before Mary fell asleep that night. When morning finally came, she awoke with the birds, still anxious in mind and feeling but little rested. There was no question of sleeping late, however, on a day that for all practical purposes held the key to her entire future existence. Rising from her bed, Mary splashed cold water on her face and then set about making a most elaborate and painstaking toilette for the day ahead.

Arranging her hair was her first concern and likewise her chiefest difficulty. She experimented with different styles, but her hair was so long and heavy and so resolutely determined against curling that her choice of hairstyles was severely limited. In the end, Mary was forced to fall back on a style that resembled her usual one, differing only in being somewhat more elaborately arranged in back and somewhat softer about the temples. She then put on her best black silk dress, reflecting with satisfaction that since today happened to be Sunday her black silk was a perfectly unexceptionable choice even without any other excuse.

When the last button was buttoned and the last hairpin in place, Mary scrutinized herself long and hard in the glass. She had to acknowledge that her appearance still left something to be desired, for the black dress was only slightly less plain and sober than her other dresses. Her face, too, appeared rather wan after her nearly sleepless night, and there were faint circles under her eyes. But even so, she looked better than she had looked at any time during the past four and a half weeks.

"And if he could propose to me looking as I did last night, then he can hardly take exception to the way I look now," Mary told herself as she turned away from the glass. The thought was reassuring, and she felt a surge of hope as she picked up her shawl and prepared to go downstairs. Becoming aware of it, Mary cautioned herself against taking too sanguine a view of the situation. There was no saying what attitude Paul would take when she met him today, after all. It would be best if she was prepared for the worst. Throwing the shawl about her shoulders, Mary opened her bedroom door and found herself face-to-face with Paul.

"Oh," she said, falling back a step in confusion.

"Good morning," said Paul, giving her a most winning smile. "I hope you'll excuse my coming here at such an ungodly hour. I wanted to have a word with you before you went downstairs. Good God, is this your room?" His eyes had gone past Mary to survey the Spartan chamber behind her. "You don't mean to say this is where you've been living all this time?"

"Indeed it is," said Mary, pulling the door shut hastily behind her. "What was it you wanted to speak to me about, Paul?"

Paul, however, was still intent on the subject of her room. "But this is ridiculous," he said, in a voice vibrant with indignation. "Ridiculous, and quite unnecessary. Why did you not tell me you were living in such shabby quarters, Mary? You must move to one of the downstairs bedchambers immediately."

Mary could not help laughing at his indignation. "I have existed in these shabby quarters for five years now, and existed quite comfortably upon the whole," she told him with a smile. "My room is no worse than the other servants' rooms, I assure you. In any case, I could scarcely complain to you about my accommodations before now. Society has a way of looking askance at female servants who approach their master on the subject of changing bedchambers!"

Paul's look of indignation gave way to a sparkling smile. "I suppose it does," he said. "But there is no reason why you cannot change now, I hope. I find it quite lowering to think that my future wife has been languishing in a shabby attic room while I reveled in mahogany and velvet below."

"I haven't been languishing in the least," said Mary, her heart soaring at those magical words "my future wife." "Don't let it disturb you, Paul. I am perfectly happy to remain up here until—well, until such time as I am obliged to move to other quarters, you know."

For a moment they merely looked at each other. "You've changed your hair," said Paul irrelevantly. "It looks very nice. You can't think how often these last few weeks I've wanted to—well, never mind." With a conscious smile, he contemplated Mary's face. "There will be time enough to go into all that later, I trust. But for now, as I mentioned before, there was something else I wanted to talk about. After you left last night, it occurred to me you ought to have a ring—a betrothal ring, you know, something to show the world we really are engaged. I thought we probably ought to take care of the matter before you went down this morning, so I had Smithson haul the family jewelry upstairs."

He gestured toward the far end of the hall. Mary looked and saw Smithson hovering there, carrying in his hands a large, square wooden box. At Paul's gesture he came forward, and when he reached Mary's side he bowed formally and addressed her in a grave voice.

"Lord Wyland has just acquainted me with the news of your engagement, Miss Grant," he said. "Let me be the first to wish you very happy."

Mary thanked Smithson with tolerable composure, but wondered nervously what was going on behind his impassive countenance. Did he think her an adventuress, marrying his master for money and social advancement? The idea made her shy, so that she hesitated to approach the box which Paul was holding out to her.

"There's a great many rings here, most of them ugly as sin, but I've found one or two that don't seem too bad," he said, opening the box and beckoning to her with an encouraging smile. "Why don't you take a look at them and see which you like best?"

Reluctantly Mary stepped forward to examine the interior of the box. "Oh, my," she said, as the full splendor of its contents came into view. There were diamonds, rubies, and emeralds; sapphires, cameos, and pearls; rings, necklaces, and earrings, all jumbled together anyhow and presenting the appearance of a veritable treasure trove. Mary was overwhelmed by the sight of such a dazzling display of riches and instinctively shrank away.

Paul shook his head with a smile. "Come, this won't do," he said. "You must tell me what you like, Mary. Do you care for diamonds? There's one or two diamond rings here that are rather pretty things, I think. Or there are some rubies and emeralds if you would prefer one of those. Heaven only knows what else is here besides. My uncle seems to have kept everything jumbled together without much concern for its value. I suppose, being only earthly treasure, he would have considered it unChristian to spend too much time or thought on mere jewelry."

"Yes, I remember he was always very critical of Lady Wyland's wearing too many ornaments," said Mary. The thought of her late employer made her shrink inside herself even more, as she imagined what would be his reaction to the news of her engagement. It was hard to know which he would have disapproved most: the idea of any virtuous woman marrying his libertine nephew, or the idea of the heir to the house of Wycliff marrying a mere governess. For a man so fond of preaching Christian humility, he had possessed some stern ideas about the kind of marriage suitable for a man of rank and consequence.

"I cannot choose, my lord," said Mary desperately, shrinking back still further.

"Paul," he corrected her, with playful sternness.

"Paul, of course—but indeed, I cannot choose."

"But you must have something. I want to get a ring on your finger as soon as possible, before you change your mind and try to wriggle out of our engagement. But of course you would never do that." There was a soft light in Paul's eyes as he looked down at Mary. "You are the most honorable woman of my acquaintance, and I would confidently stake my life on the certainty of your fulfilling any commitment you entered into. The ring is merely symbolic in this case. But of course, even symbols have their uses. I would have the other gentlemen in the neighborhood know that you're engaged to me now and keep their distance! I daresay that makes me sound impossibly feudal, but—"

"Oh, no," said Mary, almost equally overwhelmed and gratified by this speech. "But I must say, I think your worries are needless, Paul. I haven't exactly been besieged by suitors during the time I've been at Wycliff, you know."

"They must breed an uncommonly slow and undiscerning kind of gentleman around here," responded Paul, looking down at her caressingly. "Nevertheless, I'm taking no chances on one of them developing discernment at this late date. Will you choose an engagement ring, or shall I choose one for you?"

"Oh, you choose, if you please. I should much prefer it," said Mary, clutching eagerly at this suggestion. Not only would it relieve her of making a difficult decision, it would be a good way to find out the extent of Paul's feelings for her. If he chose a small, plain ring without any distinguishing features—

"This, I think," said Paul, and picked out of the tangle of

jewelry a glowing ruby in an antique gold setting. "It's a bit old-fashioned, perhaps," he went on, turning the ring over in his hand. "But the stone appears to be very fine, and it looks as though it would suit you somehow, Mary."

"Oh, Paul," breathed Mary, looking down at the ring which he was holding out to her. "Oh, Paul, it's beautiful, but it's too much—much too much, upon my word. I am not worthy of such a valuable thing."

"I would say myself that it is not worthy of you. You remember what the Bible says about a good woman's price being above rubies." Smiling, Paul slipped the ring on the third finger of her left hand, then raised her hand to his lips and kissed it. Mary, looking into his eyes, felt such a rush of emotion that she could barely keep back the tears. In that moment she forgot all about Lady de Lacey and the love versus esteem question and knew only that she was supremely, overwhelmingly happy.

"Thank you, Paul," she whispered.

He smiled down at her. "Are you ready for breakfast now? If so, we'd better be on our way downstairs. Smithson can see to putting the rest of these things back in the safe. If you would, Smithson?"

"Certainly, my lord," said Smithson, taking possession of the box of jewelry once again.

Paul gave Mary his arm, and together they went downstairs to the breakfast room. Miss Eaton was already there, spreading butter on a toasted muffin. "Good morning, my lord," she said, looking up brightly from her task. "And good morning to you, too, Mary. A lovely morning, is it not?"

"Exceptionally lovely," said Paul, giving Mary a conspiratorial smile. "And I have some lovely news for you, Miss Eaton. Or perhaps I should say rather that Miss Grant and I have some lovely news for you."

"Oh, yes?" said Miss Eaton, casting a startled look at him and Mary.

"Yes, indeed. Shall I tell her or shall you, Mary?"

"You, if you please," said Mary, avoiding her friend's eye. "You tell her, Paul."

"Very well. Miss Eaton, it is my pleasure to announce that Miss Grant and I reached an understanding last night and are now engaged to be married. Of course, we depend on you to assist us in making the wedding plans, do we not, Mary?"

"Of course," assented Mary, keeping her eyes on her plate.

Miss Eaton said nothing. Her silence went unnoticed, however, for Paul had turned to Mary, taking Miss Eaton's joy in his news for granted. "I find, unfortunately, that I must make another trip to London here in the next few days. In fact, it would be best if I left today, for my agent informs me that some matters there require my immediate attention. I expect I shall be gone about a week. Would it be possible, do you think, if we arranged to be married upon my return? Or would that be too great a rush for you? I do not know if you have friends or relatives whom you would like to invite to the ceremony. If you do, of course we would have to allow time for them to make the journey to Yorkshire."

Mary, who had yet to really assimilate the fact of their engagement, was staggered to hear Paul talking airily about being married in a week's time. "No, there is no one I would wish to invite," she managed to say, after half a minute's stunned silence. "But do you really mean you wish us to be married as early as next week, Paul?"

"Yes, is that too soon? I know it's more usual to let a month or two go by between the announcement of the engagement and the wedding, but in our case I didn't see any point in waiting. We're neither of us children, and I think we both know our own minds pretty well. I know mine, at any rate." Paul gave Mary a look that brought color to her cheeks. "And since there are no parents or other close relatives in the case whose convenience must be consulted, I thought we might as well push ahead with the business and get it settled. But I do not mean to rush you in any way, Mary. If you would rather wait to be married until later in the year, or even wait until next year—"

"No, I am of the same opinion as you, Paul," said Mary quickly. "The sooner the business is settled, the better. I see no reason why we may not be married next week." Into her mind had sprung an expression which her father's elderly sexton had been fond of quoting: "There's many a slip 'twixt the cup and the lip." While she and Paul remained unmarried, she could imagine any number of slips that might upset the cup of their engagement. It seemed best that it should be conveyed to the lips—or, to abandon metaphor, the altar—as soon as possible.

"Excellent," said Paul, giving her another glowing smile. Mary gave him a brief, shy smile in return and then dropped her eyes to her plate again, still conscious of Miss Eaton's silent regard. "Now we must settle the type of the ceremony," Paul went on happily. "Would you prefer a private or parish wedding, Mary?"

Mary thought of being married to Paul in the village church, with the whole of the parish looking on and Fanny and Sophy Rundell whispering criticisms of her dress in the Rundell family pew. "Private, please," she said fervently. "I should much prefer a private ceremony, Paul."

"Private it is, then. I'll stop by the village on my way out of town and speak to the vicar before I set off for London. And while I'm in London, I must remember to speak to my solicitor about arranging the details of the settlements. I'll have to see about ordering a new coat, too, while I'm in Town. That ought to take care of my part in the business, hadn't it? I will trust you ladies to settle the other details." He looked around the table with a smile that encompassed both Mary and Miss Eaton.

"Oh, yes, you may trust us for that, my lord," said Miss Eaton. It was obvious that she was trying very hard to sound gay and light-hearted, but to Mary's ears her gaiety rang rather false. "We must have a wedding breakfast, of course, even if the wedding is to be a private ceremony," she told Paul, with the same forced gaiety. "And we must arrange some sort of bride-clothes for Mary, too."

"I suppose you must, although I beg you won't trouble yourself with getting anything too grand. Bride-clothes are of strictly secondary importance as far as I am concerned." Paul smiled across the table at Mary. She managed a weak smile in return. Though feeble, the expression must have satisfied him. Pushing back his chair from the table, he rose and came over to her side. "I shall probably be leaving within the hour, so I'll take leave of you now, Mary, if I may," he told her, raising her hand to his lips. "I shall look forward—very much look forward—to seeing you next week. And good morning to you, too, Miss Eaton. I leave my bride-to-be in your capable hands."

Miss Eaton nodded, but made no answer. She watched as Paul left the breakfast room, then turned to look at Mary. As before, Mary was unable to meet her eyes. She pretended to be very busy breaking apart a roll which she had taken from the basket on the table. She and Miss Eaton were alone in the breakfast room, for it was the custom at Wycliff for the family to serve themselves at breakfast. Miss Eaton waited until Paul was beyond earshot, then reached out and took Mary's hand in hers.

"My dear, have you considered well what you are doing?" she said urgently. "God knows it is no easy thing to be a woman making her way alone in the world, but there are worse things, you know. To tie yourself for life to a man you do not love for the sake of money and a title—"

"But I do love him," said Mary, lifting eyes of desperation to her friend's face. "Oh, Charlotte, you cannot know what I have been enduring. I think I have loved him almost from the first moment I saw him. And yet I have had to stand by and watch the Miss Rundells and Miss Summervilles throw themselves at him, until I felt it impossible he should not offer for one of them. It seems like such a dream that he could have offered for me instead. I have to pinch myself sometimes to make myself believe it's true, but you need not doubt that I love him, Charlotte. If he were to cry off now for any reason, I think it would kill me, or drive me mad. I do, indeed."

Miss Eaton gaped at her. Mary attempted a smile and went on, her voice calmer now but no less earnest than before. "I know all this must be a shock to you, Charlotte, but I hope you will not think too ill of me for not confiding in you earlier. You know I had no idea that Lord Wyland would ever return my feelings, and so I thought it better to keep them to myself and try to struggle against them. It is such a relief not to have to struggle anymore! I have been so miserable these last few weeks, it's a wonder to me that I still have my sanity."

"Oh, my dear," said Miss Eaton, grasping Mary's hand tighter in her own and surveying her with astonished compassion. "Oh, my dear, I had no idea! I never once suspected you cared for him. Indeed, I had always supposed you rather disliked him than otherwise. But this puts a different complexion on the matter."

"Yes, it does, doesn't it?" said Mary eagerly. "Oh, Charlotte, you do not blame me for having accepted him, do you? I know it is not an equal match as the world counts such things, but how could I refuse him, feeling as I do?"

Miss Eaton shook her head slowly. "I am sure no one could wonder at your accepting him, Mary," she said. "And I am sure you have my best wishes for your happiness with Lord Wyland. But at the same time, I think you should be prepared for some of the difficulties you are likely to encounter. You know there will be people who will criticize you very harshly for marrying a man so much your superior in fortune and social position—"

"Fanny and Sophy Rundell," said Mary, making a face. "But I don't care for them, Charlotte."

"No, I daresay not, but there will be others besides them who will criticize, I'm afraid," said Miss Eaton. Seeing Mary's mulish expression, however, she abandoned this tack with a smile and a sigh. "But there, I know you are not one to let other people's opinions influence you, Mary. Indeed, I would think the less of you if you did. What concerns me more is the confession you have just made about your feelings for Lord Wyland. It sounds inconsistent, I know, after I have just taken you to task for marrying a man you do not love. But the fact remains that in any relationship between two people, it can be as disastrous to care too much as too little."

Mary was silent. Miss Eaton cast a quick look at her and went on rather diffidently. "I do not like to speak ill of Lord Wyland, but you must know that he comes from a different level of society than you and I. I do not pretend to be an expert on such matters, but it is well known that the aristocratic classes tend to hold different opinions on the subject of marriage than such people as you or I."

"Yes, sometimes a good deal stricter opinions," Mary shot back. "Look at the late Lord Wyland."

"Yes, but the present Lord Wyland is not much like his uncle, is he?" said Miss Eaton unanswerably. "Indeed, I do not wish to discourage you, my dear, but it is better that you should consider carefully before taking such a step as you are contemplating. Lord Wyland has lived in London a good many years and I daresay has picked up some of the liberal attitudes about marriage which I understand are extant there—"

"You are saying you think our marriage will be a marriage of convenience," interrupted Mary. "But indeed, that is not the case, Charlotte. I thought the same myself when Lord Wyland first proposed to me, but he assured me that he—well, that he esteems me very highly, and that he means our marriage to be a real marriage."

Mary blushed a little in recounting these words. Miss Eaton regarded her sympathetically and reached out to pat her hand.

"I do not doubt that he esteems you most sincerely, my dear. No one who knew you well could help esteeming you, and I think the better of Lord Wyland for having recognized your good qualities. But I do question whether his idea of a real marriage is the same as yours. The fact that you care for him so deeply leaves you peculiarly vulnerable to hurt later on—hurt of a very particular and painful kind. Do you understand my meaning?"

Mary sat very still a moment. At last she nodded. "Do you think—do you think I ought to break off the engagement?" she said heavily.

Miss Eaton made a helpless gesture. "My dear, how can I advise you? It seems like madness to refuse such a wonderful opportunity. And then, to turn your back on a man whom you admit to caring for so deeply! No, I could not ask you to make such a sacrifice as that, Mary. If I were to offer you any advice at all on the subject, it would merely be to go cautiously. Be careful about showing the full extent of your feelings for Lord Wyland, and if you can, try to put some kind of check on those feelings so that you are less vulnerable to hurt if his should prove inferior to your own. And be careful, too, not to set your expectations too high. If you have a realistic view of what marriage to a man like Lord Wyland is likely to be, you are less likely to be disappointed later on."

Again Mary nodded. Miss Eaton gave her another sympathetic look. "Don't think me a Cassandra prophesying doom," she begged. "I hope and trust you shall be very happy with Lord Wyland, Mary. It is only that I think you are more likely to be so if you go into this business with your eyes open. Otherwise I would not have ventured to speak, I assure you." With a painful smile, she continued, "And you know you need not pay any attention to my prosings if they offend you, Mary. I am only an old maid, after all, and I expect it is presumptuous of me to be lecturing other people on the subject of marriage."

"Indeed it is not, Charlotte," said Mary, much moved by her friend's obvious concern. "I know of no one whose advice I would rather have than yours. Indeed, I appreciate your speaking as frankly as you did, and I assure you I will consider everything you have said most carefully."

"That is all I ask," said Miss Eaton, looking herself rather moved. "I want you to be happy, Mary; that's the long and short of it."

"I know it," said Mary, and closed the conversation by giving her friend a fervent hug.

Thirteen

As might be expected, Mary came away from her interview with Miss Eaton feeling rather depressed. She was at first almost inclined to resent her friend for having so quickly brushed the bloom from her newfound happiness. But her sense of justice was stronger than her sense of ill-usage, and when she had had time to think it over, she was forced to acknowledge that Miss Eaton had merely been doing her duty as she saw it. It was only a pity that on this occasion her duty had resulted in the loss of her friend's first, sanguine hopes.

Mary's hopes would not have fallen so low if she could have been sure Miss Eaton was mistaken in her judgment of Paul's character. But of this she could not be sure, and she soon began to distrust her own more partial judgment. She reminded herself that Miss Eaton was an older and more experienced woman than herself, able to view the situation from the standpoint of an outside observer.

It was quite possible that Miss Eaton saw and judged with a clearer eye than she did.

Mary forced herself to admit this possibility, but the admission left her feeling melancholy and full of forebodings for the future. Fortunately, she had not much opportunity to indulge her melancholy in the days that followed, for she was so busy with wedding preparations that she had little free time to worry about anything but her bride-clothes and the question of whether the ceremony ought to take place in Wycliff's chapel, hall, or drawing room.

This last issue was settled with relative ease, the drawing room being fixed on as the most suitable venue for a wedding. "For the hall is so drafty, and the chapel such a plain room," said Miss Eaton, with a shake of her head. "I would never have known it was a chapel if you had not told me, Mary. Not a speck of stained glass or carving anywhere, and no cushions for the pews. How uncomfortable they look!"

"No more uncomfortable than they feel, I assure you," said Mary, with a grimace. "You are fortunate in never having had to endure them for two or three hours of a Sunday, Charlotte. There used to be cushions, I believe, but the late Lord Wyland considered such luxuries inappropriate to a house of God and had them taken out. He took out all the stained glass and carvings, too, along with one or two marbles that his ancestors had been ill-judged enough to install. His opinion, which he was happy to give to anyone who asked, was that such things smacked too much of idolatry."

Miss Eaton shook her head again, but with a tolerant air. "What a very unpleasant man he was," she said. "Only think of his desecrating his ancestors' chapel in the name of religion! Ah, well, we must hope his nephew will see about restoring it to its former state now that he has come into the property. And in the meantime, we can do quite nicely with the drawing room for your wedding. I expect that with a few flowers and potted plants, we can make it look very pretty."

Mary concurred in this, and the household staff were informed that a nuptial ceremony between Lord Wyland and Miss Grant would be held in the drawing room in a week's time. This announcement naturally caused no little stir, but since Mary had always held herself rather aloof from her coworkers, she was not troubled by any overt display of curiosity or resentment on their part.

The issue which did trouble her, and trouble her severely, was the matter of her bride-clothes. The garments she had prepared in expectation of her former marriage were no longer in existence, having been for the most part altered or adapted to suit her position as governess. Those things which had not lent themselves to being adapted Mary had ruthlessly disposed of years ago. Even if they had still been in her possession, the bride-clothes that had befitted a clergyman's wife would not have been suitable for a future countess.

"You need morning dresses, and evening dresses, and all new underthings," said Miss Eaton with authority. "Why, when the eldest Miss Summerville married Lord Barclay last summer, she had a dozen of everything, and no expense spared."

But it was no easy task to assemble bride-clothes anything resembling Miss Summerville's, given the short time at Mary's disposal. Even if her means had been equal to the task, she would have found it difficult, and as they were nowhere near being equal to it, she was forced to abandon it as a lost cause. The only money she possessed was the small sum which, through much scrimping and saving, she had managed to set aside from her earnings as a hedge against old age and illness. This was nowhere near enough to finance the kind of bride-clothes which ought, by rights, to belong to a future countess. Mary was miserably aware of the fact, but she resolved to throw everything she had into the effort nonetheless.

"Even if I don't have a dozen of everything, I can at least look presentable at the altar," she told herself. "A suitable wedding dress I must have, even if I have nothing else. And then, if I can manage it, I will need a new morning dress and pelisse, and perhaps an evening dress or two. That much ought not to be beyond my means, if I choose very plain, simple things. Then I shall need some new underthings—and a new nightdress, of course." Mary blushed at the train of thought that had inspired this last item, but added to her list all the same. "I can make up the underclothes and nightdress myself and so save a little money that way. Charlotte will help me with the sewing, I'm sure. I shall ask her to accompany me to the village this afternoon and help me choose what I need."

Miss Eaton, when consulted, was very happy to lend her assistance in this matter. Having voiced her reservations about Mary's engagement to Paul, she apparently felt her duty was done and entered into the wedding preparations with true feminine enjoyment.

"Though to my mind, you are foolish not to avail yourself of the former Lady Wyland's wardrobe," she told Mary in a low voice, as they browsed among the bolts of fabric in the village dry-goods shop. "I am sure she must have had some things that could be made over to suit you. And it's not as though you would be stealing. Her things will all be yours anyway, after you and Lord Wyland are married. It is no worse than taking over her rooms, or her carriage."

"I suppose not, but still I would rather have my own things, Charlotte, at least to begin with. I am not married yet, you know, and so Lady Wyland's old things still belong to Lord Wyland. If I were to take them now, it would be as though he were paying for my bride-clothes," Mary tried to explain.

Miss Eaton shook her head at such scruples, but made no further suggestions concerning the late Lady Wyland's wardrobe. Instead, she devoted herself to stretching Mary's small savings to cover the greatest possible number of garments.

"The sprig muslin will do for a pretty morning dress, and if you have a pelisse of the rose sarcenet to go over it, it will do for walking out, too. The ruby velvet will make a beautiful evening dress. I'm sure four yards will be enough for it, as skimpy as dresses are at present. You ought to be glad you are being married now and not thirty years ago, Mary. Back then we had to put almost that much material into the sleeves and bodice alone. Then there is the gold brocade—and the ivory crepe—and the gauze for your wedding dress. What else? Oh, yes, and the cambric for your underthings. We can make those ourselves, as you say, and leave the rest to Miss Johnson."

"But by the time I have paid for everything you've just named, Charlotte, I will have no money for a new bonnet," said Mary, lingering to look at a display of hats and bonnets near the front of the store. Since Paul had done her the honor of asking her to marry him, she was anxious that nothing about her should disgrace him, and there was no denying that her old bonnet was a disgraceful object. She could well remember Paul's pained expression the first time he had seen her wearing it. "Can we not do with one dress the less, Charlotte, and buy me a new bonnet instead?"

"No, the dresses are more important. You are getting few enough as it is, considering the position you are marrying into. Although heaven knows, you do need a new bonnet, Mary. Perhaps we could retrim your old one and make it more attractive." Miss Eaton cast a doubtful glance at Mary's bonnet. "Of course, if you were willing to use some of Lady Wyland's old things—"

"No, I am determined not to touch those, Charlotte. I will simply have to wait and get a new bonnet after I am married." With a last wistful look, Mary turned away from the millinery display. "Come, let's pay for these other things and then go over to Miss Johnson's to see about making my dresses up."

Miss Johnson, a village woman who supported herself by taking in sewing, greeted Mary and Miss Eaton civilly enough when they presented themselves on her doorstep. When they explained the business that brought them there, however, her manner became downright fulsome. She exclaimed repeatedly over the news of Mary's engagement to Paul; and Mary, knowing her propensity to gossip, resigned herself to having news of it spread throughout the village by nightfall.

The news would soon have become known in any case, for the servants at Wycliff had not been backwards about sharing such a juicy morsel of gossip among their friends and acquaintances. And when a solicitor from Paul's agents arrived on the London stage a few days later, bearing with him the finished drafts of the marriage settlements, official credulity was given to the rumors that were flying about.

Mary spent the entirety of one afternoon with this gentleman discussing the provisions of the marriage settlements. She found it altogether very heavy going. He surveyed her throughout the interview with a mixture of disapproval and lascivious interest and, without putting the matter in so many words, managed to convey the impression that she had done very well for herself.

Mary came away from this interview feeling disagreeably soiled. She narrowly missed an even more disagreeable interview the following day. Finding she lacked sufficient ribbon to trim the undergarments she and Miss Eaton were making, she made a quick trip to the village and returned to find that Mrs. Rundell and her daughters had called in her absence. Mary knew not whether they had come to congratulate or recriminate, but she was glad in any case to have escaped them. She did not escape the vicar, however, who came to call the following day to arrange the details of the upcoming wedding.

"I must say, I was quite surprised when Lord Wyland told me of your engagement," said Reverend Biddle, seating himself on the sofa at Mary's request. He was a good-looking man in his early thirties with a high forehead, intelligent gray eyes, and fair hair growing rather thin on top. As one of the few eligible bachelors in the village, he had been the favorite quarry of the local marriage-minded maidens before Paul's advent on the social scene had eclipsed his lesser light in their eyes.

Mary had always liked Reverend Biddle and had sometimes fancied that he cherished an even warmer feeling for her, although he had never said or done anything that could not be construed as mere friendly interest. Friendly he had always been, however, and so it came as a shock to her to find him surveying her now with an expression of cold disapproval.

"I was quite surprised to hear of your engagement to Lord Wyland," he repeated. "There has been a certain amount of gossip about him and the eldest Miss Rundell, I believe, but it was never so much as whispered that there was anything between the two of you—except, of course, for the ordinary relations between employer and employee. I collect it all must have come about rather suddenly?"

"Yes, quite suddenly," said Mary in a stifled voice. Once more, Reverend Biddle's gray eyes surveyed her coldly.

"I am sure I wish you very happy, Miss Grant," he said, in a voice that largely negated the effect of these words. "You have always struck me as a very deserving young woman, and your friends must rejoice to see you settled so creditably. I only hope that in accepting Lord Wyland's suit, you may not have been influenced too much by worldly considerations. However, I do not mean to criticize your decision. We are all human, after all, and sadly venal creatures when all is said and done." With a chilly smile, Reverend Biddle consulted a sheaf of papers he had just produced from an inner pocket. "Lord Wyland has approached me about performing the wedding ceremony, and of course I assured him I was happy to oblige. He mentioned this coming Thursday as a possible date?"

Mary murmured an assent and sat pleating her handkerchief nervously between her fingers as Reverend Biddle went through the other details of the wedding ceremony with her. As it was to be such a simple ceremony, these details were soon settled, and Mary was glad when he took leave of her with a stiff bow and a promise to return on the coming Thursday. His remarks about venality continued to haunt her long after he had left, however.

"Am I venal?" she agonized to herself, lying alone in her bed that night. "Not in the sense Reverend Biddle means, I'm sure. I know I did not accept Paul's offer only because he is wealthy and a lord. Why, I would marry him even if he were as poor and obscure as myself. But is it possible I have taken a merely physical attraction and twisted it into something more—mistaken lust for love, in fact? I don't think so, but how can I be sure? All I know is that I never felt so powerfully about any man before—no, not even for Francis, though I'm quite sure I loved *him,* at all events. But my feelings for Paul are so tangled up together that I hardly know how I feel about him."

The thought of her dead fiancé sent Mary's mind ranging along a different track. It had been several days since she had even thought of Francis. His miniature still lay in her trunk, untouched since the night she had impulsively put it away. Now she had entered into an engagement with another man, never once thinking of the man who had previously been so much to her. The idea made Mary feel both sad and guilty. She wondered if Francis, wherever he might be, was aware of and hurt by her neglect.

"But that's morbid nonsense," she told herself stoutly. "Francis would be the first to ridicule it if he were here. I remember him telling old Mrs. Bishop that the dead undoubtedly had better things to do in heaven than hang about spying on the living." Nevertheless the idea stayed with Mary, giving her thoughts a touch of melancholy. In this humor, it was not long before she began to reflect once more on the conversation she had had with Miss Eaton and the advice that lady had given her regarding her dealings with Paul.

"And so I am to lower my expectations and put a check on my feelings, am I?" she told herself with a mirthless smile. "The expectation part is no problem, because I really don't have any expectations. All I can do is trust that Paul means what he says and will treat me decently when I am his wife.

"But as for putting a check on my feelings—there I haven't a clue. How does one go about restraining a feeling? I might as well try to restrain the wind from blowing, or the tide from coming in. The best I can do is try to disguise my feelings for him as I did before. And oh, it will be a hundred times harder now that I've once let them out in the open. But I will try—yes, I will try. And perhaps, if I choke my feelings back hard enough and often enough, they will grow more manageable of their own accord."

This plan Mary resolved to adopt, though the thought of more self-restraint made her weary. "It is all like a great game, and one's feelings are cards which one is obliged to keep hidden from the other players," she reflected bitterly. "I wish we could all simply lay our cards on the table and be done with it. How does Paul really feel about me, I wonder? Does he miss me as much as I miss him? Or is he so busy flirting with the London belles that he has forgotten all about me? I wonder—I wonder if he will see Lady de Lacey while he is in London."

As it happened, Mary's fears on this subject were groundless. It was not flirtation but business that was occupying Paul in London. His first act, which he performed with great pleasure, was to visit Wyland House and dismiss Samuel Higgins from his position of caretaker.

Mr. Higgins raged and stormed and took his departure with a great show of injured innocence. But a subsequent search of the house brought to light some five months of correspondence which he had neglected to forward on to Paul. There was also plenty of evidence to show that the generous sums which he had drawn quarterly for the purpose of maintaining the house had gone instead to enrich his own purse.

Paul was furious at having been imposed on by the wily caretaker, but he wisely decided against spending more time and money in what would probably be a futile effort to recover the misappropriated funds. Instead, he devoted himself to his neglected house. With a new caretaker installed and a crew of cleaning women hired to clear away the dust and disorder that had accumulated during Mr. Higgins's reign, he had hopes it would be rendered habitable before his next visit to London.

"And in all likelihood Mary will accompany me on that visit," Paul told himself, as he strolled through the rooms that were now swiftly being brought into order. He found the idea strange, but at the same time alluring. He had no longer any fear that he had made a mistake in proposing to Mary. The kiss that had followed the proposal had been enough to set all his fears to rest. Every time he thought of that kiss, he felt a little leap in his heart, not to mention stirrings in various other parts of his body. And since he thought of kissing Mary a great deal, he found himself in an almost perpetual state of agitation. He was, in fact, beginning to feel very much like a man in love. And as the week wore on, and he grew more and more impatient to see his bride-to-be once again, he admitted to himself that that was exactly what he was.

He could not cut short his stay in London, however, great as his inclination was. Besides the matter of the house, he had plenty of other business to occupy him. He consulted with his agent, visited his solicitors in Lombard Street, and ordered the marriage settlements drawn up and dispatched to Wycliff under care of one of their agents. He was so anxious to get all his business transacted as quickly as possible that he spared almost no time for anything else. It was not until the last day of his visit that he happened to have a few minutes' leisure and found himself in Bond Street, having just paid a visit to his tailor to pick up the new topcoat he had ordered for his wedding.

Next door to the tailor's was a milliner's shop, a small but elegant establishment whose window displayed half-a-dozen fashionable hats and bonnets decked with ribbons, flowers, and feathers. Paul, pausing to put on his gloves outside the tailor's, threw a disinterested glance at these wares. A drooping cluster of plumes on one of the hats reminded him of those on Mary's old bonnet. Once again he thought to himself what a pity it was that such an attractive young woman should disfigure herself with such a hideous piece of headgear. Then all at once he was struck by a flash of inspiration.

"I am her fiancé, after all," he told himself. "It's perfectly proper that I buy her a new hat—or if not perfectly proper, at least perfectly allowable, considering how close we are to being married. And if she objects, I can always wait and give it to her after the ceremony as a wedding present. I'll do it, by jove. I wonder what she would like?"

With a new interest he studied the hats and bonnets in the window. There was one extravagant confection loaded with pink roses that attracted him strongly. He had little knowledge of feminine fashions, but it seemed to him everything a ladies' hat ought to be. Pushing open the door, he stepped into the shop.

"Good day, sir. I'll be with you in a minute," drawled the salesgirl, a pretty but languid-looking young woman who was engaged in trimming a bonnet at the counter. When she glanced up a few minutes later, however, and got a good look at her prospective customer, her air of languor left her abruptly. Leaving off her bonnet trimming, she came hurrying over to Paul with a seductive smile on her lips and an avaricious glint in her eyes.

"I beg your pardon for keeping you waiting, sir. Is there anything I can do for you?" she said, looking him up and down with an expression of approbation. "I'm sure I'm happy to oblige any way I can."

"I would like to buy that hat in the window," said Paul, wide awake to the innuendo in the girl's words but determined not to show it. "The one with the pink flowers, please."

"Ah, yes, the satin-straw villager. Let me fetch it in for you, sir." With a pronounced sway of her hips, the girl went to the window, mounted a set of steps, and took down the pink-flowered hat. "Is this the one, sir?" she asked, placing it atop her own head so that he might admire the effect of it against her chestnut curls. "It's a lovely hat, isn't it? Only five guineas, and cheap at the price."

"We must differ in our definition of cheap, then," said Paul, determinedly insensible to the sultry looks the salesgirl was shooting him from beneath the hat's flower-decked brim. "For myself, I should consider five guineas rather expensive for a single hat. However, it is a pretty hat and should look very well on my fiancée. Here's five pounds and a crown piece. Wrap it up for me, if you please, and I will take it with me."

The word "fiancée" had a dampening effect on the salesgirl. With a miffed air, she pulled the hat from her head, dropped it on the counter, and took up the money Paul had laid there. "Is there anything more I can do for you, sir?" she inquired coldly, as she wrote up a receipt and stowed the hat perfunctorily inside a bandbox.

"Not a thing," said Paul cheerfully. "Thank you very much for your assistance." Taking possession of the bandbox, he left the shop, happily anticipating Mary's reaction when she should see its contents.

Fourteen

"My dear, how pretty you look! Miss Johnson made a nice thing of that dress, didn't she?"

"Yes, she did," said Mary, looking down at herself. Rather self-consciously, she added, "I expect you think it odd that I should wear it today, rather than saving it until after the wedding, Charlotte. But it's such a warm day, and my old gowns are so heavy—"

"My dear, you need not make any explanations to me," said Miss Eaton, smiling. "I am sure you have the best of reasons to make yourself fine. Lord Wyland is coming home today, is he not?"

"Yes, he should arrive sometime this afternoon if nothing happens to delay him. At least we need not worry that the weather will pose any problem. It's more like July than October outside."

"Yes, a regular St. Martin's summer," agreed Miss Eaton. In a significant voice, she added, "Let us hope the weather will hold through tomorrow."

Mary made no answer. The thought of what would take place on the morrow was already causing butterfly sensations in her stomach. It seemed to her that she had never properly appreciated what a drastic business matrimony was. More than ever was she grateful that she had chosen a private rather than a public wedding ceremony. To have stood before the Misses Rundell and the rest of the parish in her present state of nerves would, she felt sure, have overpowered her completely.

Anxiously she looked at the drawing room clock. Its hands

stood only a minute or two away from three o'clock. Even as she watched, it struck the hour, then began moving inexorably on toward four. Mary wondered if Paul would arrive before that time, or if something had happened to delay him in London. She could imagine all manner of things that might cause such a delay, ranging from the downright tragic to the merely crushing. But as such imaginings tended to increase the nervous fluttering in her stomach, she put them forcibly aside and walked over to the window, trying to divert herself with a survey of the sunlit landscape outside.

It was a fine clear day, exceptionally warm for October. The sky was a deep, vibrant blue punctuated by a few fluffy masses of cloud. The sun shone brilliantly on the rocky coastline and so warmed the air that the inevitable breeze off the ocean felt refreshing rather than chilling. Mary, who had risen early that morning, had decided that such weather merited something better than one of her heavy dark serge gowns. She had therefore anticipated matters a trifle by putting on one of the dresses that had been among her bride-clothes.

The dress was a light sprig muslin patterned pink on white with a handkerchief front, full sleeves, and a single flounce. With her hair drawn back loosely and braided at the nape of her neck, Mary felt she looked altogether quite presentable and hoped Paul would think so, too, when he arrived.

The question that was troubling her at that moment was when his arrival would be. Was it possible he might not arrive at all? Once more Mary began to imagine all the possible scenarios that might prevent him from coming. She was so busy inventing tragedies that she missed the sounds that would have alerted her to Paul's arrival and thus received a shock when she awoke to find him actually standing in front of her with a bandbox in his hand and a smile on his face.

"You're looking very solemn for a bride on the eve of her wedding, Miss Grant," he said. "I'd offer you a penny for your thoughts, but I'm almost afraid to ask what they might be. You aren't thinking about giving me my ring back, I trust?"

"Oh, no," said Mary, rising hurriedly to her feet. She was sure she must be blushing. Paul took her hand in his and looked her up and down with an expression of pleased surprise.

"Well, and don't you look nice," he said. "You get prettier every time I see you, Mary, and I thought you pretty enough to start with. That's a nice dress you've got on. Is it your wedding dress?"

"Of course not," said Mary, smiling in spite of herself at this masculine naiveté. "My dear man, you cannot suppose I would choose to be married in sprig muslin!"

"Would you not? It looks perfectly fine to me," said Paul, looking down at her with warm appreciation. In a lower voice, he added, "I have missed you, you know. I never knew a week to last as long as this one."

"Nor have I," said Mary, and added shyly, "I have missed you, too, Paul." As she was speaking, she noticed for the first time the bandbox he was carrying in his left hand. Paul saw her looking at it and offered it to her with an air of smiling diffidence.

"I got something for you while I was in London," he said. "I hope you will like it, Mary."

"A wedding present?" said Miss Eaton. She had considerately effaced herself while Mary and Paul were exchanging their first greetings, but now she came over to join them, her eyes bright with interest.

"Hello, Miss E.; I didn't see you over there in the corner," said Paul, greeting her with a smile. "No, it's not a wedding present exactly; just a trifle I picked up on Bond Street. I thought that as Mary and I were so soon to be married, I might anticipate matters a day or so and give it to her now." He watched as Mary bent over the bandbox, examining its elegantly patterned exterior. She looked up at him with a glowing smile.

"Oh, Paul, I have never had anything from Bond Street before. I can't imagine what it is, but I am sure it must have been fearfully expensive, to judge from the package."

"Open it, Mary," urged Miss Eaton, quite as excited as the other two. "I believe it must be a hat. Oh, and it *is* a hat—and such a hat! You *have* been extravagant, my lord. I never saw anything so lovely."

Reverently Mary lifted the hat from the bandbox. It was a broad-brimmed villager hat of satin straw, loaded with pink roses and lavishly festooned with lace and ribbons. A broad pink silk ribbon ran over the low crown and tied beneath the chin. Looking at it, Mary felt an urge to laugh and cry at the same time. It was a beautiful hat, quite the most beautiful hat she had ever seen, but it was completely inappropriate for a twenty-four-year-old ex-governess. In her mind's eye, Mary could see clearly the kind of girl it ought to have belonged to: a girl of about sixteen, pretty, young, gay, and flirtatious; a girl such as she was not and could never be again.

"Do you like it?" asked Paul hopefully.

"Oh, Paul, it's beautiful," said Mary, blinking back her tears and smiling at him. "Indeed, it's the most beautiful hat I have ever seen. But I can't possibly wear it, Paul. The Miss Rundells would laugh themselves sick if they saw me in such a hat as this."

"I don't see why," said Paul stoutly. "I think it would look very nice on you. Put it on and let's see."

"Yes, put it on, Mary," urged Miss Eaton. "It's a perfect love of a hat, and you'd be a fool not to wear it only because you're afraid the Miss Rundells might laugh at you. I'd say myself they'd be more likely to tear their hair out with jealousy."

Slowly Mary lifted the hat and placed it on her head. She then looked apprehensively at Paul and Miss Eaton. There was a light in Paul's eyes that seemed to indicate that he, at least, found no fault with her appearance.

"You look beautiful, Mary," he said warmly. "In my opinion, the hat might have been made for you. Doesn't she look well in it, Miss Eaton?"

"Yes, she does," said Miss Eaton, with equal warmth. "It's a lovely hat, my lord. And how perfectly it goes with her dress! You might have chosen it with that very purpose in mind."

"Very clever of me, wasn't it?" said Paul, surveying Mary

complacently. "I had a feeling that particular hat might suit her. Go look at yourself in the glass, Mary, and see if you don't agree."

Mary went obediently to the fireplace and surveyed herself in the chimney glass over the mantel. "You see?" said Paul triumphantly. "It's perfect for you, Mary. Suits you right down to the ground."

Mary, surveying herself critically, could not quite concur with this extravagant praise, but she was obliged to admit that the hat was surprisingly becoming. Although youthful in style, it possessed a sophistication that kept it from looking too incongruous in combination with her no-longer-youthful face. And its colors undoubtedly suited her better than the dull black straw of her old bonnet. Indeed, it seemed to her almost as though the hat had worked a kind of magic upon her features, transforming her into a younger, prettier version of herself, more like the kind of girl for whom the hat had originally been intended. It had a beneficial effect on her spirits, too. With such a hat on her head, she felt she could face even such critics as the Miss Rundells with a smiling face and defiant spirit. And if they dared to laugh at her, she would simply laugh right back at them and go on her way undaunted.

"Yes," she said aloud. "It's a lovely hat, Paul, and it doesn't look so foolish on me as I had supposed. In any case, now that I've tried it on, I can't bear to part with it, even if it is a trifle young for me."

Paul shook his head at this modesty, but he was smiling. "Now that you've got it on, it seems only right that we put it to use," he said. "Why don't you come for a walk with me, Mary? It's such a pretty day out, we may as well make the most of the weather while it holds."

"Well, I don't know, Paul," said Mary, looking at Miss Eaton. "The wedding is tomorrow, you know, and there are still a good many things to be done. I ought really to stay and help Charlotte with the preparations—"

"Oh, there's not much to be done now, and I can easily take care of anything that does need doing myself," said Miss Eaton quickly. "You go on with Lord Wyland, Mary. As he says, it would be a shame not to make the most of this lovely weather while it lasts."

Mary made no further demur, but put on her shawl, accepted Paul's arm, and accompanied him outside to the terrace. "Where shall we walk to?" he asked, as they went down the terrace steps. "You probably know the best walks hereabouts better than I do."

Mary considered. "I think I should like to walk along the beach," she said. "The tide's out right now, so we'll have nice, smooth walking on the sands. And I always like looking at the sea."

"Do you? So do I," said Paul, looking pleased. "It's remarkable how many tastes we have in common, Mary. Let us walk along the beach by all means."

Arm in arm, he and Mary left the terrace and made for the farthest outcropping of rock where the cliffs towered high above the water. A stone staircase had been cut into the side of the cliff, offering easy access to the beach. But by common consent they bypassed the stairs and took the longer and less precipitous path that wound down among the rocks to the water's edge.

When they reached the beach, they paused a moment, looking out at the vast expanse of water that sparkled in front of them as far as the eye could see. Close to shore, the waves came tumbling in with a roar like thunder, while seabirds wheeled and screeched overhead. On the horizon, a single fishing boat trimmed its sails in the direction of the village. Paul shaded his eyes with his hand to watch its progress across the water. "What an amazing thing the sea is," he said. "There's something about it that makes one feel very small and insignificant, isn't there?"

Mary nodded. "Yes, there is," she said. "But I don't think it's an entirely bad thing to feel one's self small and insignificant now and then."

"How so?" asked Paul, looking at her curiously.

Mary looked pensively out at the tumbling waves. "For one thing, it helps put one's problems in perspective," she said. "There've been times these last five years when I've come here feeling I could not endure life as a governess one day longer. And yet, after I'd walked on the beach a little while, I found I could shoulder my burden again quite happily and carry on, grateful the situation was no worse."

Paul looked at her soberly. "It sounds as though you had little enough to be grateful for," he said. "I can hardly bear to think of all you have had to endure these last few years, Mary."

Mary shook her head, a little embarrassed by his warmth. "I don't suppose I've had to endure more than most people," she said. "Indeed, I have been more fortunate than many, I know, to have a roof over my head and a means of earning a decent living. You must not be making too much of what I was saying just now, Paul. I would not want you to think me a poor creature who spent the past five years moping on the beach and bewailing her sad lot in life!"

Paul smiled. "I don't think you a poor creature," he said.

"Well, I hope not," said Mary, smiling back at him. "It is true I used to spend quite a bit of time here when I was governess to your cousin, but that is only because I like walking by the sea so much. It is such pleasant walking when the tide is out, and one can always find something new to see. And the sea itself has so many different moods—sometimes calm, and sometimes angry, and sometimes merely playful, as it is today."

Paul assented to this, and for a time they strolled along the sands in silence, looking out at the limitless waters that sparkled beneath the afternoon sun. The offshore breeze fluttered the skirts of Mary's dress and tugged at the ribbons of her hat. She raised a hand to make sure it was secure upon her head, then glanced at Paul. He was looking down at her with the same expression of incredulous pleasure he had worn earlier.

"You do look so pretty," he said. "I can't get over the change. Not that I mean to imply you didn't look pretty before, but I always felt you were hiding most of your light under a rather large bushel. You couldn't deceive me, though. I always knew that light was there, and it is a pleasure to see it out in the open at last."

This speech made Mary blush. "Thank you," she said. "And thank you again for the hat, Paul. I did not thank you for it properly before, because I was so overwhelmed. But indeed, I am very grateful. It was kind of you to think of me in London."

Paul laughed. "I thought of very little else, I assure you," he said. "You can't think how I've missed you, Mary." Again he looked down at her. She gave him a quick, shy smile beneath the brim of her hat. Its feminine froth made an effective foil for the glossy mass of her dark hair and the smooth oval of her face. The effect struck Paul as wholly ravishing. He stopped walking and turned to face her. She paused, too, looking up at him uncertainly.

"Oh, Mary, would you mind very much if I kissed you again?" he asked in a low voice. "All week I've been thinking about it and thinking about it, and I don't think I can wait another moment."

"I've been thinking about it, too," said Mary. She had forgotten all about her resolution to keep her feelings in check. Indeed, looking into Paul's eyes was enough to make her forget everything but her love and desire for him. When he put his hands on her waist she went to him willingly, shutting her eyes and letting herself be crushed against him. His lips found hers, and they kissed, a long, leisurely kiss that seemed to take the stiffening out of her knees. "Oh," she sighed. "Oh, Paul."

He made a low noise in his throat and kissed her again. Mary was vaguely conscious of the roar of the waves in the background and the seabirds crying overhead, but the chief part of her senses was given up to reveling in the sensations which Paul's kiss was arousing in her. She felt as though she were melting inside. She was acutely conscious of the strength of Paul's arms and the solid warmth of his body against hers, and of the gentle, insinuating pressure of his lips that drew from her an ever more ardent response.

In a detached sort of way, she marveled that a mere kiss could have such an effect on her. It seemed to set her whole body on fire, making her yearn to be closer to him, to be part of him, in fact. It was growing increasingly obvious that nothing less would satisfy her. Mary was just acknowledging this fact with detached interest when Paul spoke in her ear. "We really ought to stop, you know. God knows I don't want to, but if this goes on much longer, I don't think I shall be able to restrain myself from taking the logical next step. And a beach in broad daylight is rather a public place for lovemaking when all is said and done."

"Mmm," said Mary submissively. She made no effort to disengage herself from his embrace, however, and despite his words he seemed in no hurry to release her. He held her tight against him, running his hands up and down her back as though seeking to memorize the shape of her. Mary shut her eyes again, exulting in his touch. Her emotions at the moment were an odd combination of excitement, frustrated desire, and deep glowing happiness.

"He loves me," she told herself. "I am sure he does. It cannot be that he doesn't feel what I am feeling right now. This is the happiest moment of my life." The thought was so profound that it made her shiver a little. Paul raised his head and looked at her tenderly.

"You are cold," he said.

"Oh, no," said Mary, so fervently that he laughed.

"Well, perhaps not cold. But it would probably be as well if we started back to the house now. As I said, if I stay out here with you much longer, I might be tempted to do something that would better be postponed till tomorrow night. As it is, I'm afraid I've thrown your new headgear into disarray." He reached up to adjust the hat, which during their embrace had slipped back on Mary's head.

Mary stood quietly while Paul made the adjustment. When he was done, he stepped back to look at her. "There, you look all in order again," he told her with a smile. "Give me your arm now, and we shall walk back to the house with perfect decorum."

Mary gave him her arm, and they began to retrace their steps along the beach. "Tell me what you have been doing with yourself while I have been gone," instructed Paul. "Have you been run ragged preparing for the wedding?"

"I have been busy, but not run ragged, Paul. Indeed, I hope you will find me less ragged now than I was before!" Rather self-consciously, Mary explained about her bride-clothes. "Mind you, you must not be expecting anything too grand," she added conscientiously. "I am not a rich woman, you know, and with only a week to prepare, it wasn't possible to put together anything too ambitious in the way of a trousseau."

"Of course not, and I wouldn't expect it," said Paul warmly. "My only concern is that you have strapped yourself financially to buy a lot of new things that really were not necessary. If you wanted new clothes, it would have been my pleasure to provide them for you."

Mary shook her head firmly. "No, Paul, I could not have allowed that," she said. "I don't pretend to know all the finer points of bridal etiquette, but I do know that it is not at all the thing for the bridegroom to pay for the bride's clothes. Although you see I have made one exception in that direction!" Smiling, she touched the brim of her hat. "But I could not have allowed you to do any more, after all you have done for me already."

"I don't know that I have done so very much," said Paul meditatively. "Why, there's a month's salary owing you which I might easily have advanced you if I had thought of it. I'm afraid you'll never collect it now," he added, with a mischievous sideways glance at Mary.

She smiled back at him. "I doubt I shall want for money, even at that, Paul," she said. "You must know your solicitor paid us a visit this week. I spent several hours with him, going over the provisions of the marriage settlements. You have been more than generous."

Paul looked embarrassed. "Oh, well, it's only right you should share in what I have," he said. "Considering how I came into the greater part of my fortune, I think most people would say you have as legitimate a right to it as I have. In any case, I am glad I can provide for you as you deserve, Mary. It always galled me to see you wearing that ghastly bonnet my uncle gave you and driving yourself about in the gig."

Mary laughed. "Well, you've certainly done away with the necessity for the bonnet, Paul," she said, touching her hat once more.

"Yes, and I mean to do away with the necessity for the gig, too," said Paul. "I promised to get you a phaeton and pair when I proposed to you, if you remember, and I still mean to do it. On my next trip to London, perhaps. You'll have to come with me and help me pick it out."

"Oh, Paul, you are so good to me," said Mary, feeling herself close to tears once more. She blinked rapidly, then smiled up at him. "It's not at all necessary that you shower me with gifts this way, Paul. You must know I'm not marrying you for the sake of hats, or phaetons and pairs."

"I know you are not," said Paul, pausing to look down at her. They had once more reached the path that led from the cliffs down to the beach. The staircase cut in the cliff lay a little farther on, and above them loomed Wycliff, its turreted roofline more grotesque and unlikely looking than ever in the bright sunshine. The beauty of the day served to rob the house of some of its habitual air of menace, however, and today it wore an almost smiling aspect, crouched atop the cliffs with the cerulean blue of the sky above it and the sparkle of the sea below. Paul glanced up at the house, then down at Mary again.

"I know you're not marrying me for hats, or phaetons, or for the sake of that monstrosity up there," he told her. "That is one of the reasons why I proposed to you in the first place. One of the reasons," he repeated, laying a stress on the word "one."

"Oh, yes?" said Mary, trying not to show how keenly this subject interested her. "And what were the others, if I may ask?"

Paul gave her a meditative look, but made no immediate reply. Instead, he turned to look again at the house, then at the stone staircase cut into the cliff below it. "Shall we take the stairs this time?" he said. "It must be getting close to dinner-time, and they look to be quicker than going around by the path. But perhaps the path would be safer for you, who have your skirts to manage."

"Oh, I think I can manage the stairs well enough," said Mary, disappointed that Paul had ignored her question but trying gamely not to show it. "When the wind is blowing strong off the sea, or when it has rained or snowed I would think twice about it, but in such weather as this I would not hesitate. There is a solid handrail, you notice. Your uncle had it put in when his son grew old enough to go down to the beach by himself. But even before that I never heard of anyone being injured on the stairs. And they are certainly the quickest way to get from the beach to the house."

"The stairs it is, then," said Paul, and led Mary to the foot of the narrow, rough-hewn staircase. When they reached it, he politely stood aside to let her start up ahead of him. But she had barely attained the first step when he cleared his throat. "As to what you were saying before, about my other reasons for proposing to you—," he began.

"Yes?" said Mary, turning quickly to look at him. Standing on the first step, her head was exactly on a level with his. He looked into her eyes and smiled.

"You already know them, I think," he said, and leaned forward to kiss her deliberately on the lips.

"Yes," said Mary. She felt she did know, and her heart within her swelled with happiness, until it seemed it must burst with a surfeit of emotion. Paul leaned forward to kiss her a second time.

"Mmm . . . how I enjoy kissing you," he murmured between kisses. "I think—I really do believe—that I shall kiss you once for every step in this staircase. That will slow our upward progress a trifle, no doubt, but it will make the ascent much more enjoyable."

Mary laughed aloud from sheer exuberance. "Yes, I daresay," she said. "There must be at least a hundred steps in this staircase, Paul."

"Don't think to frighten me that way," he countered, smiling. "I would be glad to know there were twice that many." He leaned forward to kiss Mary again. She submitted willingly, and in this manner they progressed up the staircase, slowly but with great mutual enjoyment.

"Seventy-six," said Paul reproachfully, when at last they had reached the top. "There were only seventy-six steps, not a hundred, Mary. You owe me twenty-four more kisses."

Mary laughed and gave him a flirtatious look from beneath her hat-brim as they started along the path to the house. Between the hat, and the kisses, and the way in which Paul had as good as admitted he loved her, she felt positively exhilarated. It was a heady sensation to find herself holding the whip-hand over Paul, as it were, while he begged her for kisses. Almost it made her feel in sympathy with the Misses Rundell. She would never carry flirtation to such extremes as they, of course, but there was undoubtedly a pleasure to be had in feeling and asserting one's power as a woman.

"If you want more kisses, you will have to wait until tomorrow," she told Paul with mock sternness. "You have had at least eighty today, counting the ones on the beach. Eighty kisses ought to be enough for anyone in one day!"

Paul found the game quite as enjoyable as she and was entranced to discover this unexpectedly playful side to his betrothed. "Well, it's not enough for me," he said. "Won't you take pity and give me one more?"

She pretended to deliberate. "Very well, one more. But not now," she said, holding up a remonstrating hand as Paul came closer. "It must be nearly dinner-time now, and even if we don't change I'm afraid we're going to be late. I shall kiss you once more, tonight, just before we go upstairs."

Paul shook his head. "It's going to be a long evening," he prophesied sadly. His manner was quite cheerful as he took Mary's arm, however, and when they parted presently in the upstairs hall to go to their respective bedchambers, he detained her a moment to address her in a low voice. "I am very glad I'm marrying you, Mary Grant," he said. "And even gladder that I'm doing it tomorrow!"

"I'm glad I'm marrying you, too," Mary told him, and ran up the last flight of stairs with her heart singing with happiness.

Fifteen

Mary slept little that night, but felt none the worse for it the next morning. When Miss Eaton came tiptoeing into her room at eight o'clock, she was sitting up in bed, looking pensively out the window where the bright sunlight cast its glory over the bleak and uncompromising coastal landscape.

"Oh, you're awake," said Miss Eaton, pausing in momentary surprise. She was carrying in her hands a tray on which rested a pot of tea and a covered plate. "I brought you breakfast," she explained, coming forward to put the tray on Mary's lap. "Just some tea and toast for now. Of course we will have the wedding breakfast later, but that will not be for some hours, you know."

"I know," said Mary, smiling at her. She was not at all hungry, but to oblige her friend she nibbled at a piece of toast and sipped a cup of tea while Miss Eaton perched on the edge of her bed and began to outline the order of the day's events.

"I thought you would like to have a bath," she told Mary. "I told the maids to bring it up in half an hour, so you'll have time to eat your breakfast first. Is your dress all ready? Oh, yes, I see you have it already laid out."

"Yes, I was looking at it last night," said Mary, with a conscious smile. Having disposed of her breakfast, she put the tray aside, rose from the bed, and came over to join her friend beside the table where the bridal garments were laid out. They stood silently surveying them for a moment, then Miss Eaton turned to smile at Mary.

"Such a momentous day this is," she said. "I feel as excited as though I were to be married myself. You have my very best wishes, Mary, and I trust you and Lord Wyland will be very happy together. But oh, there is so much to be done! When shall we move your things to your new bedchamber? I do think you ought to have taken the late countess's rooms instead of that plain little bedchamber in the south wing."

"The red bedchamber isn't so little as all that. I expect it will seem palatial after what I am used to," said Mary, with a smiling glance around her tiny chamber. "And you know if I had taken the late Lady Wyland's rooms, I would have been miles away from Paul. He was rather squeamish about occupying his uncle's old rooms and so preferred to take the south tower room. And the red bedchamber is right next door to that."

"Yes, to be sure I had forgotten he was in the tower. That does make a difference, of course," admitted Miss Eaton. "Very well, then. Shall we move your things this morning?"

"Whenever you please," said Mary. "There isn't much to move, in any case." She cast another rueful glance around the room.

"No, there isn't. I expect the best way will be for you to come down to my room as soon as you have had your bath. That way you can dry your hair in front of the fire while the maids are moving your things."

"Do you think I ought to wash my hair?" said Mary, dubiously inspecting the thick plait lying over her shoulder. "I hadn't planned on it, Charlotte. We have only a few hours until Reverend Biddle gets here, and you know my hair always takes half a day to dry."

"Oh, I expect with two of us working we can hurry it along a little," said Miss Eaton confidently. "We'll get it dry by the time Reverend Biddle arrives, you'll see. Ah, here come the maids with the bath."

Mary's tiny bedchamber was soon a scene of hectic activity, as the maidservants bustled about with bath-basin, soap, towels, and cans of hot water. Even after the bath was set up, they kept finding excuses to come into the room while Mary was bathing and washing her hair. She felt rather self-conscious to be the center of so much attention, but the maids were so obviously eager to have a part in the bridal preparations that she did not have the heart to deny them.

When her bath was done, Mary wrapped herself in her dressing gown and went downstairs to Miss Eaton's bedchamber. Together the two of them set about drying Mary's hair in front of the fire. While they were busy doing this, Ellen carefully brought down the bridal dress and accessories, then joined the other maids in transferring Mary's belongings to the red bedchamber.

With so much to do and supervise and decide upon, the morning passed quickly for Mary. She had not yet finished arranging her newly dried hair when Ellen came bursting back into the bedchamber with the news that Reverend Biddle was waiting below.

"Mind you, he told me to tell you that you needn't hurry on his account, Miss Grant. He's with Lord Wyland now, in his lordship's study. His lordship's got a new coat for the wedding and looks handsome as a prince in it. Although, to be sure, Lord Wyland would look handsome whatever he was wearing. I'm sure I never saw a better-looking gentleman. You're a lucky girl to be marrying him, Miss Grant. I do hear the eldest Miss Rundell had a fit of the hysterics when she heard you two was engaged. It's funny him choosing you instead of her, or one of the other fine ladies hereabouts, ain't it? Not but what you're as fine a lady as need be and handsomer than most, I daresay." Ellen looked admiringly at Mary in her bridal finery. "Don't you have the pretty hair, Miss Grant! I never saw it down loose like that before. Is that how you're going to wear it for the wedding?"

"Gracious, no," said Mary, then paused with a struck look. "At least, I hadn't really decided how I would wear it, Ellen. I suppose it will have to be pulled back in a knot as usual. There's not much else I can do with it, since it won't hold a curl." She looked at herself in the mirror. Her hair, fresh from its recent washing, hung smooth and glossy to her waist like a black satin curtain. Mary was obliged to admit that the effect was very striking against the white and silver of her wedding dress. "But I can't simply leave it loose like this," she said, with another dissatisfied look at her reflected self. "It would look so very odd."

"Not at all, my dear," said Miss Eaton. "The village girls often leave it loose when they are married, I believe."

"Aye, that they do," corroborated Ellen at once. "My own sister that was married last year wore hers loose with a wreath of flowers on top, and it looked pretty as a picture. What were you going to wear on your head, Miss Grant?"

Mary produced her headdress, a simple rectangle of gauze held in place by a silver wreath. She arranged it carefully atop her head, then turned to the others. "Well?" she asked. "Does it look very foolish?"

Miss Eaton and Ellen regarded her a moment in silence. "Foolish?" said Miss Eaton at last. "Oh, no, my dear: not foolish at all."

"You look splendid, Miss Grant," said Ellen enthusiastically. "Just splendid. Wait till his lordship sees you and see if he doesn't say the same."

Mary, with another glance in the mirror, was pleased enough by what she saw there to let her reservations be overruled. She was not quite convinced that she was not committing a social solecism by appearing in public with her hair *en déshabillé,* but then she reflected that she was not really appearing in public. She was getting married in front of a few friends at home, not attending a crowded ball or rout party in some village assembly room. If her appearance was a little *outrée* by ordinary standards, there would be no one present who was likely to criticize.

Consoling herself with this reflection, Mary turned away from the glass. "If you are sure I don't look foolish, then I suppose we may as well go on down," she told Miss Eaton. "It won't do to keep Reverend Biddle waiting too long."

"Not to mention Lord Wyland," added Ellen with a saucy smile. She helped Mary settle her skirts, then opened the door to let her and Miss Eaton pass through.

They found Paul and Reverend Biddle still seated in Paul's study downstairs. Reverend Biddle was composedly discussing a local woman who had recently lost her husband in an accident at sea.

"She is quite without means and has several small children," he told Paul. "We of the parish have decided to set up a relief fund to assist her. Would you care to be put down as a subscriber, my lord?"

"Oh, yes, to be sure," said Paul in a distracted voice. He looked up quickly as Mary and Miss Eaton came into the room. "Ah, here are the ladies now," he said with relief, and rose to his feet. Rather self-consciously, Mary made her way over to his side. He said nothing, but looked her over with an expression that was half surprise and half some other emotion that she could not immediately identify. Feeling more self-conscious than ever, Mary smoothed her hair back from her face and looked up at him shyly.

"You are looking at my hair, I expect," she said in a low voice. "Does it look very odd, Paul? I had meant to wear it as I usually do, but it always looks so plain that way. Sometimes I think I ought to have it cropped short so that I need not fuss with it at all."

She had spoken the words idly, but it was obvious Paul took them in literal earnest. He looked as horror-stricken as though she had proposed cutting off her head.

"Oh, no," he said, so loudly that Miss Eaton and Reverend Biddle turned to regard him in surprise. This clearly embarrassed him, but he went on speaking in an earnest though somewhat less forceful voice. "Oh, no, you mustn't think of cutting your hair, Mary. It looks beautiful just as it is. I never saw anything so beautiful." He made a move as though to touch Mary's hair, then drew back his hand quickly, looking more embarrassed than ever.

Reverend Biddle glanced at them both, then turned away with a dry cough. "If everyone is here, then I suppose we may begin," he said. "The ceremony is to be held in the drawing room, is it not? Very well. Miss Eaton, will you lead the way for us?"

"Yes, of course," said Miss Eaton, starting for the door. Smithson, who had been in the room during the discussion, but had stood apart from the others, opened the door for her and accompanied her, Mary, Paul, and Reverend Biddle to the blue drawing room. Smithson was to fulfill the office of groomsman during the ceremony, while Miss Eaton was to stand as Mary's bridesmaid.

Both attendants had argued the impropriety of their assuming these offices, the one pleading age and the other servitude as their excuse. But both Paul and Mary had been so adamant on the subject that they had eventually consented to be of the wedding party. As groomsman, Smithson wore a new topcoat of blue superfine like Paul's and a wedding favor in his lapel. His dark hair was sleeked back even more ruthlessly than usual, and his habitual air of dignity had never been more in evidence as he took his place near the drawing room fireplace, where an improvised altar had been erected.

Miss Eaton, standing opposite him, wore a new dress of violet crepe with pleated trimmings. A wedding favor was pinned skittishly to her cap, and she wore a look in which solemnity struggled with delighted anticipation. She and the maids had decorated the drawing room that morning with plants and flowers, ornamented here and there with knots of silver lace and silk ribbon. She gave a surreptitious touch to the pots of flowers flanking the fireplace, then turned to face Reverend Biddle, who had just taken his place before the altar.

"Let us begin," he said, opening his prayer book.

In a slow, measured voice, he began to read the introduction to the marriage service. Paul listened to him, glancing now and then down at Mary at his side. He could hardly believe he was, at this moment, being married to her. In the white-and-silver dress with her hair hanging loose, she looked to him as lovely as an angel, or a fairy-tale princess. His gaze kept returning to her, and more especially to the hair hanging down her back. He had never seen such beautiful hair: long, thick, and lustrous as a raven's wing. The sight of it fascinated him so much that even now he could hardly resist the urge to touch it. Resolutely he fixed his eyes on Reverend Biddle, but before long he found his gaze drawn once more to the slim white-and-silver figure standing beside him.

Mary, too, had to struggle to keep her mind on what Reverend Biddle was saying. As the words of the marriage service flowed over her, she told herself that in all the countless times she had heard these words spoken by her father and other clergymen, she had never before properly appreciated their beauty and solemnity. But even as she tried to listen, she was aware of a tightness in her chest, a growing tension deep inside of her that became more and more pronounced as the service went on. It was almost as though subconsciously, she was expecting some disaster would occur to interrupt the service before she and Paul could be wed. And when Mary considered it, she realized this was exactly the case. She had been so used to hardship and misfortune in her life that even now she could not quite believe in her good fortune. If Reverend Biddle had suddenly shut his prayer book and refused to go on with the service, or if the ceiling of the drawing room had chosen that moment to collapse upon their heads, it would have been no more than she expected.

Neither of these disasters occurred, however. The ceiling continued intact over their heads, and Reverend Biddle read the whole service through to the end in a cold, clear voice, never faltering once until he pronounced Paul and Mary to be man and wife. Even then, his hesitation was only momentary. Mary looked up at the man who had just been made her husband. He was smiling down at her, and her heart turned over at that smile. "Now I am going to kiss you again, Mary—and this time I'm not asking permission," he told her, and proceeded to do so with great gusto. He kissed Miss Eaton next, while Mary shook hands with Smithson.

"I trust you and my lord Wyland will be very happy together, my lady," said Smithson. Although the words were spoken with his customary formality, there was a hint of emotion in his voice such as was not usually present. Mary was touched by this evidence of feeling on the butler's part and returned his salute warmly.

"Thank you, Smithson," she said. "I trust Lord Wyland and I *shall* be happy, and that I will never do anything to make him regret the honor he has done me this day." She turned next to Reverend Biddle, who had shut the prayer book and was regarding them all rather gloomily. "Thank you for coming today, Reverend Biddle," she said, extending her hand to him. "We appreciate all you have done for us."

"It was my pleasure," said Reverend Biddle, giving her hand a brief salute and then turning away hastily. "I wish you very happy in your new life, my lady."

He gave these last words a faint, ironic emphasis that did not escape Mary's notice. But though she regretted his attitude of disapproval, she was too happy at the moment to let it damp her spirits. Turning to Miss Eaton, she gave her a hug that nearly rendered her friend breathless. "Thank you, Charlotte. Thank you, thank you, and thank you for everything."

"Why, I'm sure you're very welcome, my dear," laughed Miss Eaton, straightening her cap after this turbulent embrace. "Between you and his lordship, I think I've been kissed more today than I have in the last thirty years."

Ellen appeared just then, having changed her ordinary workaday calico for a gay print dress and fancy apron that were in keeping with the spirit of the occasion. "Begging pardon, my lord—and my lady," she said, shooting Mary a quick, conspiratorial smile. "Mrs. Bloomfield sent me to tell you the breakfast's all ready in the dining room whenever you care to sit down to it."

"Thank you, Ellen," said Paul. Turning to Reverend Biddle, he clapped him genially on the back. "I hope you'll stay and eat with us, sir," he told the vicar with a smile. "I know you said you had other matters to attend to today, but you needn't go hurrying off this minute, I trust."

"Indeed, I must," said Reverend Biddle, drawing sharply away from Paul's touch. Paul, whose mood at the moment was one of universal benevolence toward his fellow man, was rather puzzled by his behavior. Then he saw the rector's eyes turn toward Mary, and there was such a look of yearning in his eyes as to enlighten Paul as to the cause of his coldness. Far from offending him, this circumstance made his heart overflow with sympathy for Reverend Biddle. He could easily imagine how he would feel if their situations were reversed and he was forced not only to stand by while Mary was wed to someone else, but obliged to perform the ceremony himself. Removing his arm from about the rector's shoulders, Paul offered him his hand instead.

"I am sorry," he said simply. "Very sorry indeed. If there is ever anything I can do for you, I beg you will let me know."

Reverend Biddle gave him a startled look and seemed of two minds whether to reject this impulsive gesture of sympathy. After an instant's hesitation, however, he accepted Paul's proffered hand and shook it briefly. "Thank you, my lord," he said. "It's not very likely, but I appreciate the thought." With an effort he went on, forcing a semblance of a smile. "I have not yet congratulated you upon your marriage, my lord. Allow me to do so now, if I may. You are a lucky man in acquiring such a treasure."

"I know it," said Paul quietly.

He was a little sobered by this exchange, but not unduly so. By the time Reverend Biddle had taken leave of their party a few minutes later, his sober mood had largely passed away. And when presently he was seated in the dining room, with Mary smiling at him across the linen-draped table, he was restored to all his former exuberance of spirits.

Miss Eaton, too, was in a fine flush of spirits. "A toast!" she cried, lifting her wineglass aloft. "We must have a toast to the new-married couple, Smithson!"

Smithson, who had taken his place at the table with the same self-possessed air with which he usually waited on it, obediently raised his glass. Paul and Mary exchanged a quick smile before turning to look at him. "My lord and my lady, we drink to your health, happiness, and prosperity," Smithson told them. "May all the best blessings of heaven and earth be upon the union in which you have been joined today."

"Amen," said Miss Eaton, raising her glass to her lips. "Now, my lord—and my lady!—you must drink up your own champagne and try some of these delicious things which Mrs. Bloomfield has prepared for us. Here are sandwiches, and oyster patties, and some lovely looking tarts. And here is your bride cake," she added, looking fondly at a large frosted cake emblazoned with Paul and Mary's initials. "I saw it in the kitchen before Mrs. Bloomfield frosted it, and it looked quite luscious. I'm only sorry there aren't more of us to enjoy it. But of course the servants can all have a slice, too, when they sit down to their dinner later on. I know the maids were wanting to put some under their pillows tonight, so they would dream of their future husbands."

She continued to chatter on happily throughout the meal, pressing food and champagne on the others and consuming a fair quantity of both herself. Smithson, mellowed by the influence of champagne, inquired slyly if she intended to sleep on a slice of wedding cake herself that night. This sally produced peals of merry laughter from Miss Eaton. The two of them were soon embarked on something suspiciously close to flirtation while Mary and Paul consumed champagne, cake, and sandwiches and smiled at each other across the table. It was altogether a very joyous and festive meal. At last Miss Eaton pushed back her chair from the table with a sigh.

"Well, my dears, that was lovely, was it not? I couldn't eat anything more if my life depended on it—no, nor drink anything more, either. Indeed, I rather think I have drunk more than is good for me already. If you do not mind, Mary dear, I think perhaps I will go upstairs and lie down in my room for an hour or two, just until my head clears a bit."

"Yes, and I must get back to my duties," said Smithson, resuming his former dignified manner like a cloak. Rising from his seat, he turned to Paul and Mary. "If you will excuse me, my lord and my lady?"

"Certainly," said Paul, smiling at him. "We don't need anything more, do we, Mary?"

"Not a thing," agreed Mary heartily. "Go on, both of you, and we'll see you later this afternoon."

When the two of them had gone, Paul looked at Mary. "Well, Lady Wyland, we appear to be left to our own devices this afternoon," he said. "What shall we find to do with ourselves, do you think?"

Mary blushed at this question, which to her ears contained a distinct hint of innuendo. "I don't know," she said. "What would *you* like to do?"

He gave her a sidelong smile. "Well, given the choice, I think I'd follow Miss Eaton's example and go up and lie down for a while," he said. Seeing Mary's blush deepen, however, he laughed and shook his head. "But I suppose that would be rushing our fences a trifle. Never mind, my dear; I don't mean to tease you. We will find some polite and wholly unexceptionable way to wile away the afternoon. On the whole, I think I would like to spend it walking on the beach with you, as we did yesterday. That was a very enjoyable interlude, I thought."

"Yes, so did I. But if we go out walking on the beach, I shall have to change my dress," said Mary, looking down at her white-and-silver wedding dress.

"Must you?" said Paul wistfully. "Perhaps we had better think of something else to do, then. I hate to see you change your dress. You look so beautiful, just as you are."

He accompanied these words with a look that put Mary's cheeks in a glow once more. "Well, I don't know," she said hesitantly. "I suppose I wouldn't *have* to change, Paul. Only it will look so odd if we happen to meet anyone."

"I shouldn't think that was at all likely," said Paul. "But even if we should meet someone, and they do think it odd, what of it? I don't think I care very much what anyone may think of us today. But of course, the decision must rest with you, my dear."

As Mary sat hesitating, her ears caught the sound of wheels rattling along the gravel drive in front of the house. Paul heard it, too, and rose to go look out the window. Mary joined him there, shading her eyes to look outside. "Did Reverend Biddle forget something?" she asked. "I thought I heard a carriage outside."

"Yes, one just pulled in the drive. But it's not Reverend Biddle's rig. This looks like a private chaise—" Paul's voice broke off suddenly.

When Mary glanced at him, she saw his figure had gone rigid. "What is it, Paul?" she asked with alarm.

"I'll take care of it," he said, in a voice she had never heard him use before. "You wait here, Mary. I'll be back as soon as I can."

Not waiting for her reply, he turned and hurried out of the room.

Sixteen

Mary watched with astonishment as Paul hurried out of the dining room. When he had gone, she turned again to look out the window. She could see the carriage clearly now, a neat traveling chaise drawn by two horses and ornamented with a discreet gilt crest. As the powdered and liveried coachman brought the horses to a halt, Mary was able to get a glimpse inside the chaise. It contained but a single passenger, a woman in an extravagantly high-crowned French bonnet. Mary surveyed the woman curiously a moment, then looked again at the crest on the chaise door. A sudden, icy conviction seemed to freeze her heart.

Paul reached the carriage just as the woman was stepping down from it. At the sight of him, her face lit up. She ran down the steps and attempted to throw herself into his arms. He caught her by the wrists, however, and held her at arm's length. This harsh treatment elicited a gasp of shock from the woman, but Paul did not release his grip on her wrists. His one thought was of Mary, watching from the dining room window above. Whatever happened during the coming interview, he was determined that she at least should not suffer from it.

The woman from the chaise, having failed in her first attempt to embrace Paul, made no effort to renew her embrace. Wrenching her hands away from Paul, she fell back a step and stood regarding him with wide blue eyes that were rapidly filling with tears. "Oh, Paul, how can you be so cold?" she said in a tragic voice. "Do you still hate me as much as that?"

"I don't hate you at all, Cecelia," said Paul, smiling down at her sardonically. "I must confess, however, that I am surprised to see you here. The last I heard, you were on the verge of contracting an eligible alliance with a mutual friend of ours. Is it possible that Dunbury did not come up to scratch after all?"

The woman winced and threw him a reproachful look. "Don't be cruel, Paul," she said. "If I have made a mistake in that direction, rest assured that I have suffered for it. It is never pleasant to be jilted—"

"And who should know that better than I, Cecelia?"

"—but to be publicly jilted is harder still," finished the woman. She spoke as though she had not heard Paul's ironic interjection, although her heightened color seemed to indicate otherwise. "But of course, that has nothing to do with why I am here," she continued.

"No?" said Paul, smiling more sardonically still.

"No," said the woman, throwing him another reproachful look. "If you are determined to be cruel, Paul, then I suppose I must bear it. I daresay it's no more than I deserve, after the way I treated you. But I felt I had to come and see you at least once more, to tell you how sorry I was about my behavior this spring. Not merely because of the way everything has turned out," she added hastily, as the sardonic expression on Paul's face deepened. "The fact is, I never fully appreciated you while I had you, Paul. You were always so good to me: so kind, so generous, so *reliable*. I took it all for granted at the time, but since then—well, as to that, I will only say that since then, I have encountered a tremendous amount of deceit and duplicity in those whom I thought I had reason to trust. And that has made me appreciate your goodness all the more." She looked up at Paul hopefully.

"I am sorry to hear you have suffered, Cecelia," said Paul, in a voice somewhat gentler than the one he had used before.

"Of course it is never pleasant to be jilted. But at least you have the comfort of knowing that in this case, you were the injured rather than the injuring party. The persons who injured you may seem to have triumphed for the moment, but I'll wager that in the end they'll suffer more than you have over this affair. Deceit and duplicity generally bring their own punishment, I have observed."

Though these last words were spoken mildly, they made the woman wince again. "You are very hard, Paul," she said, eyeing him with a mixture of resentment and wistfulness. "One would think you had never loved me at all. But you did, Paul. I know you did, and I cannot believe you are as unfeeling as you seem. Oh, Paul, cannot we put all this wretched business behind us and start over again? Or better yet, cannot we pick up where we left off and behave as though these last eight or nine months had never been?"

Lady de Lacey (for it was she) paused at this question, gazing up at Paul with wide, hopeful blue eyes. The afternoon sun streamed into her face, turning to spun gold the tendrils of fair hair that peeped out from beneath her bonnet. The effect was very flattering, but less flattering was the way the strong sunlight picked out the network of tiny lines about her eyes and mouth. She looked at that moment every one of her thirty-nine years. But she was a lovely woman still, with a fine-boned beauty almost ethereal in its delicacy. Her figure, too, had an ethereal delicacy about it: despite her years, she was as lithe and slender as a young girl. Paul could not help noticing and admiring her beauty as he had a thousand times before, but the tenderness that had once accompanied his admiration was completely gone. The only emotion he felt for Lady de Lacey now was a kind of irritated pity.

From the dining room window, Mary had watched the whole of Paul's exchange with Lady de Lacey. The lady's first passionate attempt to embrace him had not escaped her, and though she had observed that Paul had not permitted the embrace, still she felt a jealous ache in her heart as she watched them talking earnestly together. As she stood looking down at them, Smithson came into the dining room.

"Smithson," she said, not turning away from the window. "Smithson, will you please come here a moment?"

"Certainly, my lady," said Smithson, joining her at the window.

"Smithson, do you know who that lady is with Lord Wyland?" she asked.

Smithson glanced down at Paul and Lady de Lacey. His figure suddenly stiffened, just as Paul's had done before him, but when he spoke his voice was carefully noncommittal. "I cannot say for sure, my lady, but I think—I rather believe that it is Lady de Lacey."

"That's what I thought," said Mary. She went on watching Paul and Lady de Lacey talking together. Smithson glanced at her, seemed about to speak, and then apparently thought better of it. After a time, Mary spoke again, in a detached voice.

"I suppose Lady de Lacey must have driven here all the way from London," she said. "No doubt she is tired from her journey. I suppose I had better go down and offer her some refreshment."

Smithson gave Mary a startled look. "You must do as you think best, my lady," he said dubiously. "But I don't think—"

"Please have some tea and biscuits sent to the blue drawing room," said Mary, continuing as though he had not spoken. "And some sherry, too, if you please. I will let you and the other staff know if Lady de Lacey plans to stay for dinner." Giving Smithson no chance for further argument, she turned and hurried out of the dining room.

Below, Lady de Lacey was still endeavoring to convince Paul that the past might be forgotten and their relationship resumed where it had been left off. He listened with only half an ear, glancing nervously up at the dining room window. He could not see Mary, but he knew she must be there watching, and the knowledge gave him the resolution to break in upon Lady de Lacey's speech. "I'm sorry, Cecelia," he said, gently but firmly. "I don't think there's any way of turning back the clock in a matter like this."

She came a step closer, grasping his arm and speaking even more eagerly than before. "But you do not deny that you loved me once, Paul. I know you did, and I cannot believe that love is irretrievably gone. You asked me to be your wife before, you know—many, many times before, but I was foolish enough to refuse you. If you still want to marry me now, however—"

"But you see, I don't want to marry you now, Cecelia," said Paul, with a harshness born of desperation. "It so happens that I'm married already."

For a moment Lady de Lacey was very still. She stared at Paul as though doubting the truth of his words. What she saw in his face apparently convinced her, however, for her whole figure suddenly drooped. When she spoke again, it was with a forced gaiety that could not conceal the bitterness in her voice.

"Ah, I have played my cards badly, haven't I?" she said. "I had no idea that you were married, Paul. You have certainly kept it all very quiet. Is that your wife there?"

Startled, Paul turned to look. Mary had just come out of the house and was making her way down the front steps. The sunlight glinted off the silver trimmings of her dress and threw bluish highlights into the glossy dark curtain of her hair. At the sight of her, Paul felt a lifting of his spirits, but this was followed immediately by a sensation of acute dismay. "Yes, that's my wife," he said. "We were only married today."

"Really!" ejaculated Lady de Lacey. Paul paid her no heed. He was too busy watching Mary's progress down the steps. It seemed to him that no man in the world had ever been in such an awkward situation. He felt he ought to do something to stave off the meeting between his wife and ex-mistress, but all power of action seemed to have deserted him. He could only stand helplessly as Mary came up to join him and Lady de Lacey beside the chaise.

"Good day, ma'am," said Mary, curtsying slightly to Lady de Lacey. Her manner was cool but perfectly self-possessed. Paul could only wish his own powers of self-possession were as great. He felt at that moment quite incapable of speech. Fortunately speech was not necessary, for after a brief glance at him, Mary turned again to Lady de Lacey.

"You are Lady de Lacey, are you not?" she said politely. "Yes, I thought as much. I am Lady Wyland, Paul's wife. I am very pleased to make your acquaintance, ma'am."

"Delighted, I'm sure," said Lady de Lacey, looking surprised but curtsying in her turn. "I am very pleased to meet *you*." She surveyed Mary with a mixture of curiosity and jealousy. "Paul was just telling me about you, and about—about your marriage this day. Allow me to wish you both very happy, Lady Wyland."

"Thank you," said Mary, curtsying again. "Won't you come inside, Lady de Lacey? You are too late for the wedding breakfast, but we could at least give you a glass of wine to refresh you after your drive. And you are very welcome to stay to dinner if you like. Did you come all the way from London?"

"Yes—yes, I did. That is very kind of you, Lady Wyland. I should like very much to stay to dinner, if I may."

Again Mary curtsied. "We should be honored to have you. Tell your servants to take the carriage around to the stables and then come into the house. I'll tell the cook to give them some refreshment, too."

Paul had stood dumb throughout this conversation, contributing no part to the civilities which Mary and Lady de Lacey were exchanging. It was quite the most uncomfortable situation in which he had ever found himself. He could hardly believe his ears when he heard Mary calmly invite Lady de Lacey to dinner, and Lady de Lacey as calmly accept. He could not help being impressed by his new wife's composure under such trying circumstances, but the prospect of dining *à trois* with Lady de Lacey was a daunting one, to say the least. He wondered what could have prompted Mary to invite her. There was no guessing from Mary's face, which was a mask of civility. It was impossible to tell what might be the real thoughts and feelings behind it.

Mary, as she led Lady de Lacey toward the house, was in fact experiencing a perfect turmoil of contradictory thoughts and feelings. She felt a natural jealousy toward Lady de Lacey and a powerful resentment toward her for spoiling her wedding day, but her chief emotion on meeting her husband's ex-mistress had been one of dismay. Lady de Lacey was not at all what she had expected. She knew Lady de Lacey was a good deal older than Paul and had unconsciously been picturing her as a coarse, voluptuous, full-blown woman, still attractive in her way, of course, but of rather a vulgar type.

What she saw, instead, was a woman of delicate, ethereal beauty, as slender as herself and appearing scarcely older. Looking into Lady de Lacey's lovely, spiritual face, Mary could not wonder that Paul had once loved her. The wonder was that after loving such a woman, he could ever have chosen to marry one of such distinctly inferior attractions. Beside Lady de Lacey, Mary felt herself to be completely eclipsed, a humble wood violet beside a rose of incomparable beauty. The idea filled her with despair. It was impossible that Paul could ever care for her as he had cared for the Incomparable who walked beside her, making commonplace remarks about the picturesque beauty of Wycliff's surroundings.

"My, what an impressive entrance hall," said Lady de Lacey, continuing her polite effusions as they entered the house. "It looks to be of great antiquity."

"Yes, it dates from the sixteenth century," said Mary automatically, her thoughts still given up to her tragic musings. "And here is the drawing room, Lady de Lacey. Would you like a glass of sherry and a biscuit?"

"Thank you, Lady Wyland, I would be happy to take a glass of sherry. No biscuits, if you please—just the sherry."

Mary silently poured a glass of sherry and handed it to Lady de Lacey. Paul accepted a glass, too, and retired to the far end of the drawing room. Out of the corner of her eye, Mary watched him as he stood there, sipping his sherry and looking out the window. She wondered if the situation embarrassed him. He had not spoken a word since she had joined him and Lady de Lacey beside the chaise. She did not know if he approved or disapproved of her inviting Lady de Lacey inside the house, but she was determined to behave civilly toward the woman whom she had so much cause to dislike.

Lady de Lacey drank off her sherry rather quickly, then turned to Mary. "I should like to freshen up after my journey, if I may," she said. "Is there a spare bedchamber I could use, Lady Wyland?"

"Of course," said Mary cordially. Inwardly, however, she wondered at the request. She could not imagine why Lady de Lacey should find it necessary to freshen a toilette that already looked perfect in every detail. And if she had made her request hoping to secure a few minutes alone with Paul, it was odd that she should have fixed on an errand that would carry her out of the room along with Mary. Mary did not voice her puzzlement, however, but rose from the sofa and turned to Paul.

"I shall be back in a few minutes," she told him politely. He nodded, but did not meet her eyes. As she and Lady de Lacey left the drawing room, she glanced at him again and saw he was gazing fixedly out the window with the half-empty sherry glass in his hand.

Mary accompanied Lady de Lacey up the stairs and showed her to the best of the unoccupied bedchambers, a large room hung with gold-and-white-striped draperies. "I hope this will be satisfactory, ma'am," she said. "If you need hot water or anything else—"

"No, thank you, my dear," said Lady de Lacey, cutting in upon this speech briskly. "I need nothing at all but a few minutes' private conversation with you." She gave Mary a twisted smile. "All that business about freshening up for dinner was only a pretext, you see, Lady Wyland. You must not think I really plan on staying for dinner. I shall be taking my leave in a very few minutes, but first I wanted to apologize for intruding myself upon you and Paul this way. I had no idea that he was married—no idea even that he was planning to marry. If I had, I would not have dreamt of coming here, I promise you."

"I believe you," said Mary, not knowing what else to say. Lady de Lacey gave her another twisted smile.

"I hope you do believe me, my dear. I would like you to believe also that I don't intend to be a nuisance to you and Paul in the future. It has never been my practice to thrust myself in where I was not wanted, and I have no intention of beginning now. You and Paul have nothing to fear where I am concerned, I do assure you."

Mary nodded, quite touched by this speech and by Lady de Lacey's evident emotion in making it. Lady de Lacey smiled crookedly once again and looked Mary up and down with a kind of morbid interest.

"I must say, Paul has shown very good taste in his choice of brides," she said. "I am sure you will make a great sensation when you are presented, my dear. Brunettes are all the crack now, you must know, and we poor blondes find ourselves quite *passé.*" With a return to her former emotion, she continued, "Indeed, I wish you all the best, Lady Wyland. I have no doubt you will be very happy with Paul. He is a good man—a very good and decent man—how good, and how decent, I only came to appreciate too late. Forgive me, I ought not to speak of that, but you will understand all this has been a great shock to me." She gestured toward Mary's bridal attire.

"I understand," said Mary, in a voice full of pity.

There were tears in Lady de Lacey's large blue eyes. She blinked rapidly, sniffed, and went on with a slight catch in her voice. "Indeed, I envy you your position, Lady Wyland. You are fortunate in being the wife of such a man. Not that I mean to imply you are unworthy of the position. Knowing Paul, I am sure he has chosen well for himself."

The tears were overflowing Lady de Lacey's eyes now. She

made an effort to dash them away with her fingers. Rather timidly, Mary offered her her handkerchief. Lady de Lacey accepted it and dabbed at her eyes, smiling at Mary through her
tears. "This is a strange situation, is it not, Lady Wyland? Like
a scene from a French farce or a comic opera. Only by rights,
we ought to be tearing each other's hair out, not sharing handkerchiefs. But I am glad I had the chance to talk with you this
once without reserve. It will probably be the last time, for I am
sure you will agree with me that it would be better for all three
of us if we did not meet too often in the future. I have been
thinking lately of doing some traveling—of making a European
tour, perhaps. They still appreciate blondes in Paris, I understand."

"Is there anything more I can do for you, ma'am?" asked
Mary, regarding Lady de Lacey with sympathy.

"No, nothing, my dear. If you will leave me now, I will try
to compose myself a bit and then see about taking my leave.
You need not trouble to show me out. I am quite sure I remember
the way, and I would rather not trouble you and Paul any further."

"Very well," said Mary. As she turned to go, she added in a
hesitating voice, "Goodbye, Lady de Lacey. I hope you will be
very happy, in Paris or wherever you decide to go."

"Thank you, Lady Wyland. The same to you, and my best
regards to your husband." Lady de Lacey flashed Mary a watery
smile. "That sounds very civilized and respectable, doesn't it?
Let us shake hands then, and if we do not meet again in the
future, we shall at least have the comfort of knowing that we
parted on perfectly good terms."

"To be sure," said Mary. She squeezed the hand that was
offered her and then left the bedchamber, affected almost to
tears herself by the unexpected gallantry of the woman she had
thought her rival.

Seventeen

Below, in the drawing room, Paul awaited Mary's return with a mixture of impatience and apprehension. He wondered if he ought to have gone upstairs with her and Lady de Lacey. The situation would have been awkward no matter what he had done, but if he had accompanied Mary he might at least have been present to intervene if Lady de Lacey became violent or abusive. The idea made him glance nervously toward the ceiling. He did not think it likely that Lady de Lacey would cause a scene, for as a rule she avoided emotional confrontations, but there was no saying whether this occasion might not be an exception. She had, after all, just made a journey of some hundred and eighty miles, only to discover it had all been for nothing. Under such circumstances a fit of hysterics might be considered an allowable indulgence.

Putting down his half-empty sherry glass, Paul walked over to the drawing room door. From here, he could command a view of the entrance hall and the first flight of the main staircase. Mary and Lady de Lacey had gone up that staircase some twenty minutes ago, and as yet neither of them had come down again. Paul wondered nervously what they were doing abovestairs. Were they still together, or had Mary left Lady de Lacey in hysterics and gone off alone somewhere, perhaps to indulge in a fit of hysterics of her own? Ought he to go see? He felt that he ought, but fear and shame held him captive. There was some comfort to be found in the unbroken silence that came from overhead, which seemed to indicate that the ladies' interview had thus far been peaceful. But still Paul was uneasy. Seating himself in a nearby chair, he took up a newspaper that was lying nearby and tried to interest himself in the latest news from abroad. But it was of no use. His mind kept straying from the paper's printed paragraphs to worry about the difficulties that still lay ahead of him that afternoon.

Chief among those difficulties was dinner. For the twentieth time, Paul wondered what had possessed Mary to invite Lady de Lacey to dine at Wycliff that evening. The thought of sitting down to dinner with both his ex-mistress and his new-wedded bride was enough to destroy his appetite altogether. Almost it was enough to make him order out his curricle and take to the roads for the next few hours, delaying his return until such time as Lady de Lacey might reasonably have been expected to take her departure.

Yet that would mean leaving Mary to deal with Lady de Lacey alone. Paul's conscience recoiled at the idea of burdening her with this task. He already felt guilty for having involved her in such a painful situation in the first place; it was unthinkable that he should simply run away and leave her with the responsibility for cleaning it up. Of all the three people involved, she was the only really innocent party, and yet it seemed likely that she would suffer most from what had taken place that day. Paul shook his head morosely.

"Quite the wedding day for her," he told himself bitterly. "If she asks for an annulment after Cecelia leaves, it's no more than I would expect. Damn Cecelia for coming here—but I suppose I ought to have expected something of the sort. If only it hadn't happened today, of all days. How does one recover from this sort of thing, I wonder? I'm sure I don't know." And he fell to wondering how best he might make his apologies to his injured bride for the mortification she had suffered that day.

He had a long time to indulge in these meditations, for Mary did not return to him until after the dressing bell had rung for dinner. She had gone to her bedchamber after leaving Lady de

Lacey, feeling the need for solitude in which to reflect upon the conversation she had had with that lady. It had been all in all a most surprising interview. As Mary thought over all that Lady de Lacey had said and done and promised during that interview, she was visited by strong conflicting emotions.

There was no doubt that Lady de Lacey had behaved very well. Mary felt that she had, but this circumstance, instead of comforting her, only made her feel worse. It was impossible to hate a rival who treated one with so much sympathetic understanding and who apologized so charmingly for having incommoded one with her presence. And if she, Mary, had been conscious of Lady de Lacey's charm, how much more must Paul have felt it, who had already proved himself susceptible to it!

Nor was Lady de Lacey's charm of manner her only attraction. She might be nearing her forties, but she was also quite the most beautiful woman Mary had ever seen. Mary was miserably certain that such attractions as she herself possessed must appear as nothing beside Lady de Lacey's astounding beauty. No wonder, then, that Paul had loved her, and no wonder if he loved her still. The idea gave Mary pain, but she forced herself to face it. By his own admission he had wanted to marry Lady de Lacey, and it was only that lady's continuing refusal that had kept him from doing so. Now it seemed that Lady de Lacey had relented, but her relenting had come too late. Paul was already married: married to her, the unfortunate Mary Grant, who was now in the position of having to decide what to do about the whole wretched situation.

Without question, the best and bravest course would be to go to Paul and offer him his freedom, so that he might marry Lady de Lacey if he chose. Mary felt this was the course she ought to follow, but her heart misgave her when she reflected that he might well accept her offer. And then where would she be?—a spinster once again, left to lead a lonely and embittered life bereft of the husband and home that had been hers for so brief a time. Mary felt she was not capable of such an awful sacrifice.

If Paul were to leave her now, after all that had passed between them, she felt she might as well put an end to her existence and be done with it. Even a life spent with a husband who loved another woman seemed a preferable alternative.

"Very well, then," she said aloud. "You seem to have made your choice, Mary. Now you may as well go downstairs and start making the best of it."

The dressing bell rang as she was going down the stairs, but when she reached the drawing room she found Paul seated near the door, still wearing the blue coat and light trousers he had worn for their wedding. He looked around quickly at her entrance and immediately rose to his feet.

"There you are," he said. "I was beginning to think you might have abandoned me."

"No," said Mary. She observed that after a single glance at her, his gaze had shifted to the doorway, as though he were waiting for someone else to appear there. Knowing who that someone must be, Mary felt a painful contraction in her heart, but she did not allow her pain to show in her face. This was but a minor sample of the sufferings she must be prepared to endure in the future. "Lady de Lacey is not coming, Paul," she said quietly. "She decided not to stay to dinner after all."

"Not stay to dinner?" echoed Paul stupidly. His expression was dazed as he looked at Mary. "You mean she is already gone?"

"Yes, or will be gone shortly. I think I hear her carriage leaving now, as a matter of fact."

"Yes, there it goes," said Paul, looking out the window. He and Mary watched in silence as Lady de Lacey's chaise rolled down the curving drive. When at last it was lost to sight, Mary turned to look at Paul. He was gazing in bewilderment at the spot where the carriage had disappeared. "I don't understand," he said. "You say she decided not to stay to dinner?"

He seemed so stunned by the news that Mary felt another painful contraction in her heart. Here was proof indeed of how deeply he still cared for his former mistress. But in spite of the pain in her heart, she forced herself to speak calmly. "Yes, she would not stay. She asked me to give you her regards, however."

"Her regards?" echoed Paul. He knew he was behaving foolishly, but it was such a relief to hear Lady de Lacey was not to stay that he felt a little giddy. "She's really gone? Well, then, that's that. It's all over."

"Yes," said Mary. She was looking at him rather somberly, Paul thought. And when he stopped exulting over his unexpected deliverance long enough to consider the matter, he thought he understood why.

"Oh, Mary, I'm so sorry," he said. With a contrite expression, he took her hand in his and looked down at her. "I hope you will forgive me for having involved you in this mess. And on our wedding day, too! I wouldn't have had it happen like this for the world, Mary—not for the world."

It was a perfectly good, straightforward apology, but Mary misinterpreted it to mean that he was sorry for marrying her when he still loved Lady de Lacey. She felt like weeping, but forced herself to speak calmly once again. "I know," she said. "You don't need to say any more about it, Paul. I understand how painful the situation must be for you."

"Lord, yes," said Paul, surprised and relieved by this understanding attitude. "I was never so close to funking it in my life as when the two of you went upstairs together. Are you sure you are not angry with me, Mary? It would be no more than justice if you were, considering the position I have put you in."

"I am not in the least angry," said Mary truthfully. Her heart was heavy with a weight of sorrow almost past bearing, but she was not at all angry. There was really no one to be angry with unless it were fate, or God, and Mary felt too weary at that moment to go railing against omnipotent powers.

Paul went on looking down at her anxiously. "You look tired," he said, with unexpected discernment. "All this has been a great strain on you, I'm afraid. Perhaps—"

He was interrupted just then by Miss Eaton, who came hurrying into the drawing room with an apologetic smile. "Hello, everyone," she said. "Did you wonder what had become of me? You know I was going upstairs to lie down for a while, after the wedding breakfast—well, I did, and I ended up falling asleep. Actually asleep! I cannot remember the last time I slept during the day. I must say, I feel quite refreshed, but I must apologize for leaving the two of you to your own devices for so long."

Both Mary and Paul made understanding noises and thought privately what a mercy it was that she had been absent during Lady de Lacey's call. Miss Eaton beamed and regarded them both fondly. "Of course, being newly married you could probably dispense with the presence of all outside people very nicely," she said. "I hope you had a pleasant afternoon?"

"Oh, yes," said Mary, not looking at Paul.

"Quite pleasant," said Paul, not looking at Mary.

"That's good, that's good," said Miss Eaton, beaming with pleasure once again. "And now here it is almost dinner time. It's a mercy the dressing bell awakened me, or I might have slept right through that, too!"

"Has the dressing bell already rung?" said Paul, looking startled. "I didn't hear it. I suppose I ought to run up and change my clothes before dinner." He shot a fleeting glance at Mary.

"I need to change my clothes, too," said Mary, avoiding his eye. As she was moving toward the door, however, Miss Eaton stopped her by laying her hand on her arm.

"No, indeed, it is not at all necessary for you to change, Mary," she said. "Indeed, speaking for myself, I should prefer to see you in your bridal finery. And there is no reason for you to change, either, my lord. We are all among friends here, and to my mind you both look splendid exactly as you are. Let us go on and sit down and see if Mrs. Bloomfield has conjured up as good a dinner for us as she did a wedding breakfast."

The dinner was indeed very good, beginning with clear soup and stewed eels and progressing to a roast of mutton with mashed turnips and caper sauce. These dishes were followed by a second course that included braised partridges, a dish of carrots and celery, an omelet, a soft pudding, and a dish of apples, pears, and damsons.

It was not a meal that held much enjoyment for Mary, however. She tried to eat what Paul and Miss Eaton put on her plate, but her throat was so tight that she could swallow scarcely anything.

"You shall wither away to nothing, Mary, if you don't start eating more than you have today," scolded Miss Eaton playfully. "My lord, you must persuade her to take a little of this omelet. I am sure she needs it, and I expect you have more influence with her than I do!"

"Indeed, I wish you would eat a little more, Mary," said Paul gently. "If you do not want the omelet, perhaps you would prefer some pudding? Or one of these apples, perhaps? I'll peel it for you—how will that be?" Having peeled and sectioned an apple, he deposited it on his own dessert plate and pushed it toward Mary. She meekly ate a few pieces, which satisfied her two dinner companions, and then the three of them adjourned to the drawing room for tea and coffee.

It seemed a long evening to Mary as she sat beside Paul on the sofa, listening to him discuss the latest news from abroad with Miss Eaton. The two of them initially made strenuous efforts to include her in the conversation, asking her questions and consulting her opinion on the probable fate of Napoleon and the progress of the Viennese congress. But her answers were so abstracted that they finally let her be and began addressing their remarks to each other over her head.

Mary hardly heard them. What she was most aware of was Paul's hand resting lightly on hers as they sat together on the sofa. He had taken her hand when they had first sat down; and she, supposing that he was seeking to atone for the day's earlier painful occurrences, had made no effort to withdraw it from him. It was comforting to feel his touch now, even though she knew his heart belonged to another. So Mary sat and let him stroke her fingers between his as he and Miss Eaton argued and expounded and derided each other's opinions on international politics in the most good-humored way.

At last the clock struck ten. Miss Eaton glanced at it, then looked at Paul and Mary. "I suppose you two will be wanting to go upstairs before long," she said. Her voice was determinedly matter-of-fact, but there was a tinge of pink in her cheeks as she went on, addressing herself to Mary. "Mary, dear, I thought perhaps you might like me to help you get ready for bed tonight. The maids are all very nice girls, of course, and I am sure they would be happy to assist you, but you know they tend to be rather free-spoken on these occasions. It would probably be less embarrassing for you if I were to be your ladies' maid, just for tonight."

Mary waited a moment before replying. It would have been inaccurate to say she had forgotten tonight was her wedding night, but after all that had happened that afternoon, the matter had assumed a secondary importance in her mind. Indeed, she felt it quite possible that Paul would not care to come to her that night after the painful scene that had taken place between him and his ex-mistress.

Nor was she altogether sure that she cared to receive him if he did come. Mary shot a quick, troubled look at Paul. He was regarding her with half a smile on his lips, waiting for her to reply to Miss Eaton's question. Catching her eye, his smile became slightly embarrassed, but he did not look away. Instead, with great deliberation, he took up her hand which he was still holding in his, lifted it to his lips, and kissed it.

This seemed to settle the wedding night question. Mary supposed she must be lacking in proper pride to welcome the caresses of a man who would rather be with someone else, but still the misery in her heart was eased a little by Paul's gesture. She turned back to Miss Eaton. "You are very kind, Charlotte, but I think I can manage for myself this evening. Thank you all the same for offering."

Miss Eaton shook her head disapprovingly, though her face wore a resigned smile. "You cannot always do everything for yourself, Mary, you know," she said. "You are a countess now, and someday you will have to start accepting the consequence that is due your position. However, we need not make an issue of it tonight. Good night, my love, and good night to you, too, my lord. I think I will get a book from the library and read for a while in my bedchamber before retiring."

"I will come up with you, Charlotte," said Mary, gently disengaging her hand from Paul's grasp. Rising from the sofa, she added, "Good night, Paul. I will see you later upstairs." She was careful not to look at him as she spoke.

"Good night," said Paul, in a voice that held both consciousness and amusement. Mary could feel his eyes upon her as she left the room with Miss Eaton.

Upstairs in the red bedchamber, Mary found all had been made ready for her occupancy. A fire was burning in the grate, the bedclothes were turned down, and her best nightdress was laid conspicuously on a chair near the bed. Mary blushed a little at the sight of it. With swift fingers she removed and folded away her wedding dress and undergarments, then went over and began to button herself into the nightdress.

This particular nightdress was of her own making, for she had been too embarrassed to entrust the construction of such a private garment to the local sewing woman. She knew Cliffside and its ways well enough to be sure that half the women in the village had found excuse during the past week to drop by Miss Johnson's home in order to look over the future Lady Wyland's bride-clothes. It was intolerable to think of them looking over her bridal nightdress, too. Therefore, she had made the nightdress herself, fashioning it from the finest of lawn and embellishing it with ribbons, tucks, and a trimming of narrow lace.

It was a pretty nightdress, and Mary thought she looked appropriately bridal in it. Yet as she stood before the glass, tying the ribbon that bound it at her throat, she was overcome by a sense of futility. It seemed years since she had stitched that ribbon in place, in a happier, more hopeful state of mind. To be sure, her prospects had not been cloudless even then, but they had seemed so compared to the ones that faced her now. Then Lady de Lacey had been only a name. Now she had a face as well as a name, and such a face, too! Mary felt her own must fade to insignificance beside it.

Turning disconsolately away from the glass, she picked up one of the brushes that lay atop her dressing table and began brushing her hair with long, methodical strokes. When she was done, she did not plait it as was her usual custom, but merely smoothed it back from her face. She then extinguished the candles that were burning in the wall sconces and got in bed.

As she lay in bed waiting for Paul to come to her, she found herself dwelling unhappily once again on the changes that the last few hours had made in her situation. Only this morning she had been looking forward to this night with an eagerness that was almost unmaidenly. Now she felt more fatalistic than eager, although she still retained a certain impatience to get the business over and done with. In some obscure way, she felt that she and Paul would not really be husband and wife until their relationship had been physically consummated. Until then, the tie between them would be a fragile thing, abstract and insubstantial and insufficient to prevent him from going back to Lady de Lacey.

The thought of Paul's former mistress continued to haunt Mary as she lay there in the darkness. Especially was she haunted by the image of Paul and Lady de Lacey together. She tried to push these images aside whenever they grew too disturbingly explicit, but still they remained on the fringe of her thoughts, recognized but unacknowledged.

"I don't care," she told herself defiantly. "I am married to him now, and he has sworn to love and honor me—me and only me. That is all that matters. I'm not going to hand him over to Lady de Lacey, just because she has changed her mind and decided she wants him for herself after all. He is my husband, and this is our wedding night, and so long as he is willing to come to me, I'm not going to turn him away. He belongs to me now, not Lady de Lacey, at least as far as the world is concerned."

With such speeches as this Mary tried to reassure herself, although her efforts were not completely successful. In some far corner of her mind she was still plagued by the suspicion which had occurred to her earlier, that she was lacking in proper pride.

"Well, and what if I am?" she demanded, facing the idea at last in an effort to vanquish it once and for all. "What good is pride to me? Being proud all these years never brought me love, or money, or happiness. Better I should take what I can get and be grateful. I am in a position most women would envy, and I'm not about to throw it all away just because things are not exactly as I would have them. I daresay I will become reconciled to the situation in time."

She continued to brood, however, and to argue the matter back and forth as she lay there in the dark. It occurred to her to wonder what her former fiancé would think of her dilemma. Francis had wholly disapproved of marrying for worldly gain.

"But I didn't marry for worldly gain," Mary told herself unhappily. "I married for love. Or rather, I married Paul because I loved him and thought he loved me, too. I suppose my mistake was in not finding out the extent of his feelings for me before I accepted him. I expect he would have told me if I had asked. He has been quite open and honest about his relations with Lady de Lacey whenever I questioned him before." Then Mary sighed and smiled wryly to herself in the dark. "But I'm afraid I would have married him all the same, even if I had known he did not really love me. Oh, dear, what a weak, spineless creature I am. I'm sure Francis would be disgusted if he could see me now."

These last words were only a passing thought, but as soon as they had occurred to Mary they seemed to take on a life of their own. She found herself wondering uneasily if her first bridegroom might not be watching her from some heavenly region. It was not a comfortable thought to bear her company there in the dark, while she waited for bridegroom number two.

"I wish Paul would hurry up and come upstairs," she fretted inwardly. "If he doesn't come soon, I'm afraid I'm going to lose my nerve altogether. What can be keeping him such a time? I'm sure it's been an hour since I left the drawing room."

At that same moment, Paul was experiencing a few nervous reservations of his own. He had come upstairs only a few minutes after Mary, but even after Smithson had assisted him in changing his coat and trousers for his dressing gown and had bade him good night in a significant voice, he delayed going to his bride. It was not because he was not eager to make love to her, as he assured himself. He was very eager, but at the same time rather intimidated, for he had never made love to a woman who was a virgin before.

He knew, of course, that the basic technique ought to be the same. Yet it seemed clear that he must also make allowance for his partner's inexperience, and perhaps for her reluctance as well. And no wonder if she were reluctant! Paul had always understood that a woman's first experience of that kind was generally attended by pain, and even by blood if all he had heard and read was true. Yes, it was all rather intimidating. Paul ran his fingers through his hair. He wondered if he was capable of rendering Mary's first experience an enjoyable one. He hoped he was, but his hopes had a definite tinge of doubt. Lady de Lacey had always assured him that he was a wonderful lover, but unfortunately Lady de Lacey had not been distinguished for the honesty and candor of her speech. It was possible that she had lied about this as she had about other matters.

Paul sighed and ran his fingers through his hair once more. He had hardly thought of Lady de Lacey since she had left Wycliff that afternoon, except to marvel that her appearance had caused so little trouble between him and Mary. The understanding Mary had shown over the whole affair seemed to him downright miraculous. But as the miracle was one so much to his advantage, he was not inclined to overanalyze it. He was more inclined at the moment to worry about his prowess as a lover.

It was true, of course, that Mary would have nothing to compare him with. Although she had been engaged before, he felt sure she never would have granted herself the freedom of the country girls, who were apt to consider a reading of the banns license to indulge in the full panoply of conjugal pleasures.

Yet he found the thought of Mary's previous engagement disturbing all the same. It was odd to think that if things had turned out differently, she would now be married to another man instead of him. And when he reflected that she had undoubtedly loved her former fiancé and had perhaps kissed him with all the ardor she had shown in their own embraces, he felt such a wave of primitive, unreasoning jealousy that for a moment he literally saw red. Then it struck him how foolish he was to waste time being jealous of a dead man when his beautiful flesh-and-blood bride waited for him in the room next door.

"I'll go to her this instant," Paul vowed to himself. Tightening the cord of his dressing gown about his waist, he slipped out into the hall.

Mary's door was only a few yards down from his. "If we keep occupying these rooms, we shall have to have a communicating door put between them," Paul told himself, as he eased open the door to Mary's room. "It is very inconvenient to have to go around by the hall, not to mention very embarrassing. I should look no-how if one of the servants should come by just now. One would prefer not to advertise one's intentions to one's employees quite so openly!"

Inside Mary's room, it was so dark that Paul had to stand still a moment until his eyes became accustomed to the darkness. Even then, he could barely distinguish the shadowy mass of the curtained bed lying ahead of him. It was impossible to tell if Mary were in it. Some sixth sense told him that she was, however, and that she was awake and waiting for him, even though she made no sound to acknowledge his presence.

Walking carefully to avoid obstacles in the dark, Paul made his way over to the bed. As he drew aside the curtains, he felt rather than heard a small movement within. By straining his eyes, he could just make out Mary's form lying beneath the bedclothes and the dark gloss of her hair spilling across the pillow. He reached out to touch it and felt her shiver a little, but still she said nothing. Paul began to find the silence unnerving. "Mary?" he whispered.

She made a soft noise that might have been an affirmation. Somewhat encouraged, Paul pushed the curtains further aside and got into bed beside her. He could see her more clearly now, her slim form motionless beneath the bedclothes and her face a white oval against the dark cloud of her hair. She appeared to be asleep, but as he eased himself down beside her, her eyes fluttered open, and she turned her face to look at him.

Her expression was solemn—even, Paul thought, a little fearful. He found this so touching that he wanted to gather her into his arms straightaway. He desisted, however, not wanting to frighten her by seeming to go too fast. Reminding himself of the need for gentleness, he instead contented himself with kissing her very lightly, first on her forehead and then, when she showed no signs of resistance, on her lips.

Mary shut her eyes and let herself be kissed. She was at that moment torn between two distinct and contradictory emotions. Paul's kiss, gentle though it was, had contrived to send a tingle of excitement down her spine. It was incredibly arousing to be lying in the dark beside him, feeling the warmth of his body beside hers and the intimate, insinuating touch of his lips on hers. Yet though her inclination was to abandon herself to his caresses, part of her resisted. She had thought she was willing to take whatever he would give her and be grateful, but now, as he kissed her, a small voice in the back of her head reminded her that she was only his second choice and that he must all the while be comparing her with another woman and finding her wanting.

The idea nagged at Mary's thoughts, even as her body grew more and more aroused. It was a struggle not to respond to the growing ardor of Paul's kisses, but she forced herself to do so with a self-discipline that was truly heroic under the circumstances. As Paul put his arms around her, drew her closer, and proceeded to ravish her mouth with his own, she felt like swooning. But she continued to hold herself motionless in obedience to that spirit that was part pain, part perversity, and part pride—perhaps most of all pride. For she discovered that she did, after all, have her share of proper pride. Her body might be ready to accept passion without love, but her mind could never be content with such half-measures. With a feeling of despair, Mary acknowledged the truth: if she were to succumb to her baser urges now, she would forever lose her own self-respect.

Paul was surprised by his bride's lack of response. He had expected that she might be shy or reluctant, but that she would be cold had never occurred to him. She had always been enthusiastic in returning his kisses before. Now, as he continued doggedly with his caresses, he felt as though he were kissing a statue. The slim figure in his arms was not so hard and cold as marble, but it was quite as unresponsive.

Paul found this phenomenon very disconcerting. He could not imagine what he was doing wrong, but he was definitely not getting the response he was looking for. He kissed Mary again, stroking the back of her neck with his hands and running his fingers through her hair. He had been longing to do this all day, and the feel of her hair between his fingers was just as delicious as he had imagined, but the enjoyment he had expected to receive from it was diminished by Mary's own seeming lack of enjoyment. He persevered further, even venturing to untie the ribbon at the neck of her nightdress and press a kiss on her bare shoulder. He thought he heard her sigh faintly, but this was all the response he got for his trouble.

Paul was in a quandary. The idea of going further without

some sign of acceptance on her part was unthinkable. He had entered into his task with enthusiasm in the beginning, aroused not only by her beauty and by the deliciously feminine scent and feel of her body, but by the idea that, in spite of her virginal qualms, she desired him as much as he desired her.

Now he was beginning to doubt seriously whether she desired him at all. He had no wish to force himself upon her against her will. Indeed, after having spent some twenty or thirty minutes in labor as unremitting as it was unrewarded, he was beginning to fear he lacked the physical capability of doing so.

Within a few minutes, his fear had become a mortifying certainty. This, as far as Paul was concerned, was the final straw. He released Mary abruptly and got out of bed, drawing his dressing gown and the tattered shreds of his dignity around him.

"I'm sorry," he said in a low voice, and left the room without a backward glance.

Eighteen

The suddenness of Paul's retreat took Mary by surprise. Sitting up in bed, she looked after him with consternation. Even after the door had closed behind him, she could not believe he had really gone, and for nearly an hour afterwards she lay waiting for his return before finally accepting the fact that he was not coming back to her that evening.

To say that Mary was devastated by this turn of events would have been an understatement. She had felt badly enough when she had supposed Paul wanted her without loving her. Now it seemed that he did not even want her. It was an idea Mary found both humiliating and painful. Nor was her pain all emotional, for she had also to endure the pangs of unfulfilled desire which her body now saw fit to torment her with. Overcome with frustration, mortification, and the weight of her own misery, she turned her face to the pillow and cried herself to sleep.

Paul, in his room, was feeling miserable, too, but to his misery was joined a deep indignation. He felt Mary had not played fair by him. She had certainly acted as though she loved and desired him before they were married, he told himself as he paced up and down his room. But no sooner had the ring been put on her finger than she had changed her tune and started treating him as though he were something distasteful.

"To lay there like an iceberg and let me kiss her for half an hour, without ever once kissing me back," Paul fulminated to himself as he paced. "It's clear as glass that she never cared a groat for me. It was the title that she was after all along—the title and the money."

The realization was an exceedingly bitter one to Paul. He was forced to face the fact that his new wife was, at heart, no different from the Misses Rundell or Lady de Lacey or any of the other women who had been chasing after him ever since he had succeeded to his uncle's position. The only difference between Mary and the others was that Mary had been subtle enough to make him think he was the one doing the chasing. Running his fingers savagely through his hair, Paul chastised himself for his stupidity.

"I ought to have known better," he told himself. "I certainly ought to have known better. I've seen it happen often enough in the past, God knows. Why, I laughed myself sick last year when old Hutchins made a fool of himself by marrying that predatory Taylor girl. And then what do I do? Let myself be taken in like every other gudgeon who thought he was marrying for love, only to find out his bank account was his real attraction. Women are all alike, I do believe. They don't care for a thing beyond money and social position."

He was, at that moment, filled with a deep resentment toward the opposite sex. Most particularly was he resentful toward the member of that sex who was lying in the chamber next to his. "She's got what she wanted, and now she's making it clear she doesn't want anything more from me," he reflected bitterly. "And what's worse, I don't suppose there's anything I can do about it, unless I behave like a brute and force myself on her. And I'm not quite desperate enough to do that, thank you very much. There are other women in the world—and other places I can go, too, if it comes to that. I'm damned if I'm going to stay here and let her treat me as she did last night. One dose of that treatment was enough, by jove. I'd leave this minute, only it would look so peculiar to the servants and Miss E. There's no sense in causing a scandal, I suppose, though God knows it would serve her right if I did."

After spending some minutes more fulminating on Mary's

duplicity, Paul settled down to make serious plans for the future. He made up his mind that he would leave Wycliff first thing in the morning. "And I'll never set foot in Yorkshire again," he vowed. *"She* can live here, and I'll divide my time between London and Wyland Park. Quite the nice living arrangements for a newly married couple, I don't think! Of course there's plenty of precedent for it, but somehow I never thought I'd be in that position myself."

And with a disconsolate heart he went to his dressing room, the sofa of which he proposed to occupy in place of his bed that night, so as not to cause gossip among the servants. There he disposed himself as comfortably as possible and tried to take what rest he could in preparation for his journey on the morrow.

Mary arose heavy-eyed the next morning, a good hour before her usual time. She felt far from rested, but so miserable had been her endeavors at sleep that she left her bed with alacrity.

All night she had been trying to decide what she ought to do. Should she go to Paul and ask him openly why he had left her the night before? She wanted badly to be reassured that he did not find her physically unappealing. But it was possible that he would have no reassurance to offer her on that score, and Mary did not think she could stand to be rejected again as she had last night. Moreover, her pride rebelled against taking such a humble course. *He* had left *her,* after all, and if he changed his mind and decided he really did want her, it would be for him to seek her out, not the other way around. This idea somewhat bolstered Mary's sagging self-esteem.

"I shall not go begging him for his favors," she told herself, with a proud lift of her chin. "I'll be perfectly polite to him when we meet, but he will have to make me some sort of explanation for last night before I shall let him near me again. Yes, he shall have to explain himself, and then after that—we'll see. There'll be time enough to cross that bridge when we come to it."

Having made up her mind in this regard, Mary began to make her toilette for the day. Rejecting the pretty new dresses in her wardrobe, she put on her old gray serge dress and pulled back her hair severely rather than arranging it in the new, softer mode she had lately adopted. She was determined to look as plain and uncompromising as possible. After all, it had been Paul who had left her, she reminded herself, not she who had left him. To attempt to look fetching under the circumstances might be interpreted as an attempt on her part to win him back. Mary was resolved that from now on, the advances should all be on his side. Only then would she be certain that he wanted her. Having surveyed herself in the glass and assured herself that she appeared quite as plain as it was possible for her to look, she left her room and went downstairs, resolving to greet Paul in a manner that was at once cool and dignified.

She found him already at the table, in conversation with Miss Eaton. He glanced up as she came in and arose to assist her into her seat. "Thank you," said Mary, in a voice she trusted was extremely cool and dignified.

"You're welcome," he replied, in a voice fully as cool and dignified as her own. He then reseated himself at the table. Miss Eaton gave Mary a sympathetic smile.

"You poor dear," she said. "Lord Wyland was just telling me that he is obliged to take leave of you this day and journey down to London. That is hard luck when you were only married yesterday, is it not? I was just telling him that he must sometimes wonder whether it is worthwhile to have great wealth and estate, when they make such unreasonable demands on his time."

Mary's eyes flew to Paul in startled inquiry. He was very much absorbed in dissecting a slice of ham, but he looked up and met her gaze for an instant before answering Miss Eaton's question. "Yes, it is a great nuisance, ma'am," he said. "But I have quite resigned myself to the fact that wealth and high estate carry with them as many disadvantages as advantages."

"Even so, I doubt many of your cottagers would hesitate to exchange places with you," said Mary dryly. Her heart was almost breaking with sorrow and misery, but she was determined that neither he nor Miss Eaton nor anyone else should suspect it. As she forced herself to pour a cup of coffee and take a sip of it, she told herself that her plight was even worse than she had supposed. Not only did Paul not want her, it now appeared that he meant to abandon her and return to London, where he would doubtless resume his relations with Lady de Lacey. It took all Mary's resolution to remain at the table calmly drinking coffee when what she really wanted to do was burst into tears and run out of the room.

Miss Eaton had taken up the conversation again, not giving Paul any opportunity to respond to Mary's remark. "Yes, it is a great shame that you must leave the very day after your wedding, my lord," she said, with a shake of her head. "And especially so when one considers you only got back from London a few days ago! It's a pity you couldn't have seen your way clear to go with him this trip, Mary. It's a long journey, of course, but quite a nice season for traveling, and I am sure there must still be plenty of amusement to be found in London even if it is growing rather late in the year."

"I would much rather remain here," said Mary with emphasis. She took another sip of coffee, addressing Paul with an air of unconcern. "Will you have to stay as long in London this time as last, do you think?"

"Probably quite a bit longer," he returned, without meeting her eyes. "Have you any commissions for me in Town?"

"No, none," said Mary, and with those two words resigned all her hopes to the grave.

"You ought to have him buy you some dress goods," said Miss Eaton, looking her over critically. "I am sure they must have finer things in London than the village shop carries, and you could really use a few more dresses, Mary. I see you're wearing one of your old ones again this morning—"

"Yes, I thought it quite suitable under the circumstances," interrupted Mary. Turning to Paul again, she said in a voice of finality, "I want nothing from London, thank you."

He bowed. "Very good, ma'am. I suppose I ought to go see if Smithson's done packing my things." To Miss Eaton, he added, "I thought I'd leave Smithson here at Wycliff, at least for the time being. I can manage without him well enough for a week or two. Of course, if I find I must be gone longer, I shall have to look into hiring someone else to valet me. This business of making him double as butler works well enough when I am here, but I can see it's going to be a problem if I am away from home a great deal."

"Let us hope you need not be away as much as that," said Miss Eaton, smiling. "I am sure there are other considerations than Smithson that make your presence here desirable." She looked significantly at Mary.

"Just so," said Paul, rather dryly. He rose from the table, saluted Miss Eaton's hand, and then, after a moment's hesitation, bestowed a similar salute on Mary's. "Goodbye to you both," he said. "I'll write and let you know what my plans will be." Having bowed to them both once more, he turned and left the breakfast room. Mary, watching him go, wondered despairingly if she would ever see him again.

The efficient Smithson had already seen to the packing of Paul's bags, so that he was able to leave Wycliff less than an hour after taking leave of Mary and Miss Eaton. Over the next two days, he traveled more or less constantly, pausing only when absolutely necessary for rest, food, and fresh horses. He was in no hurry to reach London, yet he could not bear to dally about the business of getting there, and it was a relief when at dusk on the second day he finally reached the environs of Hanover Square.

He found Wyland House considerably improved in appearance since his last visit there. Its brick facade had been freshly scrubbed; the rooms had all been cleaned; and most of the renovations he had ordered were either complete or well on their way to being so. Several cleaning women were still pottering about, putting the finishing touches on the rooms, and Paul gratefully accepted the offer of one of them to make up a bed for him. That night, for the first time, he slept at Wyland House, full master of his inheritance. Yet though he was glad to have finally achieved this position, and glad also to be spared the necessity of staying at a hotel (which he had been dreading for fear of encountering some acquaintance who might know and question him about his marriage), he also felt singularly depressed.

It was depressing to be staying alone in London once again, when he had been confidently supposing that on his next visit he would be accompanied by his wife. It was depressing to be staying in the house which he had been preparing for her reception; to lie alone in the bed which had been redraped and refurbished in a style he had thought would please her. It was depressing to reflect that his marriage had ended less than twenty-four hours after it had begun. This last reflection, in particular, was depressing to Paul. Here he was, irretrievably tied to a woman who neither loved nor wanted him, feeling more lonely even than he had felt when he really was alone.

"God, what a mess I've made of this business," was Paul's inward, despairing summing-up. He thought of how calmly Mary had taken the news of his departure. Yet when he relived their last conversation together moment by moment, it seemed to him that for a fleeting instant there had been a different look on her face when Miss Eaton had first broached the subject of his leaving. It had been a look that was shocked, almost lost. Paul told himself that he must have been mistaken, but the idea haunted him in spite of his efforts to disparage it.

"She never said a word about wanting to go with me," he reminded himself. "Indeed, she made a point of saying she would rather stay at Wycliff. And then the way she was dressed—and the way she had her hair screwed back in that damned spinsterish style! That was meant to be a slap in the face for me, I have no doubt. And she did that before she ever heard a word about my leaving. No, she was glad enough to see me go, I'll warrant, and that being the case, I'll just oblige her by staying away. Still, it's going to be a damned awkward business when all's said and done. The announcement of our marriage will have appeared in the papers by now, and everybody I meet will be wanting to ask me about it. It's enough to make me wish I'd gone to Wyland Park instead."

In this latter respect, things did not turn out so badly as Paul had feared. London was so thin of company that he encountered scarcely anyone he knew during the first week of his stay. The few inquiries he received about his marriage were brief and formal, and were satisfied with replies of equal brevity and formality. Indeed, after a week spent skirting the fringes of society and dealing almost exclusively with members of the legal profession, Paul was so hungry for human contact that he ventured to dine at his club. Here he hoped to meet someone who would show a genuine interest in his affairs, even if it was an inconvenient interest.

But there was no one at White's who had been among his particular acquaintance. The club's sole occupants were a military man or two, and a few hardened gamesters who lost all interest in him when he declined to join them in a game of high-stakes whist. The solitary beefsteak and bottle of wine which he took that evening did nothing to raise his spirits, and he departed from White's feeling more melancholy than ever. A long evening lay ahead of him, and he had no idea how to fill it.

"I'll drop in at Drury Lane, perhaps, and see the farce," decided Paul, after hesitating a few minutes outside of White's.

The evening was fine, so he decided to walk to the theater instead of taking his carriage. He hoped the exercise might tire him and enable him to sleep better than he had during the past few nights. Accordingly, he set out to traverse the network of busy streets that lay between White's and Drury Lane.

As he passed a narrow court between two buildings of flats, a voice came out of the darkness.

"Sure, and it's a fine evening for a walk, ain't it, sir? There's nothing I like better meself than a little stroll in the evening."

The speaker of these words, a dark-haired woman clad in a shabby red satin dress, emerged from the shadowy region between the two buildings. Smiling boldly at Paul, she went on in an insinuating voice, "But what's a fine gentleman like yourself doing out all alone, sir? Sure, and it's not natural to see a handsome gentleman out walking without a lady on his arm. I'd be glad to bear you company, sir, if you're looking for a bit of fun."

Paul had recognized the woman's profession at a glance, but he nevertheless paused to look at her. She had been a handsome woman once and was handsome still, though clearly no longer in her first youth. Her rouged cheeks were a trifle thin and haggard, and there were a few threads of silver in her glossy dark hair. Her eyes were blue and merry, however, and her smile disclosed a set of white, even teeth such as many a society woman would envy. She flashed them again in a seductive smile as she moved closer, laying a hand boldly on Paul's arm. "Go on, sir, and let's have a bit of fun, shall we?" she coaxed, with another provocative smile. "I've a place round the corner where we can go to be private-like. You won't regret it, sir, that I promise you."

Paul, looking down at the woman's face, felt a sudden reckless impulse to accept her offer. He had never had dealings with the muslin company in the past, not even after Lady de Lacey's cavalier behavior had freed him of any obligation to abstain on her account. This was partly because of the principles he had been raised with; partly because he feared contracting some venereal illness; but perhaps most of all because his own fastidious nature could not stomach the idea of consorting with women whose function was akin to that of a public convenience.

At the moment, however, he felt strongly inclined to abandon all such fastidious reservations. Here was a woman, and a good-looking woman, too, who really seemed to want him. Why should he not indulge himself this once as other men did? He had very nearly made up his mind that he should, when the woman spoke again. This time there was a new note in her voice, a note which Paul recognized as desperation.

"Please, sir, won't you come round to my place?" she begged. " 'Tis only a step, and I'll do me best for you when we get there, upon me word I will. And if it's the price that's worrying you—why, you can set your own price, sir, after we're done: whatever you think I'm worth. There now, you can't say fairer than that, can you, sir? I'd take it as a great favor if you would. I'm in a bit of a spot, as it happens, and I do need the money in the worst way."

This speech promptly shattered all Paul's illusions. Gone was his image of a woman who really wanted him for himself, and in its place was the all-too-familiar one of a woman interested only in his purse. Paul smiled bitterly at his own credulity. Yet as he looked down at the woman's anxious face, he found himself unable to reject her plea for assistance, as was his first impulse.

"Why do you need money so badly?" he inquired, in a not unkindly voice.

This was all the encouragement the woman needed to embark upon a long, voluble speech detailing her various financial woes. There was, it seemed, a mother in Ireland who had recently fallen ill and needed nursing. "And there's no one could do it so well as meself, sir, if only I could find the money to pay me passage over. But business lately hasn't been but enough to barely keep me. I'm getting a bit long in the tooth, as you've no doubt noticed for yourself, sir, and the gentlemen don't come around so eager as they used to once upon a time."

"I find that hard to believe," said Paul gallantly. The woman flashed him a grateful smile but shook her head.

"Sure, and you've a kind heart to say so, sir. But by the Holy Cross, 'tis enough to drive me distracted, knowing me mither's ailing and I can't be there with her. I wasn't just what you might call a good girl growing up—wild and willful in me ways, and causing her many a sorrow, as the good saints could testify. The

matter's been weighing heavy on me conscience these many
years now, and when times was flusher I used to send her a bit
of money now and then by way of making up for it. But it's me
she wants now, and it seems to me that nursing her'd be a way
of squaring me debt once and for all. I don't know if I make
meself clear, sir—"

"Indeed you do," Paul assured her. "I quite understand your
feelings, ma'am. Of course you would want to go to your
mother if she is ailing. And I expect, too, you would like to see
your own country again after being away so long."

"Aye, that I would," said the woman with a sigh. "Even before Mither fell sick, I was thinking about going back to Ireland—and of trying to turn over a new leaf, perhaps. There's
Gerald Fitzpatrick, as good a man as ever breathed, who was
ready to marry me when I was sixteen, only I was fool enough
to think I could do better for meself in London. Well, I've heard
Gerald was still a bachelor, and me mither wrote me in her last
letter—her last letter before she fell ill, you understand—that
Gerald was asking after me. And I thought perhaps that if I
could see him and talk to him again, something might yet come
of it. Of course, there's no saying that he'd still want me if he
knew what I'd become." The woman looked down at her shabby
finery with a sad smile. "But even if he didn't, I'd rather be in
Donaghmore than here, especially with me mither so bad off.
And so you see, sir, if you was to oblige me by coming back
to my place—"

"I'm afraid I can't oblige you in that manner, ma'am," said
Paul with great firmness. Seeing the woman's face fall, he shook
his head and gave her a sympathetic smile. "However, that's not
to say I wouldn't be happy to finance your passage back to Ireland." Taking out his purse, he produced a couple of banknotes
and handed them to the woman. "Will this cover it?"

The woman looked at the banknotes wonderingly, as though
she had never seen such objects before. "Aye, and then some,"
she said fervently. "But never say you're giving me all this
money, sir? Not without taking anything for it?"

"Indeed I am," said Paul with a smile. "I want nothing in return, I assure you."

The woman looked at him, then again at the money in her hand. Then reluctantly, but with great determination, she handed the banknotes back to Paul. "Here," she said. " 'Tis very kind of you, sir, but I'm not desperate enough yet to accept charity. I would rather earn me money honest while I can."

Paul could hardly keep from smiling at the woman's rather twisted notion of honesty. He liked her all the better for her scruples, however, and racked his brain to think of a way to remove the stigma of charity from his bequest. "I'm sure you are not desperate," he said. "If I were a bachelor, I would not hesitate to avail myself of your services, I assure you, ma'am. But you see, I am a married man. Under the circumstances, I cannot think it right that I should—er—patronize you professionally, but I hope you will accept this money as a token of my admiration." Again he pressed the banknotes in the woman's hand.

She eyed the money longingly, and after a moment's consideration divided the two banknotes, stowing one carefully in her décolletage by way of a pocketbook and returning the other to Paul. "Here," she said. "Sure, and I don't need but the one to get me to Ireland, sir. You take the other and go buy that wife of yours a new bonnet. She's a lucky woman," added the woman in a sober voice. "A very lucky woman."

"I doubt she would agree with you," said Paul with a wry smile. He repocketed the banknote, however, and advised the woman to be off to the shipping office immediately, so that she might secure passage on the next packet to Ireland.

"And I trust she may not squander the whole sum in some gin-shop before she reaches the shipping office," soliloquized Paul, as he continued down the street. "However, she seemed earnest enough about wanting to return to Ireland. And of course if she had only been trying to impose on me, she might have taken all the money instead of only half."

As Paul continued on his way to Drury Lane, he reflected on

the woman's advice about buying Mary a bonnet. "I don't suppose she'd accept it from me, even if I did buy one," he told himself, pausing beside a milliner's shop whose shutters had not yet been put up for the night. "She said she wanted nothing from me."

Yet the idea stayed with Paul as he continued on his way to Drury Lane. It was an odd circumstance, but his encounter with the woman in red seemed to have given him a more hopeful outlook on his personal affairs. He began to think that he might have been too hasty in dismissing his marriage as moribund after so short a trial. Was it not possible, just possible, that if he went to Mary and spoke frankly about his concerns, they might yet be able to salvage their relationship?

After all, she had not actually rejected him on their wedding night. True, she had not received his advances with any enthusiasm, but this might only have been due to timidity or terror. Perhaps he had been unreasonable to suppose she would welcome his presence in her bed as eagerly as she had welcomed his kisses. Perhaps she had been stiff with fear rather than distaste.

Looking at the matter from this point of view, Paul began to think that perhaps he *had* been unreasonable. It was only natural that she should have been a little stiff with him, considering the demands of her role and her lack of experience. And when he had gone so far as to admit this alternative explanation for Mary's behavior, it occurred to him for the first time that her encounter with Lady de Lacey earlier in the afternoon might also have had something to do with it.

He himself had been quick to dismiss the Lady de Lacey episode as a mere annoyance. But it was just possible that Mary had seen it differently. How would he have felt if their situations had been reversed and it had been *her* former lover who had shown up in the midst of their wedding festivities? The mere thought sent a quiver of jealous rage through Paul's body. He began to feel a very real and lively sympathy for what Mary must have suffered that afternoon. Of course, she had assured him afterwards that she harbored no resentment for what had happened, but he had been foolish to take such assurances at face value. An angel in heaven might have been pardoned for feeling resentful about such an untoward occurrence. It was only natural that the humiliation Mary had suffered that afternoon should have colored her treatment of him that night.

"I have been a fool," said Paul aloud. A couple of apprentices seated in a nearby shop doorway gave him a startled look and sniggered loudly. Paul paid them no attention. He stood stock-still a moment, then turned and started back the way he had come, at a greatly accelerated pace.

"I have been a fool," he told himself again, as he threaded his way purposefully among the loiterers, pedestrians, and street merchants who had also chosen to walk abroad that evening. "And there's no saying that my foolishness hasn't already done an irreparable damage. But I'll give it another try and see if I can't straighten things out. I wonder if that milliner's shop is still open?"

The lights were just being extinguished in the milliner's shop when Paul arrived. The milliner was very glad to relight the lamps, however, once Paul had explained his errand. He left the shop a few minutes later with a neatly tied bandbox on his arm and a faint light of hope dawning in his heart.

"I'll give it another try," he told himself. "After all, I've nothing to lose by trying, and perhaps everything to gain. I'll go back to Wycliff and see if I can't patch things up with her."

Nineteen

Like Paul, Mary found her feelings undergoing a change in the days that followed upon their disastrous wedding day.

She had at first been as much angry as desolate, and this emotion she tried to encourage as being the less painful of the two. She reminded herself of how Paul had abandoned her on their wedding night, and how coolly he had taken leave of her the next morning. These remembrances were useful in whipping up her anger, but she could not live at a fever pitch of indignation all the time. In spite of her best efforts, feelings of sadness, longing, and regret had a way of creeping in.

Although she tried to assure herself that the whole blame for the situation rested on Paul's shoulders, she could not rid herself of a suspicion that her own role had not been completely blameless. Paul had certainly abandoned her on their wedding night, but not until after he had spent a considerable time kissing and caressing her. Was it possible that her own behavior that night had had something to do with his abrupt withdrawal? Mary's conscience prickled a little when she recalled how she had forced herself to lie still and unresponsive to his caresses. That had not been behaving honestly, for she had wanted him in the worst way—quite as badly as he had seemed to want her, in the beginning.

Mary tried to counter these arguments in a variety of ingenious ways. She reminded herself that according to all she had heard and read, men were different from women: strange, brutish creatures who were very well able to dispense with a woman's enthusiasm so long as they had her compliance. Sometimes they were known to dispense even with that. She, as a woman, was not expected to go along eagerly with the physical aspects of marriage. It might even be considered unladylike for her to do so.

But still, the feeling that she had behaved dishonestly continued to trouble Mary. In fact, when she looked back on all she had said and done throughout her acquaintance with Paul, she was able to trace a continuing theme of dishonesty. This was very galling to Mary. She had always prided herself on maintaining a frank, forthright character, whatever else the fickle workings of circumstance might have deprived her of over the years. Now it seemed that her pride was little warranted.

"But I really could not have been completely honest in this situation," Mary argued to herself. "If I have been less than frank in my dealings with Paul, it was only in the cause of self-preservation." To which her conscience responded by demanding what she had preserved by her behavior on her wedding night. Certainly it had not been the integrity of her marriage.

"Perhaps I did drive him away. Perhaps I should have let him make love to me that night and tried to be content," Mary told herself unhappily. "But could I have been content, knowing he didn't love me? Probably not . . . no, probably not. Still, it's an even question whether I would feel any worse than I do right now."

The idea continued to haunt Mary as she wandered desolately about the house, trying to occupy herself in Paul's absence. This was difficult to do, for Miss Eaton was careful to guard the dignity of her friend's new position by forbidding her any work apart from the lightest sewing and needlework. Nor was the weather such as to encourage exercise out of doors. Clouds had begun to gather on the afternoon of Paul's departure, and before the day was out, the balmy St. Martin's summer which they had been enjoying had given way to a spell of stormy weather. Day after day, the coast was lashed by high winds and driving rain, and waves crashed furiously against the cliffs on which Wycliff stood. Mary could hear the pounding of the surf at night as she lay in her solitary bed. It seemed to her that the weather was perfectly expressive of her own disturbed state of mind.

One morning a little over a week after Paul's departure, she awoke to find the worst of the storm had passed. But though the sun was out, the sea was still running high, and the grounds and garden were too sodden to make walking an inviting exercise.

"What shall you do today, Mary?" inquired Miss Eaton, as the two sat sewing together in the drawing room after breakfast. "I hope you don't intend to sit moping about the house all day, as you have for the past week." Rather archly, she added, "I suppose Lord Wyland will be returning to us soon, and then you will have no reason to mope."

"I would not be moping now, Charlotte, if only you would allow me to make myself useful," countered Mary tartly. "It's enough to make anyone mope, being condemned to work chair-covers and embroider handkerchiefs all day long. As for Lord Wyland, I am quite sure he has no thought of returning to Wy-cliff at present. Nothing would surprise me more than to hear he was coming here anytime soon."

"Then prepare to be surprised, Mary dear," said Miss Eaton, looking out the window. "For if I am not mistaken, I see his carriage outside right now, and him in it."

"You must be mistaken, Charlotte," exclaimed Mary. Dropping her needlework, she rose from her chair and hurried to the window.

One glance was enough to show her that her friend had not been mistaken, however. The carriage was certainly Paul's carriage, and as Mary watched she saw Paul himself step out of it, carrying a bandbox in his hand. The pale sunlight gleamed off the fair hair beneath his hat-brim, making it shine like new-minted gold, and in his form-fitting pantaloons, tailored topcoat, and many-caped greatcoat, he made altogether an impressive figure. Mary admired him automatically, even as she wondered what he was doing there. Was it possible that his business in

London had been real after all and that he was returning to her as a matter of course? Was it possible she was to have a second chance at happiness after all?

"Aren't you going to go down and greet him?" said Miss Eaton, regarding her curiously.

Mary shook her head and sank back in her chair once more. She suspected her knees were incapable of carrying her downstairs, even if she had wanted to go. "No," she said faintly. "I think I will wait and greet him when he comes up here, Charlotte."

He appeared a few minutes later, still hatted and great-coated and carrying the bandbox. On entering the drawing room, he looked about as though searching for someone. Mary felt certain he was looking for her, but she shrank back in her chair and remained seated while Miss Eaton hurried forward to greet him.

"My lord, what a delightful surprise this is! We had no expectation of seeing you today. In fact, Mary was just saying that nothing would surprise her more than to hear you were returning to Wycliff anytime soon."

"Where is Mary?" asked Paul. Mary knew she ought to come forward, but her knees still felt rather watery. She had forgotten what a physical effect he had on her. The mere sound of his voice was enough to reduce her to a state of quivering weakness, and she had already been weakened by the shock of seeing him again after having given him up for lost. And when to this one added all the stress and strain she had suffered during the past week, Mary could not think it surprising that her knees did not feel particularly trustworthy.

Miss Eaton answered Paul's question by smiling and nodding toward Mary's chair. "There she is, my lord, tucked away in the corner over there. I hope your presence may do her good. She has been sadly pulled down by your absence, I assure you."

It did not seem to Paul that Mary looked particularly pulled down. She was a little pale, but her face and manner were quite composed as she rose to her feet and came toward him. Such was her composure, indeed, that Paul felt an inward chill. He had experienced a spontaneous rush of pleasure at the sight of her, but if she felt any reciprocal pleasure, she was disguising it very well. It stung him that she had not even risen to greet him when he came into the room. "Hello, Mary," he said, putting aside his first disappointment and trying to greet her in a friendly manner.

"Hello, Paul," she said, and gave him her hand after a little hesitation. Paul noticed the hesitation and resented it. She really did not seem at all glad to see him. For the first time, he began to wonder whether he had been foolish to seek a reconciliation. He was willing to go halfway to meet her—more than halfway if necessary—but that would do no good if she was not willing to give some ground, too. Her attitude at present was hardly encouraging. If she would only smile at him, or say a friendly word, it would have been enough, but she only stood there, looking at him somberly. Faced with this discouraging treatment, Paul could not even summon up the courage to give her the new bonnet he had bought her in London.

"I hope you have been well," he said, turning away from her with a feeling of frustration. "It looks as though you have had a good deal of rain while I was away."

"Yes, it has been rather rainy," replied Mary. She seated herself in her chair once more and took up her needlework. As she began to set stitches, she added in a calm voice, "I trust you had a pleasant journey up from London?"

"Yes, very pleasant," said Paul. He stood a minute longer, hoping still to obtain some word or gesture of encouragement, but having received none, he left the room with a sensation of defeat.

The rest of the day was equally discouraging for Paul. From the time he arrived at Wycliff until the time he retired to bed that night, he found no propitious moment in which to approach Mary for a confidential discussion. She clung like a shadow to Miss Eaton throughout the whole afternoon and evening. And though she became somewhat less reserved as the day wore on and even made an effort to join pleasantly in the conversation during and after dinner, Paul thought she was finding it a strain. He observed that she tensed whenever he spoke to her, and that even when she was thanking him for serving her with some dish or declining his offer to help her to another, her manner toward him was both watchful and wary.

He was not mistaken as to the wariness, but he misinterpreted its cause. Could he but have known it, Mary's reserve was only a mask for uncertainty. She was fearful of exposing herself and her feelings for Paul after the rejection she had suffered on her wedding night. In her first joy at seeing him again, she had jumped to the conclusion that he had come to resurrect their marriage, but it had subsequently occurred to her that he might equally well have returned to seek an annulment or divorce after consulting an attorney in London.

This dreadful possibility had naturally thrown Mary into a great flutter. She surveyed Paul apprehensively throughout the afternoon and evening, wondering what he would say to her when at last they were alone. She sensed he wanted to talk privately with her, but not knowing what the subject of this talk would be, she was anxious to postpone it as long as possible. There would, however, be nothing to stop him from coming to see her that night in her room, if he so desired. Mary knew this, and she told herself it would be a test of their relationship. If he came to her that night, the interview would most likely be a positive one and would very likely end in the consummation of those relations which had ended so abortively on their wedding night.

This idea also put Mary in a flutter, so that she was nervous and distracted throughout the evening. When she retired to bed that night, she took special pains with her appearance and then got in bed, where she lay tensely waiting to see if she would presently be joined by her errant bridegroom.

Paul was strongly tempted to come to her. Even in spite of the prim dress and severe hairstyle which, perversely, she had chosen to wear that evening, he found her attractive. He knew by this time that beneath that uncompromising facade was a very beautiful and alluring woman. He was eager to speak with her and set straight the misunderstandings which he felt were keeping them apart. But he felt nervous now about approaching her in her bedchamber. Having once retired broken from that particular field of battle, he was not eager to return to it.

"I'll wait and talk to her tomorrow," he decided at last, and cast a wistful look at the wall that separated him from Mary. As barriers went, that single wall did not appear very formidable, yet it was so strong and solidly built that it had stood now for several centuries. In all likelihood it would stand for several more without any great strain. Paul, reflecting gloomily on his difficulties, felt it to be a fitting analogy for the wall of misunderstanding which had arisen between him and his new wife.

If he had supposed that wall high before, he was soon to discover that it could attain heights heretofore unsuspected. Mary, having waited all night for Paul to appear, arose the next morning in a mood equally compounded of anger, sorrow, and determination.

It was clear now that he did not want her, or he would have come to her during the night. No doubt he had returned to Wycliff in order to obtain an annulment or divorce from her, so that he might be free to marry Lady de Lacey. Mary told herself she ought simply to accept the situation and retire from the scene with dignity, but when she reflected on what her life would be without Paul, her heart rebelled against this civilized course. There was probably no way she could prevent him from obtaining his freedom if he really wanted it, of course, but she resolved that he should not obtain it with any assistance from her.

That being the case, it was obviously in her interests to avoid any *tête-à-têtes* with him. He would naturally prefer to discuss so sensitive a matter in private, but she would not allow him to adopt this craven course. He would have to speak out before Miss Eaton and the servants if he wanted to depose her for Lady de Lacey. Meditating on this theme with gloomy satisfaction, Mary rose from her bed and rang the bell for the maidservant.

Ellen appeared promptly in answer to the summons. "Here, I am, Miss Grant—I mean my lady," she corrected with a self-conscious grin. "Never will get your title straight, will I? Here's your hot water, and I brought you up a cup of tea, too. Do you need me to help you dress?"

"Yes, stay with me, if you please," said Mary, refreshing herself with a sip of tea. In an elaborately casual voice, she inquired, "Is Lord Wyland down yet?"

"His lordship? Aye, he came down a little bit ago. He was asking after you, too, now that you mention it. That's part of the reason I asked you if you needed help dressing just now. I thought, as he was so eager to see you—"

"You may carry my compliments to his lordship and tell him I shall not be down this morning," said Mary, breaking in upon this speech with determination. "I have decided to have a bath, so I shall be breakfasting in my room. And I shall wash my hair, too," she added, mentally congratulating herself upon this piece of cleverness. The act of washing and drying her hair alone would, she calculated, occupy all of the morning and give her an excellent excuse to avoid Paul's company during that time. And when afternoon came, she could no doubt find another excuse.

Accordingly, she dallied all morning in her room, receiving frequent bulletins from Ellen about Paul's activities downstairs. "His lordship has sent for his bailiff and is seeing him in his study," Ellen reported about one o'clock. "Would you like to go down to nuncheon, or shall I bring you something up here?"

"I think my hair is dry enough to go down," said Mary, laying a hand to her head as though appraising its condition. Her hair had in fact been dry an hour ago, but she had chosen to linger upstairs until she was sure Paul was out of the way. The news that he was with his bailiff pleased her very much. Attending to his estate business ought to keep him occupied for at least an hour or two, she calculated, and would give her time to obtain some nuncheon and escape the confines of her room for a little while. With Ellen's help, she twisted up her hair and dressed herself in her oldest serge, so that he should not suppose she was trying to attract him if he happened to come away from his interview early.

This proved to be a wise precaution. Mary had only just begun to fill her plate from the assortment of cheese, cold meat, fruit, and biscuits that stood ready on the sideboard when Paul appeared in the breakfast room doorway. "Ah, so you're down at last," he said, looking her up and down rather grimly. Mary was glad when Miss Eaton came bustling into the room, sparing her the necessity of answering.

"Oh, there you are, Mary," said Miss Eaton gaily, taking up her own plate and joining Mary at the sideboard. "I haven't seen you all morning. Ellen said you were washing your hair?"

"That's right," said Mary. With a defiant look at Paul, she carried her plate to the table, sat down at her place, and began to eat.

"Such a nice day out today," said Miss Eaton, helping herself lavishly to grapes and Stilton. "Not so warm as it was a week ago, but still quite pleasant for October."

"Yes, very pleasant," said Paul. Still looking at Mary, he added, "I was thinking of going for a walk. You wouldn't care to come with me by chance, Mary?"

"No, I think not," said Mary. She managed to speak calmly, but it was an effort, for her heart was beating rather fast. She had never seen Paul look so grim.

"Very well," he said shortly, and turned away. As he was leaving, Mary nerved herself to speak again.

"Aren't you going to have some nuncheon?"

"No, thank you," he said, without turning around. "I've no appetite just now." He left the room, and a few minutes later Mary heard the sound of hoofbeats pounding across the drive beneath the window. Miss Eaton turned her head to look out the window.

"There he goes," she said. "He must have decided to go for a ride rather than a walk. You ought to have told him to wait and gone out with him, Mary. I'm sure you could use the exercise after being shut up so much this last week."

"I have no desire to go riding today," said Mary with great finality. Under pretense of helping herself to more cheese, she rose and went to the sideboard. Glancing casually out the window as she passed, she saw in the distance a rapidly vanishing figure on horseback. She lingered long enough to watch the figure leap the front gates in a singularly reckless manner before turning north along the coast road.

Mary knew this direction would take Paul away from the village rather than toward it. The seed of a new plan began to take root in her mind. "I think I shall drive into the village this afternoon, Charlotte," she said, returning to the table with her plate. "I can get my exercise looking for bargains in the village shops. Would you care to come with me?"

"Yes, I would," said Miss Eaton, then instantly contradicted herself. "Oh, but I can't, Mary. I must stay and see to preserving the last of the damsons. But of course you can take Ellen if you want company in the carriage."

"No, that's not necessary. I was planning on driving myself in the gig anyway."

Miss Eaton pulled down the corners of her mouth in a manner that was becoming very familiar to Mary. "You know that is really not at all seemly, my dear," she said. "Women of your position do not commonly go out driving alone in gigs."

"Yes, I know, but I intend to all the same," said Mary, rising briskly to her feet. "Have you any commissions for me in the village?"

Miss Eaton sighed. "I suppose you intend to wear that old fright of a bonnet, too," she said sadly. "You're such an odd creature, Mary. I don't see why you never wear that pretty new hat Lord Wyland bought you. It really looked quite lovely on you."

"I'm saving it for special occasions," said Mary shortly, and repeated, "Have you any commissions for me?"

"No, I have no commissions, my dear. You go on and enjoy yourself in the village. And while you're there, take my advice and buy yourself a new bonnet—one you won't mind wearing for everyday!"

Twenty

Having ordered out the gig, Mary drove to the village and spent several hours canvassing the village shops. They were not particularly enjoyable hours. She knew herself to be an object of gossip to those around her, and it made her shrink inside to see the nods and significant looks being exchanged among her fellow shoppers wherever she went. Still, she resolutely lingered in each shop as long as she could, inspecting the different goods with great though spurious interest.

This was tiring work, however. By the time four o'clock had rolled around, Mary could endure no more of it. She knew that by returning to Wycliff so early she ran a risk of running into Paul before dinner, but this consideration no longer seemed as important as it once had. She was footsore and weary, and with her weariness had come a sense of fatalism. Her efforts to stale-mate Paul's plans by making it impossible for him to talk to her privately seemed all at once both childish and futile. If he was really determined to obtain his freedom, he would eventually find some way to speak with her, after all. At most, she could only hope to delay the inevitable by a few days.

"I may as well get it over with," said Mary aloud. Mounting the gig, she took up the reins and turned the old horse's head toward home.

In half an hour she was back at Wycliff. Having turned over the gig to the stableman, she entered the house. As she passed the drawing room door, she was not surprised to be hailed by Paul's voice. "Is that you, Mary?"

"Yes," said Mary. She was pleased to hear that her own voice sounded cool and calm, in spite of her rapidly beating heart. Paul came to the drawing room doorway. He was still in his riding clothes, carrying his riding crop in his hand, and he looked both windblown and irritable. This did nothing to diminish his natural good looks, however. Mary felt the familiar flutter in her heart as she stood waiting for him to speak.

"I wonder if I might talk to you privately a few minutes?" he said formally.

"Of course," said Mary. She followed him into the drawing room and tried not to shudder as he shut the door behind him. It seemed to her especially portentous that he turned the key in the lock before turning to face her.

For a moment they only looked at each other. "Where have you been?" Paul asked at last.

"To the village," said Mary, still striving to sound cool and calm.

"You said nothing about going out earlier," he said, and his voice held a note of accusation. "When I asked you to walk with me earlier this afternoon, you turned me down flat."

"I changed my mind after you left," said Mary. She felt intensely uncomfortable under Paul's unsmiling scrutiny. To gain a few minutes' respite, she turned to the mirror over the fireplace and began to remove her bonnet. "What did you want to talk to me about?" she asked, untying the strings with fingers that trembled slightly. "Or did you merely wish to quiz me about my business in the village?"

Mary meant this last question as a feeble joke, but to Paul's ears it had the sound of a taunt. He watched with growing frustration as she laid aside her bonnet and, with seeming absorption, began to tidy her hair. The sight of the bonnet sitting on the mantelpiece added further fuel to his frustration. It appeared that she liked him so little that she preferred wearing an unsightly object like that to the new and expensive hat he had given her.

As a gentleman, he could not take his rage and frustration out on Mary, but there was nothing to prevent his taking it out on the bonnet.

"Oh, damn it all," swore Paul aloud. In one swift motion he snatched the bonnet off the mantel and hurled it into the fireplace.

A fire was burning in the grate, for the day, though fine, was by no means warm. The bonnet smoldered an instant or two, then burst into flame. The room was immediately filled with the stench of burning feathers.

"Paul, you idiot," cried Mary, gasping and choking and retreating from the fireplace with the utmost rapidity. "Why ever did you do that? Good heavens, what a smell! Open a window, Paul—a window, for heaven's sake!"

Paul, choking also, ran to the window and threw it open. Mary rushed to join him, and they stood side by side, coughing and choking and gasping for breath as the room gradually cleared. When at last the atmosphere was breathable once again, Mary wiped her eyes with her handkerchief and turned to look at Paul.

"Really, Paul, that was rather unnecessary, was it not?" she said, but she was smiling. Paul took courage from this circumstance and spoke out with a mixture of laughter and humility.

"Yes, highly unnecessary," he said. "Oh, Mary, I'm sorry about your bonnet. I *am* an idiot—I don't know what came over me."

"Oh, but Paul," Mary began, with a startled look. She was shaken by another paroxysm of coughing, however, which prevented her from finishing the sentence. When her coughing subsided, she shook her head and looked at Paul with a watery smile.

"Oh, Paul, it's I who am the idiot," she said. "Don't apologize about the bonnet. It was a hateful thing, and I am glad to see it gone. Good riddance to bad rubbish, as my father's sexton was used to say."

"No, but I *am* sorry, Mary," said Paul, grasping eagerly at this opening. "I'll buy you another bonnet. In fact, I've got another one for you upstairs. I brought it back from London with me and would have given it to you before, only—well, only that there hasn't seemed to be a proper moment for it yet."

"You bought me a bonnet?" said Mary, looking at him wonderingly.

"Yes, I'll get it right now," said Paul, turning eagerly toward the door. Mary caught him by the arm, however, and stopped him.

"No, don't, Paul," she said. "I don't deserve any more hats and bonnets from you. I don't deserve anything after the way I've behaved."

Paul, turning in surprise, saw there were tears in her eyes which had nothing to do with burning feathers. "But you haven't done anything," he said. "If anyone has behaved badly over this situation, Mary, it has been I." Drawing a deep breath, he went on quickly. "About what happened on our wedding night, Mary. I'm afraid I wasn't very understanding that night. You must know I would never force myself on you. We can go as slowly as you please, and if you still find you are repulsed by me—well, there are such things as annulments, I suppose."

Mary's tears were falling faster now. "Paul, stop," she said. "It's not like that at all. I am not in the least repulsed by you— quite the reverse, in fact. But after meeting Lady de Lacey—she is so beautiful, Paul. And you had spoken earlier of how you loved her and wanted to marry her. And it appears now that she wants to marry you, too. I could not help thinking that—well, that you might rather be married to her than me."

Mary paused and looked at Paul timidly. He was staring down at her in blank astonishment. After a moment she went on, in a diffident voice. "I can understand how it all came about, Paul. It was nobody's fault, really. The thing now is to try to set matters right as far as we can. If you want an annulment so you can marry Lady de Lacey, I will not stand in your way."

Paul continued to regard her in silence for some minutes more. "Lord, but I *have* been a fool," he said at last, in a devout voice. "Mary, I don't want an annulment. I haven't the least desire to marry Lady de Lacey. Everything between the two of us was over months and months ago, I assure you."

"But you said you wanted to marry her," Mary reminded him. "You said you asked her over and over—"

"Yes, so I did," agreed Paul. "But that was in the early stages of our relationship, before I came to know her as well as I do now. If you only knew how I—but perhaps I should not speak of it. The subject must be a painful one for you." He paused, looking down at Mary uncertainly.

"You may certainly speak of it if you want to, Paul," said Mary, trying to disguise her eagerness. "Honesty is always the best policy, I think, and I doubt the truth can hurt me more than my imagination has done. I hope we may always be honest with each other after this, Paul. I'm afraid this whole situation has come about mainly because I haven't been honest with you in the past. I have felt wretchedly about it, I assure you. I have always prided myself on being a person of integrity—"

"And so you are," interrupted Paul. "I could tell it as soon as I met you, Mary, and that was part of what attracted me to you in the first place. Honesty and integrity are qualities which I particularly admire—and qualities which were sadly lacking in Lady de Lacey, as I eventually discovered. That, more than anything, was the reason our relationship came to an end. She has many admirable qualities, of course—it does not become me to speak ill of her, but as I came to know her better, I could not help seeing that she was incapable of anything resembling honesty. And it was that realization which finally destroyed my love for her. I don't hate her, you understand. Indeed, I cannot help pitying her, for by all accounts she has been having an uncomfortable time of it these past few months. But I trust I am transgressing no Christian precept if I say I would prefer never to see her again."

A smile had begun to tremble on Mary's lips. Paul reached out and took her hands in his. "Oh, Mary, I hope you can forgive me," he said. "This business must have given you a poor idea of my character, but I beg you will believe I am not an immoral man at heart. I have the greatest possible respect for matrimony and the married state. When I vowed last week to love and honor you and only you till death do us part, I meant it from the bottom of my heart. Because I do love you, Mary. I love you, and I've been miserable this week, thinking you despised me."

Mary made a small, inarticulate sound. Paul looked down at her searchingly. "You do care for me a little, don't you, Mary?" he said. "A very little will do, to begin with. You mustn't think I expect you to return my feelings all at once. That's why I've been so shy up till now about saying how I feel about you. I've wanted to, heaven knows, but I didn't want you to feel pressured to say you loved me, too, until you honestly did."

Mary laughed shakily. "Oh, Paul, what a comedy of errors," she said. "I think I've loved you almost from the first moment I saw you. I have, Paul," she asserted, seeing his look of astonishment. "As soon as you smiled and spoke to me that first day at the door, it was all up with me, I promise you!"

Paul looked only half convinced. "You certainly didn't act like it," he said dubiously. "When I think of the pains you took to avoid me—"

"But don't you see, that was only because I was so attracted to you," explained Mary. "You were my employer, and it would have been very inappropriate for me to let such feelings show. And then, too, I'm afraid your uncle didn't give you a very good character, Paul. What with one thing and another, I thought it better not to put myself in your way more than I had to."

"Yes, I'm sure my uncle painted me black as Lucifer," said Paul, looking rueful. "And of course, this business with Lady de Lacey must have tended to confirm your bad opinion of me. But I am glad to hear it did not keep you from caring for me—"

"From loving you," corrected Mary, giving him a look half shy and half ardent. "I got past merely caring for you in the first five minutes after I met you."

A bemused smile spread across Paul's face. "Do you know, I still can scarcely believe that," he said. "You really and truly mean to say you fell in love with me the first minute you saw me?"

"If not the first minute, within the first hour," Mary assured him. "And oh, you can't know what a battle it's been to hide it, Paul. There've been times when I—" She broke off and looked at Paul, a bright flush staining her cheeks.

"Times when you've what?" prompted Paul, regarding her with a look of awakening interest. "Go on, Mary."

"Well, times when it was harder than others," said Mary. Her blush had deepened, and she had trouble meeting Paul's eye. He held her gaze deliberately with his own, however, so that she could not look away.

"Would our wedding night have been one of those times?" he asked.

"Yes," admitted Mary. She felt she must be scarlet as a poppy. Paul was smiling at her, but when he spoke again his voice was both serious and profoundly relieved.

"Well, thank God for that," he said. "I can't say how glad I am to hear you say so, Mary. I've spent the last week wondering whether you weren't simply giving me a hint that me and my attentions were unwelcome to you."

This made Mary laugh in spite of her embarrassment. "Unwelcome! Oh, Paul, nothing could be further from the truth. In fact," she went on, determined to make an entirely clean breast of the matter, "if I am to be perfectly honest, I must confess that I have wanted you and your attentions quite desperately, right from the beginning. Do you remember that second evening you were here, when we were going over the accounts together in the drawing room?"

"Of course," said Paul, regarding her with fascination.

Mary took a deep breath. "Well, all the time that we were sitting together, I was wishing you would tear off my clothes and ravish me right there on the sofa. I *did,* Paul—and it made it very difficult to concentrate on the accounts, I assure you!"

"Indeed," was all Paul said, but the way he said it spoke volumes. He regarded Mary a moment, then turned to look at the drawing room sofa. He then looked at Mary again, and she observed with alarm that there was a speculative light in his eye.

"Oh, no," she said, falling back a step and folding her arms instinctively over her chest. Then she laughed and spread them wide in an attitude of resignation. "That is—yes, Paul. Yes, if you want to."

"I do want to," said Paul. Taking a step toward her, he swept her masterfully into his arms.

Things progressed rapidly after that. Mary made no further attempts at resistance. When Paul kissed her, she kissed him back; when he caressed her, she caressed him back; and such was the abandon of her response that Paul entirely forgot her lack of experience, as well as his own intention of proceeding with gentleness and caution. It was not until matters had reached a very critical stage indeed that he was reminded of both by a small outcry from Mary.

"Oh, my love, I'm sorry. Did I hurt you?" he said, remorsefully wiping away a tear from her cheek.

"Yes. No. A little, perhaps," said Mary, tremulously lifting her face to his. "But don't stop, Paul. As you love me, do not stop." Putting her arms around his neck, she drew him to her once again.

Thus encouraged, Paul went on to acquit himself with both energy and enthusiasm. As they lay afterwards in each other's arms, Mary sighed and stretched herself with an air of luxurious enjoyment.

"I'm sorry, am I crushing you?" said Paul, raising himself on one elbow to look at her.

"Not at all," she said, smiling up at him. "To speak truth, Paul, I have never felt so comfortable—or so happy."

"Me, either," said Paul, burying his face in her hair. "It's a wonder to me how you continually surpass my expectations, Mary. I must confess I had some doubts about this marriage business to begin with, but now I begin to think there might be something in it after all. Have I mentioned lately that I love you?"

"Not for at least five minutes," said Mary, stroking the hair back tenderly from his brow. "It's very remiss of you, upon my word."

"I'll make it up to you," promised Paul, kissing her cheek. "Only give me another chance."

Mary laughed. "As many chances as you like, my love," she said, and drew a contented sigh. "Oh, Paul, I feel positively voluptuous. This is a delightful way to spend an afternoon, isn't it?"

"Delightful," agreed Paul, burying his face in her hair once more. "Deliciously degenerate, yet morally irreproachable. You are my wife, after all. My wife," he repeated, with an air of intense satisfaction. "And if I choose to ravish you upon the drawing room sofa, no one can say a word about it."

Mary laughed again. "I don't know about that, Paul," she said. "If one of the servants were to come in just now, I expect they would have quite a few words to say about it. The servants' hall would probably be buzzing for weeks afterwards. But there, I'm forgetting. You locked the door when we first came in, didn't you?"

"One of the doors, at least. And I think the other was already locked. I think it was—I am almost sure it was. However, perhaps it would be prudent if I made sure of it." Rising from the sofa, Paul went to the door that communicated with the dining room and tried it cautiously. "Yes, it's locked, too."

"Good," said Mary, stretching luxuriously again. Paul returned to the sofa and stood a moment looking down at her. She smiled up at him lazily, making no effort to conceal her state of undress. "You look like the sultan's favorite," he said. "Or like a cat stretched in front of the fire."

"And you look like Apollo," she responded, looking him up and down with appreciation. "What a handsome husband I have got, to be sure. It's really a pity you have to wear clothes."

Paul grinned as he seated himself beside her. "I might say

the same about you, wife of mine," he said. "If I had my way, I'd make you go around with no garment for your modesty but your hair, like Lady Godiva. It would make a very effective garment," he added, reaching out to stroke the long locks of hair lying loose on her shoulders.

Mary smiled and sat up, making room for him on the sofa beside her. He settled back against the cushions, putting his arm around her shoulders and pulling her close against him. "Oh, Mary, I am so happy," he said. "Now that I've got you, it seems as though there wasn't anything in the world left to want. I do love you so much."

"And I love you, too, Paul," she said, turning to kiss his cheek. "What a fool I've been, wasting time being jealous when I could have been doing this."

Paul laughed, but there was a light of understanding in his eyes as he looked down at her. "You need never be jealous on my account, Mary," he said. "Indeed, I might more justly be jealous on yours. Jealous of your former fiancé," he explained, seeing her look of puzzlement. "When you spoke of him earlier, that first evening after we met, I could tell how much you still cared about him. And I must confess that it made me feel rather envious, even before I had come to know how much your regard was worth."

Mary was embarrassed but spoke honestly. "Yes, I do still care for Francis, Paul. But indeed, that's not something you need be jealous of. Everything that happened between Francis and I was in the past. It's a closed book now, and there can be no future for us, as there is for you and me. I expect it's no different really from the way you used to care for Lady de Lacey."

Paul shook his head. "Ah, but 'used to' is the critical phrase there," he said. "I used to care for her, but now I cannot even think well of her. Whereas you will probably always care for your Francis. I don't mean to be unreasonable, however," he added, bestowing a kiss on Mary's brow. "As long as I have you, I will try not to be jealous of your first love."

Mary gave him a quick sideways smile, then looked into the

fire with a thoughtful expression. She was fairly sure that however much she had loved and respected Francis, she could never
have felt for him quite the distinguishing degree of passion she
felt for this man. But it did not seem to her that conjugal unre-
serve required her to offer up this reflection, so she only kissed
Paul's cheek and told him he had nothing to worry about. "Unless
it be how we're going to get upstairs without the servants seeing
us," she added with a laugh. "You can put on *your* clothes again
easily enough, but I don't know what I'm going to do. I'm afraid
my dress is pretty well destroyed, and my chemise, too."

"You said you wanted me to tear off your clothes," reminded
Paul, looking complacently at the forlorn heap of serge and lawn
lying on the hearth rug. "Anyway, I always hated that dress."

"Yes, my love, but your having destroyed it puts me in an
awkward position. I don't care to emulate Lady Godiva, however much you may admire her. Do you think you could run
upstairs and bring me down a different dress if I wait here?"

"To be sure," said Paul, rising to his feet and reaching for
his clothes. Having put them on, he kissed Mary, bundled up
her discarded dress and underthings, and told her he would be
back with fresh ones in no time at all. Mary accompanied him
to the door and remained there, watching through a narrow
crack as he ran up the stairs with a buoyant step. She then
relocked the door, returned to the sofa, and sat smiling to herself
as she awaited his return.

Paul returned only a few minutes later, carrying a bundle of
red velvet in his arms. "I was pleasantly surprised to see that
your dresses are not uniformly dark and concealing," he said,
putting the bundle in her arms. "This looked very pretty. You'd
better dress quickly, for I heard the dressing bell ring while I
was abovestairs getting your things."

"Oh, Paul, you goose," exclaimed Mary, surveying with
laughter the bundle he had brought her. "This is a formal evening
dress. Miss Eaton and the servants would think me mad if I wore
this to a simple family dinner. But then, who cares if they think
I'm mad," she added quickly, seeing Paul's look of disappoint-

ment. "It is a pretty dress, as you say, and since it pleases my husband that I should wear it this evening, I shall do so."

Paul looked so gratified by this speech that Mary felt repaid for her small concession. Rather to her embarrassment, he insisted on helping her dress, and seemed to take great pleasure in unraveling the mysteries of feminine attire. "I can see I have made a fundamental error in my dealings with women so far," he said, stooping to kiss Mary's neck as he did up the buttons down the back of her dress. "Before, you know, I had a mistress but tried to treat her like a wife. I can see now that the proper thing to do is get a wife and then treat her like one's mistress. Altogether a much more satisfactory system."

"Mmm," said Mary, shutting her eyes to enjoy the kiss.

"Much more satisfactory," repeated Paul, gently turning Mary around and surveying her with pleasure. "You look beautiful, my love. I shall be so proud to show you off when we go to London in the spring. I hope you've no objection to spending the Season in Town? I have a mind to shock the world by taking my uncle's seat in Parliament—the first time it's been occupied in twenty years at least, I'll be bound. All those political debates with Miss Eaton have fired me with a desire to try my hand at the real thing!"

Mary's only response to this was an absent smile. Paul stooped to kiss her again before going on in a reflective voice. "And then there are some changes in my rental properties which I've been turning over in my mind. My agent convinced me this spring I'd be better off selling than making any major renovations, but since then I've wondered if I made the right decision. There's a buyer who's made an offer, but the sale hasn't gone through yet, so I still have a chance to change my mind. You must come down with me and see what you think I should do about it, Mary. I would be very glad to have your opinion on the subject."

"Oh, yes, certainly," said Mary, in a preoccupied voice. Paul stooped again to kiss her on the forehead.

"My love, you are not attending," he scolded affectionately.

"Your eyes are on me, but your thoughts are obviously miles away."

"No, I heard everything you said, Paul. You spoke of taking me to London—and I should like very well to go to London. Then you spoke of taking your uncle's seat in Parliament—and I should be very proud to see you take your seat in Parliament. And then you spoke of your rental property—and of course I would be glad to see it, and give you my opinion on the subject if you want." Mary gave Paul a saucy smile. "You see, I *was* attending, my lord!"

Paul shook his head darkly. "You have your answer very pat, ma'am, but I still suspect your thoughts were on something besides London and Parliament and property," he said. "You were looking at me very particularly a minute ago."

Mary laughed and colored. "Actually, I was wondering when we could make love again," she said naively. "Must we wait until tomorrow, or can we do it again tonight?"

Paul gave her an astonished look, then began to laugh. Gathering her in his arms, he kissed her long and thoroughly. "You are a woman in a thousand," he said. "And it is not at all necessary that we wait until tomorrow night. Indeed, I could do it this minute, only I'm afraid that would make us rather late for dinner. On the whole, I think it would be better if we waited until this evening. With your permission, I think I shall ravish you in a bed this time, as a more comfortable alternative to the drawing room sofa."

"I did not mind the drawing room sofa," said Mary, smiling up at him. "But I would be most happy to enlarge my experience to include bedrooms."

"I shall ravish you in every room in the house before we're done," Paul promised recklessly. "That's what—forty or fifty rooms?"

"Let me see. There are sixteen rooms on this floor, and at least twenty on the one above it. And then there is the attic floor—and the basement. I do not count the servants' quarters, you understand, but—"

The dinner bell rang as Mary was speaking. Paul, uttering an imprecation upon its ill-timed summons, released her from his arms and straightened his neckcloth while she gave her hair a last hasty smooth in the chimney glass. When she was done, he offered her his arm, and together they went down the hall to the dining room. As Paul opened the door for her, she gave him a smile brimming with mischief.

"Fifty-two rooms," she said in a low voice. "I make it out at exactly fifty-two rooms, Paul. That should keep us occupied some little time. And after that . . . hmm. I wonder how many rooms there are at Wyland Park?"

"At least seventy, I should think," said Paul with a conspiratorial smile. "And another thirty or so at Wyland House."

"And shall you ravish me in every one of them?"

"Every one of them," promised Paul, and set a seal to his promise by kissing her again, right there in the doorway.

WATCH FOR THESE ZEBRA REGENCIES

LADY STEPHANIE   (0-8217-5341-X, $4.50)
by Jeanne Savery
Lady Stephanie Morris has only one true love: the family estate she
has managed ever since her mother died. But then Lord Anthony Rider
arrives on her estate, claiming he has plans for both the land and the
woman. Stephanie soon realizes she's fallen in love with a man whose
sensual caresses will plunge her into a world of peril and intrigue . . . a
man as dangerous as he is irresistible.

BRIGHTON BEAUTY   (0-8217-5340-1, $4.50)
by Marilyn Clay
Chelsea Grant, pretty and poor, naively takes school friend Alayna
Marchmont's place and spends a month in the country. The devastating
man had sailed from Honduras to claim his promised bride, Miss
Marchmont. An affair of the heart may lead to disaster . . . unless a
resourceful Brighton beauty finds a way to stop a masquerade and
keep a lord's love.

LORD DIABLO'S DEMISE   (0-8217-5338-X, $4.50)
by Meg-Lynn Roberts
The sinfully handsome Lord Harry Glendower was a gambler and the
black sheep of his family. About to be forced into a marriage of convenience, the devilish fellow engineered his own demise, never having
dreamed that faking his death would lead him to the heavenly refuge
of spirited heiress Gwyn Morgan, the daughter of a physician.

A PERILOUS ATTRACTION   (0-8217-5339-8, $4.50)
by Dawn Aldridge Poore
Alissa Morgan is stunned when a frantic passenger thrusts her baby
into Alissa's arms and flees, having heard rumors that a notorious
highwayman posed a threat to their coach. Handsome stranger Hugh
Sebastian secretly possesses the treasured necklace the highwayman
seeks and volunteers to pose as Alissa's husband to save her reputation.
With a lost baby and missing necklace in their care, the couple embarks
on a journey into peril—and passion.

*Available wherever paperbacks are sold, or order direct from the
Publisher. Send cover price plus 50¢ per copy for mailing and
handling to Penguin USA, P.O. Box 999, c/o Dept. 17109,
Bergenfield, NJ 07621. Residents of New York and Tennessee must
include sales tax. DO NOT SEND CASH.*